MW01101159

CITY OF SINGLES

CITY OF SINGLES

JASON BRYAN

SICKLOVE STUDIOS

VANCOUVER
BRITISH COLUMBIA
CANADA

Copyright © 2013 by Jason Bryan

All rights reserved. No part of this publication may be reproduced,distributed, or transmitted in any form or by any means, including photocopying, recording, or other electronic or mechanical methods, without the prior written permission of the publisher, except in the case of brief quotations embodied in critical reviews and certain other noncommercial uses permitted by copyright law.

For permission requests, write to the publisher, addressed "Attention: Permissions Coordinator," at the address below:

Sicklove Studios
55 Cordova Street East
Vancouver, British Columbia, Canada
V6A0A5

www.sicklovestudios.com

Cover Design by
Stephanie Vachon

Book Design by
Fresh Ink Foundry

To Alex, Diana, and Stephanie

I couldn't have written this book with you,
I couldn't have written it without you.

Contents

Bellum omnium contra omnes

1 Disconnection

A lazy blue haze hangs in the air. Smells like an Indian temple in here. Never been to India, but I've eaten a lot of curry. Tamarind and cumin play inside my mind before last night's good idea pulls me back to reality. Chest pressed against cold concrete, odours of urine, garbage and stale beer. How did I end up on the floor today, and what time is it?

Mashed potatoes and gravy, these go together like Yaletown and pug shit. A flash of old memory percolates through my substance-mangled mind; a hand extending out, in its grip a steaming dish of food.

"Would you like some yam, Dylen?"

"Yes, please."

The dish is pretty hot, better put it down. Careful now, you know how these fancy people eat, utensils, no talking, elbows off the table. Sit up straight. Did everything like I was supposed to up until this point, serving myself and then passing the food to the other guests. First mistake, taking a bite of hot sweet potato, my greedy tongue should have waited. It burns, slurping in cold air, choosing to convulse in my seat rather than spitting it onto the table. To think; just a few hours ago I was licking my girlfriend's asshole on the floor of her living room, half of her family was ten feet away watching the hockey game highlights on the kitchen TV. A pinch on my arm lit up my face, saying grace should be done before anyone eats, I'm reminded. Hope they don't think this is rude and all, slamming my entire glass of wine to soothe seared taste buds.

Twenty minutes. On the fucking floor for twenty minutes. My whole life I haven't been able to sit still for this long, and now I can't even move. Wish there was a pillow under my head right now, or breasts. Speaking of girl parts, there's some soft snoring somewhere behind me. Not the baritone snore of a fellow, but the slow, rhythmic sighing of a petite female. The lady from the night before is the tramp on my couch this morning. Flaps on the table, whose cocaine was it anyways? Did I buy it in a haze again? Lying to myself wasn't just a good idea anymore, but more of a habit. Thought I made a promise that I wouldn't get involved with that shit; guess when the liquor is flowing like a hemophiliac on her rag, excuses become wingmen.

Sitting up wasn't such a good idea. The world is dancing under me and I can't see straight. The floor will quickly become my destination again should these party legs try to stand up. Come on man, one hand, other foot, now another hand, another foot. We spend such a small amount of time crawling as children, then again as alcoholics. Her hazel eyes remind me of Kentucky bourbon after a few cubes melted in a tumbler. Wonder if she has a tumblr. Did we meet last night? Fuck this. The whole room is spinning, that's never good in an open concept loft. It's not possible to stare at anything for too long without a rolling ocean wave throwing my eyes off. There are shiny floors for light to play tricks on, high ceilings for that vertigo, no soft carpet to cushion a fall. My skin's sweaty in the way a smokie sausage blisters over flame. Something's coming up, fuck. Retching is never fun. That first gag hits your mind like the phrase 'We need to talk,' or 'Have a seat over there.' Posting up on one arm, never thought a little jiu jitsu would help me get to a toilet to puke faster. Throw my feet under me, go! The wet smacking sound of clumsy meat hitting concrete, my mind went silent for a few nervous steps. Almost, almost, just a couple more. With precise timing of chin pimples before first dates, gravity acts up to throw me shoulder-first into the bathroom sink.

Back on the floor and in worse shape, my foot stings, warmth. get a wiggle to see if they're all still there. Hot moist grime betwe toes, and my heel sticks to the floor. A curious eye flutters open, my world now a bear spray kaleidoscope of nausea and pain, chunks of vomit ski forehead slope into quickly unfluttered eyelids.

I'm a pile of old scars.

A rough beating heart quakes inside my chest while head-on car crashes pile up endlessly between ears. Textured discomfort of tile floor presses into skin, a stale drain pipe giving off that burp smell in my face. Must have pin-balled off the sink and fallen into the shower. The rim around the base that holds in the water is now firmly planted in my lower ribs. Reaching up, probing fingers find the shower handle. My ribs hurt, so much. Shallow breaths to slow my pulse.

Maybe this is what Jesus felt like, minus the hangover.

A cold blast of water, thank you. Ah, feels good. Guess it is times like these that remind me I'm still alive. Blink. Blink. Still stings. Tile floor grinds hip bone, rolling from my right side onto my back, the shower jet spray hitting me directly in the face. A barely-caring wipe clear of bits, grease finds its way to slick my fingertips. Chunks in my hair, those aren't supposed to be there. Finally able to see, I glance at my foot, a nice crescent moon shaped gash between the little toe and fourth toe. Ugly feet are usually the colour of peanut butter gone bad. Through the blur of steam, banged up foot resembles five fat hogs dining on a trough leaking strawberry jam. Focus seeking eyes find it on the floor outside of the shower, an orange donut shaped puddle of vomit. Did I fall, hit my head, and projectile vomit straight up and somehow not choke to death? At least rockstars die like that. I can't even die with the style I like these days.

Hung over souls find soothing comfort in nursing envelopes of warm water. Relief runs across my body in a hug that doubles as a handy wipe. I gag and barf on myself a few more times, half-digested food doesn't even have a chance to be identified before swirling into the abyss. Wonder if my organs are having a meeting inside of me right now, all huddled around the liver, asking it just what the fuck happened. The punch drunk stomach screams "Fuck YOU guys!" through bloody lips, storming out of the meeting. My lips are numb. Must be the nasally ejected vomit mixing with last night's devil's dandruff, a fresco of party running from my nostrils.

There is not a lot to do when you're in a shower, retching. At least now it's just gagging and not actually throwing anything up. A chunk is stuck in my chest hair. My arms feel too heavy to lift, so to dislodge it I move more into the water jets. A small, grey cube, maybe it was meat. Who knows how much effort the farmer put into his crops, how much gas and oil went into transporting the raw ingredients. The chef who prepared it applied his art to make it taste good, all to be doomed to reside in my chest hair, like some sort of half-digested vagrant. The piece tumbles and slides down into what's left of my pubes. Groin dressing is usually kept trim to avoid a 70's pornstar look. Lately I've been running low on fucks to give, so it looks more like what I imagine as a postcard from the deathly hollows. Chewed, acid-burnt, struggling for purpose outside of nourishment. Barf is stuck in my crotch fur. Well, I guess that's as good of a place as any, not like it belongs inside my stomach right now.

After what seems to be an eternity, counting tiles and inspecting my genitals for sex barnacles, the water loses its appeal. Being alive but looking dead, my fingers are as wrinkled as a set of long, plump prunes. With a twist of the handle, my sanctuary from reality thrusts me back into the thick of the shit. Water drips from the showerhead while a shivering, cold, nude and wet me looks for a towel. The floor is soaked with water, mixed with vomit and blood, a Van Gogh with smeared oranges and reds.

Cracks in concrete wearing bodily fluids can remind one of an oak tree in fall.

Steady now, no repeats Dylen. At this point if I fall again, might as well just stay down and try again tomorrow. No time for that though, what's this girl's name anyways? A delicate pink purse lounges on my purple couch, doing its best impression of a rectangular breast with a swollen pink nipple. Grabbing a towel to dry myself off, putting a half-assed effort in gets a quarter-assed result out; my first steps are wetter than in the shower. Barely dry and shivering still, I try my luck resting on the ottoman while waiting for fresh hints of nausea to pass. My nose is busy smelling nothing but sniffles while bloodshot eyes spy popcorn and a bra on the floor here.

Lacey. Niiice.

The purse is already yawning wide open, if it's good for the dentist it might get a lollipop. Papers, tampon, lipstick, pepper spray, panties. Panties? Panties. License, check. She's Katelynn, born in 1988. She's got the face of an angel, pure, happy, relaxed. Flashbacks of going to church youth group and time spent fingerbanging curious good girls behind the gardener's shed.

Legs push the earth down and shuffle me to my computer. My addiction to the internet took root a long time ago. At the speed of light and through phone cable, you can make connections that you'll never make in the meat world. Shaky hands poke a switch on the monitor. The brilliant white of Facebook's background blinds me for a moment, my mind conjures up an image of the crew of the Enola Gay, somber and quiet on the flight home. Refreshing Facebook, I uploaded a photo of my urine stream at some bar again. Only three likes.

Ripping the mouse down to the Taskbar, it lazily slides up to give me a peek at the time. Fuck you Windows. It's 3 PM. She's asleep and it's 3 PM.

With my tired head perched on palms and both elbows on the table, I drift back to the yam-thermite experience. Could go for some gravy. Nothing cures a hangover like some grease. Reaching up to feel what hurts on my scalp, touching a smarting goose egg on the back of my head just pisses me off. I'd ice it, but I probably used the ice for drinks. The last time I used a bag of frozen peas for medical purposes, the bag had a hole which lead to a fruit fly apocalypse for weeks. Maybe someone should have swept them up. Maybe, but I didn't care. A gentleman would have already found out how Kate's doing, but status updates are more important.

The studio is a long, open rectangle, separated by set of curtains in the middle. Remembering the first time I saw this place, the afternoon sun blanketed exposed brick in a layer of gold. It usually makes for a happy and well-lit artist's space, today it reminds me of dirty piss. An overcast grumpy sky shown through stale warm Corona. Stepping through the archway from the business section to the pleasure dome, Kate is slumbering away. Her dark and thick messy hair drapes over the side of a pillow as moss. With eyes half open as she sleeps, a drug slug-trail peeking out from her lower nostrils. Moving deftly to avoid disturbing the sleeping beauty, quiet feet tip toe the long way around my steel cube coffee table. Post-It notes litter it as evidence of prior floor-bound hangovers, messages from spirits of friends gone by.

An older man wearing only a towel approaches a younger girl asleep on a couch. Where have I seen this scenario before? A blanket mostly covers her, my towel barely covers me. Moving to sit down, taking care to lift her feet slowly and place them on my knees. The leather of the couch is soft and warm. Her feet must have been stretched out earlier. Maybe she's cold now? Gently tucking the blanket in around her, an approving soft sigh escapes her throat. Her face is lily white, cheeks of rose. Faded mascara leaving a bluish tinge around her eye sockets, the same hue as a toilet puck a few flushes from dissolving. Caring instincts brush loose strands of hair out of her face, neatly tucking them behind her petite ear. For a moment those same feelings picture her and I together, a girl I didn't even remember the name of mere minutes ago. Now those same feelings are asking myself; how could I forget?

Remembering a girl's name shouldn't be hard.

Forgetting and letting go wasn't always as easy.

I grew up watching my grandparents in love, a Pepe LePew cartoon where the cat loved him back just as much. Together for fifty years, they witnessed their final sunset within hours of each other's passing. If their path was walked with a gentle tangerine sunset at their backs, mine is ran with fluorescent light blasting from every direction. Does the stallion ever miss a mare after his owner studs him out? A caged mouse with white coated friends, you learn pretty quickly that the lever will always bring another slice of cheese. All of our curious pink little rat faces, a phalanx of white whiskers on each side and a twitching nose hunting for more. The squeaking little guy gets his fill over and over, never appreciating the acquisition of another meal. The next is just a pink paw press away. Now this rodent has had its fill and is satiated for the time being. My cage a wasteland of unfettered indulgence.

Her smell wafts into my nose, somehow having fought its way through the snot and blood now protesting last night's cocaine use. Lavender and Du Maurier accompanies sweat and musk, a bouquet of the both of us. Her head rolls over and cracks open a slow crooked smile. The softest rattle of 'morning' croaks out to acknowledge me. The opening to her mouth is flakey and dry, a pair of dead worms awkwardly spooning on a pretty girl's face. Her tongue stabs away saliva dried on corners of puffy lips, another lick resurrects arousing qualities. They're a youthful pink again, matching beard burn down her neck. She turns over slowly and the blanket lifts up for a moment, my eyes feast on her budding left breast.

3 AM would have that nipple in my mouth.

3 PM would have it in a taxi out of here.

Wet whiskey-tinted eyes close as she stretches her legs out across my own. The back of her knees brush against my raw cock. My right hand moves to the blanket and rests on her upper thigh. Feeling less human, more an animal of pleasure. Her right hand slides over and covers my own.

"I don't ... usually I am not the kind of girl that leaves with a guy," Katelynn giggles, "I am going to catch so much shit from Josh!"

"Who's Josh?" I hope she didn't hear the hesitation in my voice.

"My manager, he cut you off last night remember?"

"Yeah-" I grunt, nodding.

She sits up, her heel brushes tender foreskin, subtle and smooth as steel wool on fire. Katelynn snorts back snot, throwing her hair over shoulders as the blanket falls to her waist.

"That shit wasn't too speedy, I liked it." She ties her hair back in a braid.

Festive sniffles bully silence.

Empty flaps on the table are party origami. It's nearly 4 AM, or what I call 2nd delivery hour. We're naked and sweating, the fucking paused briefly to make like urban anteaters. An old gym membership card is used to crush the rocks up, a fine whitish yellow. I hate when it's humid and sticks together too much. Fuck, just need this in my fucking nose to get back to fucking her doggystyle. The heart shape originally came from what a woman looks like bent over forwards, it has nothing to do with love.

Soft blanket ruffles quietly as it goes to cuddle the floor, my eyes focusing back into the real world. A lithe ivory body displayed fully standing and stretching in front of me, my last glance at her tight labia powers lust up my spine. A little variety would be nice, she's just another girl who waxes it all off. Thongs always make the same snap when they're pulled up. She takes her Blackberry and strolls off in the direction of my bathroom.

Katelynn fumbles around looking to illuminate the can. "Which switch for the light again?"

My thoughts scream middle with each distant click. She finds it herself and closes the door.

A solitary soldier rests on its side. The noble 26 ounce bottle of tequila, what I refer to as a twixer, rests with only a shot or two left. The glass feels slippery and cold in my clammy hands. I tilt it back, drink the last shot, and put it upright on the table. It's important to show respect for the poison, saluting the empty bottle with my free hand while warm fumes of alcohol pour from my nose. Cracking and popping noises in abused sinuses, a disqualified nose protesting last night's uphill skiing championship. Liquor entering my stomach mimics Norm at Cheers, every ulcer happily waving. This time the hard bar is less welcome than masturbation in a mall food court. The next five minutes is spent making promises in my head to not drink anymore today if the stomach agrees not to turn inside out. We make peace mentally, kiss, and make up.

Normality isn't normally around here, and while normally I wouldn't just smoke first thing in the morning, it is neither morning, nor normal. I sit by one of the only two windows of the studio. Flick. Bubble and breathe. A deep inhale, a seagull cries out. Do seagulls prefer one type of French fry to another? I certainly do prefer McDonald's fries to most others. Golden grease sticks with the power to magically cure nearly every ailment. Try having a chocolate shake and French fries and being mad. You can't. Clown food is gaudy edible comfort, the ghost of meals changes your style, dresses you in those unfashionable lipids. This bong sticks my worries onto the wings of a gull and carries them away from Cordova Street. Maybe later that gull will shit my worries out on some unsuspecting tool biking the seawall. Sharp echoes of an angry voice mixes with hard wheels of a shopping cart pushed down the alley. Wish I could give that poor cart a toke, I can't imagine how it's been treated.

A flush and a door opening signals the return of my visitor, girl skin creamy under bathroom spotlights delivering a reason for pied eyes to remain open.

"Shit! Why didn't you fucking say it was nearly 4!" Katelynn bellows, putting her hair up. "I told you I had to be at my parent's for this afternoon, I fucking told you!"

Tiny girl feet make more noise than they should across concrete loft. She bends over to pick up her skirt, bra and t-shirt. Right now loving the way her breasts hang there, a solid C cup. A dirty mind drift is recalling her riding me, grabbing her breasts and licking both of those nipples together. My back arched as much as it can, hips tensed forward to poke her guts. Her sweet, soft moans when I hit the top of her cervix.

"My earrings, where are my earrings?" Katelynn says with a growl, her little feet dragging her in circles around the studio.

"I can't find the other fucking hoop!"

"Dylen ... Hello?"

I could have told her honestly that I didn't hear her. I hate to lie, but I did anyways.

When my bathroom mirror isn't full of myself, it would probably gossip that it's seen this before. A crisis of dressing to put on a face fit for the public. She never did find the other hoop. Her exit is a dull door thud. Sober brain can't remember swapping numbers with her, and my phone has no records of her name. What I do possess is twenty unchecked voicemails dating back two months, six Facebook updates, and eight texts from other people. Sorry. Details get lost in the cadence of my life. What would we do now anyways, date?

The rest of Saturday is spent surfing the internet and playing video games. Reading that gold just hit $2,000 US an ounce makes uneasy future visions eclipse any relaxation found. Don't really know what affect that will have on my life, but it sucks anyways. The wealth gap between rich and poor is higher than during the great depression, putting me now into depression. Cat pictures, fucking cat pictures. Reddit made me hate cat pictures. I download some mods for a game that allow me to replace the face textures of some characters. Skyrim was designed by aliens as a human hamster wheel. It takes me two hours just to get it to load properly after thinking my video card's memory was full, but it was just a version conflict. Finally the game starts and I'm eager to forget this morning.

An extra hard finger, rigid with purpose to push on plastic squares, moving myself through the virtual world. The anticipation has me focused like a Zen Master trying to catch a fly with chopsticks. I move around the wall of a castle represented by pixels on a glowing rectangle. This is my life, sighing to myself in my head. Excitement drops once the characters with facial textures replaced are found. Ugly noses too big to look real, the ears don't line up right.

The tits are too big on this orc bandit.

I don't even hit escape, an alt-tab and right click ends my digital escape.

Bed.

2 No Sunset

Ash grey clouds roll and flatten out over a bruise purple sky. Old fashioned Gastown streetlights above lengths of black chain, dividing street from sidewalk. These voyeuristic white orb sentinels peer out into the night while damp links reflect a pale luminance through gloom. A flapping of fabric is barely audible over the din of wind, smothering what could be soft tapping of small raindrops.

She stands in the street with her black hair pressed against her face, rising up and obscuring her eyes with each gust. The half block stare-down ends when she turns away, stepping deep into the misty veil ahead. Pursuit. Willpower. Taking the hardest step of my life. That single footfall turns into many, legs burning and shaking with each step. Further into the thick of the fog, time gets lost too. Her figure shimmers in the distance, raven hair curling, tossed by currents. The world glides under me slower than test results on a late train, her languid pace matching my own.

Old brick stones shine rain slick, reflecting an increasing glow of flickering neon. The left storefronts hold torn awnings, shadows cradle untouchable strewn garbage.

Discarded underwear.

Wadded up napkins.

Old newspapers.

Peeling paint greys and boarded up doorways. These dirty abandoned places used to hold people together seeking some commonality. Low throbbing bass rumbles in the distance. The street keeps pulling me along. New stores full of gyrating, naked women cloaked in neon pinks and reds. Gentrification for the gentleman's soul.

Slogans promise release. They blow kisses at me, dancing seductively they press their asses against the glass and spread their cheeks wide. Turning my head like trying to twist steel with muscles of warm butter. She's walking away from me, followed by a gossamer shroud of vapors, a dark and mystic wedding train.

Malevolent bass begins to drown out my thoughts. It's impossible to tell if my legs are moving me forward, or if my world is in undertow. Out of the grey soup ahead, she steps around a dark figure. Drawn closer to it, I've lost sight of her, slamming bass jarring every ounce of flesh and bone.

A motionless obelisk.

Not until I'm almost walking into it can I recognize what it is, a three meter high stack of beer bottles in coffin shape. Brown and glossy, thousands of little glimpses of my life fill each bottle.

A new girl in my life.

Going to a party.

Being sick after.

Fucking some pretty girl.

Cashing a paycheque.

Getting high.

Discovering.

Learning.

Laughing.

Having fun.

Being carefree.

Being miserable.

Being broke.

Being alone.

I can't stop myself from crashing head first into the stack.

A single crack is heard, followed by silence, a roar of shattered glass crashing to the street. Stunned eyes shut while staggering a few steps, anticipating the blackout. Sounds of countless social memories blare from everywhere around me, the echos reverberating down endless city blocks and becoming part of the dream DJ's mix.

Eyes open.

I'm standing in the middle of a four-way intersection, brown shards of bottle form a crater of smashed glass around me. Dancing nude girls move seductively while backlit in pink, they fill every window of oppressive grey skyscrapers which rise forever into an inky heaven. Heavy bass notes of generic electro-trash thumps away sync'ed with gyrations of the beauties everywhere around me. I'm holding a drink. She's gone. I die.

3 Sailing Through Sunday

Having a smooth face and neatly combed hair once fostered a great sense of pride. The point was to look friendly, wanting to appear trustworthy and stable. Today's feature look is halfway between whatever and dumpster. It doesn't seem to matter how you present yourself when the goal has nothing to do with presentability. Darkly lit house parties or bars don't judge over a few days growth, pants sagging as per usual, beltless and worn with dirty shoes. Twenty dollar graphic shirt splashed with sparkling metallic fabric. Add a hoodie and it makes a Vancouver tuxedo. In fact, one can argue that the less you give a fuck, the more you'll be rewarded.

I don't have any tattoos. It's hard to find enough faith to believe in anything, let alone something to inspire putting ink under my skin. Hard to not find a coincidence that almost any self-aggrandizing musician or pseudo artist will be covered in sleeves of modern empty icons. Praying hands and religious symbols for those of little to no faith, dice with playing cards for those who need to show they game the system. Men inked with messages of love towards family while not paying support, raising children without the guidance they publicly profess. Screams to the world through symbolism and external expression, meanwhile the inner voice of these same people remains silent; often only listening to echoes of what the popular narrative is. Imagine the Pope, the Dhali Lama, and the Sihk gurus covered in tattoos, wearing slogans to convince themselves of messages they don't even believe in.

Ink can become a very real god to those seeking salvation through art, only this canvas dies.

Stale loft air wringing out every last drop of dopamine from my brain.

Leaving bed or dying are the only options left. A wet back against satin sheets works better than any alarm. Here we go again, shuffling through my routine on autopilot. Taking a shower, brushing teeth and shaving my neck to not look like such a loser. I'm bored. The sky outside a brilliant electric blue. Mornings don't really exist in my world, just light or dark.

I get dressed in some cheap jeans that hug my crotch, a pretty nice bulge for the women to check out. Ex-lover female friends have told me that they leer at men as much as they get leered at. I'm too caught up with the thought of having some plaything to hang out with tonight to remember to put on underwear. Couch leather groans and stretches, the weight from six feet and two hundred pounds pressing into it. This little bit of spare tire should be a gut given what I eat, drug-filled nights and mornings spent emptying organs serve to keep calorie counts down.

A silent vibration muffled by the couch, reminding me of a fart crushed into an office chair. Sometimes I forget to turn my cell phone ringer back on and people wait outside my building in the rain. It's not funny, but sometimes I giggle when soaked bodies walk in. The little switch on the side clicks on as my eyes catch the latest pop-up, it's a notification of an invite to a beach party through Facebook. The list of people going is looking grungier than a Pabst Blue Ribbon clearance sale at Commercial and Venables. Envisioning the scene I frown at the thought of doing this again, listening to self-absorbed people talk about meaningless shit, a social jousting of bragging and men trying too hard to get laid.

Electronic music spun by backwards-hatted 40 year-olds, shitty bass with warm beer, listening to blackberry owners talk about LV, BBM, and YOLO.

Now rewind ten years ago, the pussy was a little harder to get, the crowds were smaller, and I didn't mind making new friends. Deja vu happens all too often, I can predict the conversations and how I'll get my dick sucked if I speak to a girl's insecurities. It's not that I don't enjoy it; it's less effort and cash to get a girl to come over and fuck me without leaving home.

My thumbs are little robots putting together a car on an assembly line. Texting involves no hunting and pecking, only cold precision. They know where to hunt and find each letter of 'drink' and 'patio' with my eyes closed. Custom programmed auto-correct heaps silver tongued sour speech into little mounds of filthy prose; text seduction is my A-game. Phone penetrates pocket while sauntering to the kitchen, looking to raid Yummyland to tide me over until someone wants to go out. The cupboard is stocked with utility foods and not much else today. Greasy kettle BBQ chips and protein powder form a snack odd couple. Devouring a handful of almonds, Apple's bells on my phone signal the next meal.

Misha is first to reply. A girl with some pedigree, she loves to climb down onto anything different. A lawyer by trade, you would never guess it by the way she lounges around in a hoodie or yoga pants. When ready to party, the dresses and personality comes out with aplomb, her attitude is half consumer, and half get-me-high-now-and-fuck-me. Polite and outgoing, she'll also slide your hand up her skirt at sushi before you're through your miso. She's a turbo BMW with seats made out of a piss-soaked potato sack. The prettiest apple, but too many worms have eaten all that's good inside; nothing clicks with her outside of the realms of sex, liquor, or drugs.

She wants to meet up for a drink, and she's bringing her best friend. I don't mind since they're both interesting to talk to, albeit a bit vapid. Her friend's name is Kayla, otherwise known as Kiki to her friends. Her body and femininity have always allured me with her natural charms, too bad she's so apt for pursuing plastic vanity. Last time we hung out, she was talking about getting a tit job and reading 'How to meet your millionaire match'. Her idea of romance is to date men who usually procure their income from less than legal means. She was shocked that her ex would threaten her once they broke up, snakes do bite.

This is sure to get interesting.

I tell her to text me once she has a table, the phone carefully laid down to tidy up my place a bit. After nearly half an hour, there's enough of a significant dent in the debris of my life to call it acceptable. Found a pair of panties and tied my curtains up with it. Add a little light to this place. Dozens of wet baby sheet-ghosts fill the kitchen sink. That's what happens when you can't cook egg whites very well, and clean them up even worse. You wash the frying pan off afterwards and it looks like Halloween had abortions in your drain. The teapot is pitted, the silver mixing with rust and decay. Patches of brown and beige craters are autumn on metal. My phone sings a text dingle.

Having thrown on a light olive coloured coat, I exit the studio. The hallway has a geometrical pattern of cubes on the carpet, could be a Lego ad when high. The elevator takes its sweet ass time to serve me, its minutes before I'm at ground level. Leaving the sanctuary of the filtered air building, I'm immediately standing in a cauldron of rancid ether, the blend of so many different smells lights up my brain and furrows my brow in repulsion. Piss, scat and exhaust are the strongest to orbit my senses. A burst of loud, thick coughing to my left. A shoeless, crooked body shuffles by on the other side of the gated fence. Fingers dip inside and explore pockets for protection from public people pronto. A fumble or three, a clawed hand reaches in to pull out headphones and sunglasses; this makes walking around here a breeze. I put on some mindless electro-trash, slide dark lenses in front of my eyes, and forget the world around me.

The patio of the local chic restaurant is a caricature of a caricature of Gastown. Even the flowering potted plants have cigarette butts in them, proving that everyone and everything on street level runs on some sort of chemical stimulation. Geeky tourists mingle with homeless crazies in rags. Wayfarer-wearing hipsters pose for the scene in fedoras while gorgeous women sprinkled about through the crowd are doing what good looking women do best; looking good. Exotic bird coloured dresses remind me of a bowl of Froot Loops. Did I smoke weed today? I can't really remember. Misha and Kiki's laughs can be heard over everyone else sitting, they certainly know how to be seen.

I'm starving. My stomach sends a stab of nausea to remind me of its needs. I don't bother to take my sunglasses off. Pointing at Misha and Kiki at their table, the hipster host responds with some flippant acknowledgement. Misha is in a bright yellow dress, a change from her usual faire of flower prints. Kiki is wearing a leopard print halter top that looks painted on her perfectly round breasts, two monolithically large Caesars sit in front of both women. The human brain amazes me sometimes. Corked away inside of this lump of flesh is a massive network of connected synapses, more complex than anything else in the universe, yet it seeks big tits and a source of inebriation.

My ass crashes into a chair with loose fitting red padding on the seat and arm rests. The black iron frame hot from sitting in the sun, I can't help but see myself as a human waffle.

"Dylen!" Misha greets me with enthusiasm, "You look so skinny!"

Misha remembers me from when I still drank sugar and fat loaded mochas. I would sit at my desk and laugh myself to tears at the gas a mocha and sausage breakfast sandwich would create. A toxic cloud that you could smell in the hallway sometimes, it would chase me from my desk.

"Dill?" Kiki had been trying to get my attention. I must have daydreamed off in public again.

"Yeah, it's all that broccoli!" Blurt out from the idiot hole on my face. Not sure if that fit the conversation, but I'll know soon if it did.

Kiki's face lit up as she leans forward. Her breasts squish together to touch in the middle.

"We are on the soup-only diet. It totally works." Kiki says with a beaming smile.

"Strange thing is, Caesars are considered a soup on this diet. No really!"

She takes a long suck from her straw. Her pillow lips fit around the tube and leave a burgundy hued ring.

Her nude, on top of me, my hands grip her hips to be able to thrust deeper.

A gaunt and pale arm moves in front of my face. The waiter is pointing at a drink on the menu in front of me. His lips move but nothing registers, I'm just picturing Kiki getting fucked.

"Yes one large, please!" I always speak out of turn.

Drink is ordered. Misha and Kiki both order more Caesars. My inner self grins as it recalls the last time Misha and I drank together.

We ended up alone in the kitchen of a late night party, slid my hand up the front of her blue vintage dress. I brought her to a shrieking orgasm against the granite counters in the kitchen, surprised we weren't caught.

Noise of seagulls and crows mix in with the sounds of passing cars, laughter, and conversations on the patio. A green bean hitting me in the face snaps me back to reality.

Misha quips with a giggle, "More late nights there, eh buddy?" She's wiping her guilty throwing fingers on her napkin.

"Getting you to talk used to be easy, you'd never shut up." Misha always loved it when I would bite her neck.

"Kiki and I haven't seen you in ages, and you're just zoning out!"

The waiter is almost at the table, if I can just wait until a little liquor floats in my system before I have to talk, that would be great.

My drink arrives, its honey coloured with two ice cubes. Eager lips lead to an oral flood. Trap door views from the roof of my mouth, the tongue is a fat red whale. Bristling with caramel-toned rum, it surfaces for air while alarms ring in the liver. Down the hatch it goes, I almost choke. Straight rum burns. Somehow by not listening, I ended up ordering a full glass of rum. They must know me here.

"Misha, you're fucking gorgeous, and Kiki; you're a babe." I emphasize 'you're' and point at Kiki while saying this.

I completely ignore talking about my lack of talking.

"I haven't seen you guys either, and when I did, I was stunned. You're both looking so goddamn good." They both smile.

"Kiki decided against getting boobs!" Misha says before a sip of Caesar. Kiki bounces up and down in her chair, smiling and proud of herself.

Living in a cartoon only gets easier with time, or it could be all that kush. The fabric of her tube top looks under so much stress, her breasts collide together in the middle and try to push each other out of their cups. They're the only two sumo wrestlers I'd like to see greased up. I throw my hand in the air to signal a round of high fives, followed by a toast and another large mouthful of rum. I'm glad Kiki didn't get her breasts enlarged even more, and that Misha never got a pair of ugly bolt-on tits. Women with grapefruit sized implants on surf board chests can look like an ugly parody of a woman, a twisted cartoon object of non-femininity. Mental visions of Misha with ruined boobs gives way to that old familiar buzz. The warm, slower talking sensation starts to wash over me. Hard to believe I was celebrating a girl not butchering her perfectly natural body.

Raising my glass in the air, "Another toast, my dears." The girls raise their glasses high. "To not shitting my pants today."

Clink.

The conversation begins to ebb and flow over the topics of food, Kiki's dog and how she needs a new purse. I daydream off with sunglasses on. Eyes relax as golden fall sunshine lazily drapes over my arm and face. Vanilla people bathed in yolk orange rays of light, moles in pale doughy skin as little chocolate chips. Getting a lot of sun could lead to cancer, but mostly just pretty Instagram photos. Long deep breaths purge fumes from my nose. In go several wafts of garlic, seafood and fresh breads as waiters busily pass by. Nodding occasionally to questions over who has cuter shoes, or which perfume smells better, enjoying the moment in every way possible. Misha's leg presses against mine under the table. She is leaning it against me. I move my leg over to push onto her legs and they feel smooth, feminine, and very soft. While Kiki babbles on about herself, my eyes lock with Misha's, we're thinking the same thing.

Kiki excuses herself from the table and clip-clops her way off the sun soaked patio. Misha smiles at me. She's gripping the arm rest and squeezing it tight.

"I didn't think I'd end up hearing from you today." Misha says, as she lets go of the armrest to take her drink in both hands.

She takes a long pull from the straw and empties the glass. The silence of enjoyment is ended with the hollow sucking of dead drink.

"Well, I'm a busy guy, Misha-I think it's been about two weeks since we saw each other last?" I reply.

She is sitting to my right with Kiki's empty chair in front of me. Misha shifts her weight onto her arm rest and whispers softly into my ear:

"Two weeks since I've been fucked properly."

She leans back into her chair, her eyes in a cocky squint. In an instant comes response from my southern brain. She *is* thinking what I'm thinking. My drink magnetizes itself to my hand and my mouth bathes in straight rum.

More clip-clopping shoes herald the return of Kiki. Picturing her as a giant walking pigeon, her awkward steps are only second mate to her captain'ing breasts that lead the rest of her body.

"Mish!" Kiki exclaims, maneuvering her prime booty into her seat. "Guess who texted me?"

Oh the suspense.

"Jorden Vosh!"

Misha is in the middle of having a sip, her brow furrows and she puts down her drink with conviction.

"Jorden called me fat! That guy is such an *asshole*."

I remember Jorden Vosh. He's a local gay male model, one of the city's best. He's a total professional with looks chiseled from marble, my own molded from clay. Met that guy at a party once, his completely friendly and effeminate demeanor hides how he is so socially cold to females competing for attention. I learned what the term 'frenemy' meant to girls after meeting that cruel homo.

Misha spouts off about Jorden for the next ten minutes. Kiki hops in to defend him throughout her rant, but is quickly sorted out through Misha's quick use of her index finger. Her technique to point in people's faces is her often overused method of saying "No, no, NO!" to stagger any verbal duelist. I always found it so fascinating that one person can suggest to a girl that she's overweight and she will bear that cross for eternity. Maybe some women tie in their weight with their sense of self-worth. Recalling the shitty and worthless feeling when I'm broke, and it all makes sense. Lonely ice cubes rotate freely as the last of the rum slides down my throat, just in time to hear Kiki blurt out a frustrated "Oh my fucking god Misha!"

The girls have been bitching for over ten minutes about the context of how Jorden called Misha fat. She has a very nice feminine body. Her toned upper abs could be in a jeans ad. Those tits are a bit saggy in her late 20ies, but look gorgeous watching from below when she is on top. I prefer being on her, with those soft, long tanned legs on my shoulders. Making out with her in my car is one of my most fond memories of her. My hands crept up her inner thighs, feeling like silk on my fingertips. Her jean shorts soaked, her fragrance filling the air. Kiki is intensely texting on her phone, stone faced with glass eyes.

Kiki sighs. "Well, Jorden is not meeting us here anymore. I'm going to walk up and meet him at the Starbucks." Kiki dumping bucket loads of disappointment in her voice.

Misha has her legs crossed, and her elevated leg is kicking the air slowly, half obscured by the table.

"Misha, what are you going to do?" Kiki rarely talks in her serious voice.

It's hard to believe a six month old comment has these two women mad at each other.

"Mish, you should come and check out the new Wosk collection." I casually suggest that in my most sophisticated tone.

I think I slurred the word collection. My mind slips off to think ahead to Misha naked, and I feel my pants squeezing tight against my wedding tackle.

"Do you have any more drinks? I kind of feel like getting fucked up today," Misha says through a sly grin.

My left eyebrow rockets up and I ask her if a leprechaun pimp would own anything green or gold. She chuckles while digging through her purse to pay her bill. Kiki thanks me for coming out and puts barely her share of money on the table. I'll have to cover the tip again. No karma lost in lacking cash as long as you're beautiful. The clothed reed-like waiter collects the money and drops off a few vanilla mint hard candies. They make this particular crinkle when you open them, forever reminding me of satisfied stomachs. I unwrap one, toss it in the air and catch it in my mouth. Lingering rum mixes with candy, a cold sweet vanilla breeze.

Walking up the street together, Misha's bright dress contrasts sharply against unwashed awnings and the grimey sidewalk. A bum in camo pants and a stained green sweater is pawing through trash, his greasy hair stays flat on his head as he turns and spots Misha. A yellow smile hides in a ring of matted fur and tangled beard. Bob the painter must have found a happy little crack pipe. Misha ignores him with a polite but not very kind smile in the opposite direction; as we pass by a waft of intense BO assaults my senses. I tend to bitch about the smells and people I'm subjected to by living in a neighborhood like this, yet the raw nature is refreshing. In a world of plastic trees, photoshop, warm lighting, and flawless skin, it's an oasis of unadulterated humanity.

Misha almost dances as she walks, passing by a patio and heads are showing an obvious focus on her. Around the corner and quarter block in, we arrive at my building. A beep greets me as my hand swipes the key card and the metal gate unlocks. Misha goes first, my drunk hand pats her tight little ass on the way in. Through the courtyard to the front door of the condo block, beep, and the steel doors of the elevators gleam in the otherwise dull former warehouse.

Blood-coloured light erupts from the 5 button, and the elevator hums to life. Refurbished lofts don't feature German engineering, the elevator rides a little smoother than square wheels down a hill during an earthquake. Swaying and shuddering, the old lift matters less as Misha lures me in with beckoning eyes. My shoulder brushes up against the side door. Two lights up on the elevator's display screen. In the corner, Misha holds onto both railings, one long leg slides up onto the bar to her right. Barely covering her upper thighs, Misha's bright yellow dress rides up to reveal a hint of panty. Tucking her chin down towards her chest, those big green eyes beam sensuality.

"What about this have you missed?" She says with a pout. My eyes lock with hers.

I straighten up my back against the wall, as much as someone who drank a glass of rum on an empty stomach can.

"I miss watching you slide up and down me, while I watch it in the mirror."

Her tight little ass and how hot it was is still fresh in my mind, the way it bounced up and down in the reflection. Her right leg is laid out on the railing, her tiny red painted toes wiggling with excitement. I don't waste a moment of time, hormones and ego force me down on one knee to kiss her thigh softly. My right arm reaches over and helps her left leg onto the other rail. Looking up at her face and she has her eyes closed with her head tilted up. Horny bodies breathe shallow, teasing sensations sigh deep. Pulling her skirt up a few inches and my tongue runs along her inner thigh. Exhaling slowly as I go, blowing soft puffs of cool air on the tongue's trail. Slowly now, breathing hot air onto the same spot.

Moving my mouth to her right leg, my tongue finds the outside seam of her panties. Her natural fragrance is intense and sweet smelling. Flicking tongue darts between panty and skin, just enough that I taste her. She must have been needing this. The elevator stops, soon after Misha jumps over me in an awkward leapfrog.

"Ereaak!" Misha half-giggles, half-yelps.

Springing to my feet and I have no idea how long we've had an audience. A couple is standing in front of us and waiting semi-patiently. Who knows if it was our obvious adult elevator play, or my stark erection, but their faces disapprove without speech.

When drinking my steps change styles while words become slurs more spit than spoken. Feet lose their utility to find style and swagger in strutting. Everything changes a little on the sauce, smiles curl deeper as eyes dart below necklines. Drunken walks through the building have my feet seeking to step on only green squares of the hallway's patterned floor. On my first walkthrough before renting here I thought it was a schizophrenic chess board. Misha watches in amusement as I stretch, hop, lunge, and bounce around the corridor. Insane pawn movement disobeys all the rules of adult behavior. Just before we get to my door, I stop, turn to her, grab her hand and spin her around. Her dress flows around her body and her face beams with a grin.

Reaching inside my pocket for the keys, the silver one is a snug fit in the lock. There's irony in keys, much like my penis, they are meant to be put inside things. My dick makes a poor key, fitting inside many locks but never opening anything. Keys without purpose keep doors closed. This jagged metal finds its home, the door opens, and Misha trails behind me. An old pair of my underwear sits by the front door. Without any surprise, spaced out people sometimes space out on this shit. Fuck it. An obvious high step over them and maybe she'll smile.

A hasty beeline to the fridge and from the freezer emerges a twixer of spiced rum. Tucking the bottle under my arm, two spare hands find bottles of orange juice and a club soda. Misha is sitting on a bar stool patiently. An eager slide through the curtained border between business and pleasure, an important delivery for sure. Eye contact kept as I walk up to put the bottles down on the black glass bar. One might wonder what a bar is doing in an office space, but when you work with artists, liquor and drugs are frequent and close co-workers. Misha picks up a crystal glass and rubs around the rim with her finger. It hums and she twirls the glass intently. I don't have time to waste waiting for her to put it down. My head rocks back for rum, a mouthful straight from the bottle. Warmth felt. Two fingers of mine pinch the vessel from Misha's hand and pour her a Gastown Punch. Half orange juice and equal parts club soda, add spiced rum. I pour one for myself, no cherry garnish as alcohol aesthetics aren't important when you're trying to get shitfaced.

A clink of glass and a toast to nothing we've discussed. Popsicle-like flavour washes over my mouth, tangy and sweet, perfect for kissing. Stumblean posture pulls me down over the bar and my lips find Misha's. She kisses me back hard before giggling after our lips touch for the third time. When her mouth opens her soft tongue thrashes around against mine. She reaches forward and pulls on my shirt, a faint moan erupts from her. Our lips unlock and she breathes out heavily. My war spear rigid with the anticipation of the moment it will be coated in bitch dew. Misha doesn't hesitate, and slams her drink back in two mouthfuls. Mine is downed in three. She slides out of the barstool and looks around the room.

A purple leather couch is directly in the middle of the business section, facing a large computer monitor. I must have been doing a presentation again that I forgot about, the middle of the room is usually reserved for art. Misha slowly walks over to the couch and crawls onto it seductively. She is on her elbows and knees, looking back at me with a coy smile from over her shoulder. It's time to see if there is still some fire to all of this smoke.

4 Tastes Like Copper

Three beeps of the alarm, two seconds of dead air and a single thud marks the passing of tonight's girlfriend. Whipping my arm around and releasing, the fluids-rag flies overhand into the laundry basket, nothing but net. The couch is folded out and I'm sprawled across it nude. The leather under me is warm, I must have fallen asleep. The only sound a whirring of the bathroom fan. A louvered saint of exhaust, I owe those spinning blades so much for putting up with my shit. Sometimes its switch gets neglected and it drones on for days.

I'm cold. My mother always used to tell me to put on a sweater and socks if I thought the house was chilly. That kid grew into a teenager and began thinking of this as a sign of poverty. A perpetually young adult living on his own and discovering a toasty house can cost a few hundred bucks per month.

This man shivers.

Cool air settles on my chest and face. As the colours dance on my eyelids, I try and hold onto the endorphin high from sex a little bit longer. Imagination theater or a memory tour, the curtains that serve to keep both hidden are pulled apart by fatigue. They open when my eyes are closed, in moments I recognize green iron and the white lights of the Lion's Gate Bridge.

It's late and I'm driving, she's riding with me. You know which one Dylen, the one with the haunted eyes and demure movements. If a cat could ballet, she would be a Persian in point shoes. My little Dark Heart would put a black swan to shame.

My balls itch. The remnants of my date and I form a cracked and flaking shell of lust on my pelvis and thighs. Waxing poetic just felt so wrong when I'm covered in another woman. My head falls to one side as I exhale a little deeper, my chin sand papering my shoulder. Only a little while ago her moist and bronze legs held that space, shaking and pushing against me with each thrust. Flashes of the sex I just had battle my muse for attention, swollen rose ruffles of Misha's vagina lips fade to midnight and city lights.

I've tried to forget how I stopped the car in the middle of the bridge. There were no cars in sight, nothing in my rearview. Hard to believe what she had just said. She told me she felt guilty that I always paid for the gas to drive around with her. No way did I believe my ears. How could she think I didn't like to drive with her? It was always my pleasure to have her company. The shit she said next still shakes chains in my attic. "I would be here with you without a car, even if you had to double me on a bike, or walk with me, I just like your company." She must have had too much to drink. I can't remember if she even drank much that night. It's easier on my conscience believing she had.

Sticking your tongue inside a girl is always a game of Russian roulette. You almost never quite know when she showered last, or what sort of diet she has kept lately. Vegans and vegetarians, now they have a light, pleasant taste without the same thickness meat eaters have. This one takes care of herself. Vivid visions of just fucking Misha swim and mix with missing what felt like was a former part of me. Leather and sharp nails, Misha grabs the back of my head and her body shudders. She accidentally brings her heel down hard on my back, I cough into her groin. She giggles. My tongue finds the hood, ducks inside, and does its best flag in a gale. My left arm reaches up to knead one soft breast. She bites and gently sucks on my index finger. A rock hard nipple pokes into the center of my palm. Animalistic instincts guide my body against hers.

They say if you have a real bad trip on acid, you never quite recover. I'm getting over being lovesick with every little fuck, or at least I think I am. Now I only reminisce about her after fucking another girl, and not every time I drink anymore.

I still don't remember turning the car off, only that I had silenced the radio so we could talk. Images from the past boil in the cauldron of a drowsy mind. I hear the sounds of the ocean below, the breeze from the open sunroof plays with my hair. Leaning in and kissing her. Lips of heat and concentrated sensuality, warmth of her love spreads through my face. Touching her cheek, thumb brushes her ear, and back through her black hair. There was always some energy when I felt her, genes feeling friendly to her essence of being. I don't know how long this spontaneous passion lasted, but when we unlocked our faces, neither of us could catch our breath. Two genuine smiles. Headlights in my mirror hint to move the car.

The soft leather steering wheel in my hands turns into feminine hips. I'm behind Misha's beautiful and round ass. These cheeks have just enough bounce and wiggle for Surrey yet small enough to fit in around Yaletown. Earlier I put baby oil on my hands and slapped her bottom a flush pink. The lights above give off a shine on each cheek. Memories of headlights casting loving silhouettes of our embrace, the moment was interrupted but never forgotten.

I post my right arm down and reach for a handful of hair. She moans as I begin to thrust extra hard using my grip on her as leverage. She reaches back and jabs her nails into my leg. Hot razors accompany her moans that almost growl at me. She sits up and back, forcing me to sit on my heels. The baby oil is slippery enough she can grind my lap with lustful ferocity. She's frantic and losing her rhythm, I push back with force and keep the tempo up. She reaches back with her other hand and digs another sex claw into my upper thigh near the hip. I'll bleed from this one for sure.

Her head tilts up and she gasps, her body starts to shake. I seize the moment and push her forward, one leg over her hip and fuck her. I give her a pounding as deep, hard, and fast as I can. She shakes and cries out one last time as we both come to a sweat soaked, spent finish. There is no condom because she's on the pill, neither of us caring about ourselves enough to bother with rubber anymore. I used to dread getting tested, I laugh at clean results and dare myself to fuck dirtier.

The drive to her house was lost under a black moon. A long ago blur of emotion stepped on with time. Maybe the peak moment stuttered my brain into forgetting the next hour. I dropped her off, kissed her goodnight, and drove home stunned. Was I being gamed? Who says that to someone after so little time of knowing them? Surely something was wrong with her. After all, at this point, we hadn't even fucked. We just really liked to talk and make out. We talked about everything together and hid nothing, maybe except for how she made me feel. Hours and hours spent in bed that night trying to block her out proved useless. I didn't need that in my life. My life, not hers, or ours, mine.

I'm alone again now. A single drop of water hits tile in my shower. Leaking slowly, I could imagine it on my forehead ten thousand times. Sitting up and the sticky leather laments me with a fart-like pfft. Even my furniture is disappointed in me. Where are my pants? Found my underwear next to the couch. Lacking any energy, my best effort is to slowly elevate them up my leg. Short shorts bring me back to the yodeling climber on The Price is Right. Loved that game show as a kid, keep your pets spayed and neutered. I attempt a yodel and pull the elastic band up to my belly button, it crushes my nuts and I laugh. A few ball smashing steps into my kitchen and the elastic band gets yanked down to my hips.

My dry tongue seeks some relief in glasses of cold water. Then another gulped back. The musky female scent is on me, and it turns me on a bit. Finishing my second cold glass, I step over to the toilet to complete the process of converting rum to urine. Takes me two minutes to brush my teeth and pick a small zit off my neck. I look content yet empty. Sometimes she still crosses my mind. Where could she be? Can't help but start laughing about why it was so easy to fuck a girl I don't like, and so hard to think about one I do. An army style salute to myself in the mirror followed by a fucked up thumbs up, what an accomplishment. Way to go buddy. Fuck it all, I'm going to bed.

5 A Thing For Redheads

Morning sounds like Apple when waking up to messages incoming. My eyes are reluctantly awake as a giant fart bloats inside of me ready to rip out. No hangover, yesterday's mission successful. My iPhone lights up with a half dozen texts, one from a particular redhead I've been missing. Finally a reply, been weeks since I've heard from her.

I met this girl after Game 2 of the Stanley Cup final, both of us riding the high of the win. Her and I aren't big into sports, but love to be immersed in the sea of euphoria coming from joyous Canucks fans. My bill that night was over two hundred dollars, my friend Dougie's nearly twice that.

We took a bunch of people to my house after the bar closed and we partied all night. She tried M for the first time, her moans woke up the few remaining stragglers passed out on the studio's opposite side. I kept getting text messages from my friends asking me who the hell that was after sneaking out of my place during our bawdy early morning romp. We woke up, threw on clothes, and walked through a light rain to a luxurious cafe called Medina. An orgy of breakfast ensued, butter and maple syrup covered waffles so light that they melt in your mouth the way a fresh baked Krispy Kreme does. Washed down with orange juice, the last bite was perfectly filling to the point where I considered never eating again. The bill was pretty big, but I soon forgot about it when she suggested returning to the studio for a post-waffle fuck.

She was downtown for when the Game 7 riots kicked off, her worried voice on my phone sprung me into action. I found her alone after she got split up from her friends near Richards and Dunsmuir. There were fights going on everywhere, glass breaking and fires started. Mobs ran wild in an urban battlefield, sacking and looting what they could. What a rush it was to kiss her in doorways, hidden from mobs of police and disaffected youth. Tear gas watering our eyes, the danger making it that much more exciting.

We meandered back down to Gastown, acrid air biting into our noses, our ears filled with sirens, screaming, and chaos. Back to the safety of my studio, we enjoyed cold beer, joints, kissing, and live coverage on CTV. As the stream played on detailing the destruction wrought by modern barbarians, her moans filled the studio as I vandalized her vagina. Remembering that night, her passing out naked on my chest, her hair smelled of smoke.

We kept seeing each other off and on towards the trailing end of summer. I'd pick her up late at night after work, the windows down letting in a luke warm autumn breeze. Stealing kisses when she got in, strawberry chapstick had me wanting more. Many times we ended up in her bed smoking joints and watching Flight of the Conchords, playing scrabble and having sweaty sex. We'd drink morning coffee and share the newspaper; she always poured mine in the broken-handled mug.

A couple days ago I received a notice from BMW that my car lease was almost over. It's pretty cold out, so recapturing her hair blowing softly while embraced in a kiss wasn't going to happen. At least I don't have to take a cab to see her just yet.

Her text reads: Hey D, I've been soooooo busy with work. I'd love to see you tonight if you could pick me up at 11. I'm going to be SO tired so we're going to have to go to bed pretty fast, but at least we can spend some time together right? Let me know ciao.

Happy fingers text her back and confirm I'll be there.

Maybe I should be excited, but I'm not. My face visits with the razor and a long shower de-stinks me. Thoughts are wandering all over the place but eventually come back to the realization that I'm just killing time. Yeah, she is a pretty good looking woman and intelligent enough to stimulate my mind, but the interaction we have is completely unromantic. Sure, we kiss, make out, embrace, cuddle, fondle and fuck, but so do hookers and johns. The assumption that this means anything beyond pleasurable fluid swapping can be thrown out in this modern, meaningless hookup age we live in. Me myself and I are going to need some liquor to slow these bursts of anxiety down. I wash my hair and the fragrances bring me a little calm. Nice work focus group. Sitting cross legged in the shower and breathing slow, haven't tried to meditate in years and my mind is far too derailed to start now.

Twisting stainless ceases the shower. While stepping out to dry myself, my dulled reflection catches my eye in the steamed mirror. A pinkish blob of nondescript features stare back at me.

Hair, arms, legs and cock, this could be anyone.

I comb my hair back with the towel around me and wonder, how many other men are getting ready to visit a girl they have no real long term interest in? My hairline has receded over the last few years and I'm going grey. My bank account has retracted while my waistline expanded, the implications of this are that I should be glad that women pay any attention to me or my dick at all. Without a goal or shared cause of society, we're all just out for our own motivations. There's no current to guide me. No soft hand on my shoulder giving me direction, or even any pressure to do anything but drink and fuck. There are no taboos except for speaking up on the suicide of western exceptionalism. What are we doing, and what is the plan?

Everything feels like a race for the bottom, I wish I had the integrity to care. Instead, even I sell porn and fuel the commodification of women and erosion of traditional femininity. Women seen as less than our sisters, mothers, daughters and more as things to stick our cocks into. Making money has never been easier either, playing to their insecurities to profit from, porn snatching cash from leering voyeurs, tits and ass promoting products and lifestyles. The fact that I'm visiting this girl as something to do and not someone to romance feels wrong, but I can't stop.

Fresh underwear, dry socks, and day old clothing fit the bill for tonight. I'm not quite clean shaven, but my facial hair is shorter than it normally is. It wasn't my plan—I tripped over the electric razor cord while drunk and broke it. Facebook and Twitter are great ways to murder time, as I have hours to waste before picking her up. Glancing through articles on Vancouver–cuts to the park services, partitioned basement suites in East Van are selling for six hundred grand, an article on how Vancouver is still a great real estate investment. Has anyone else noticed it was written by Real Estate agents? Picturing the Marlboro Man telling me to smoke cigarettes, they're healthy for you, while dying in a bed of emphysema. Embers of a slowly burning white cigarette poke out from a hole in his neck, to defile your temple like that makes for some elegant death erotica.

A woman posts a photo of her closet. Stacks of boxes full of high-end shoes show off status as comments of unabashed sycophancy follow in the comment stream. Yes, those are real Jimmy Chus. Yes, she has 30 pairs. No, she can't decide which to wear tonight. It used to be a mystery to me why anyone would need or want dozens and dozens of expensive shoes. A few lessons on how socializing works and the social ranking she gets from those shoes will become unmistakable.

Someone posts a link about Chris Brown hooking up with Rihanna. I'm not surprised. Chris Brown could spend the rest of his life offering to fly women from all over the world to meet up with him, and fuck a new beautiful girl daily, perhaps hourly, until he dies. This power, this allure to Rihanna, must be all-encompassing. Women like her would never want the stable provider beta, or even a low status ultra-alpha. They want the danger, the status of being one of his chosen ones in the inner stable of available poon. The threat of being beaten just means he likes you and cares enough about you to hurt you if you leave. That mystical power of the highest status men, once a woman has a taste of it, no other man is good enough for her. Picturing a date with Monica Lewinski, I laugh a little. Once she's sucked off the president of the most powerful nation on earth, no other lowly male could ever live up to that.

Most of the bullshit posted by people just disgusts me. All I want is one link, maybe a 'Cure for cancer found' or 'Mars colony ship under construction', instead finding myself whipping the scroll wheel faster and faster. Childish memes, many posts shitting all over religion, men posting images of nearly naked women and people drunk while giving the camera the middle finger. This is my generation, and these are the role models for the next.

Are there any consequences to such a lowest common denominator? Everyone seems to agree that drinking, drugs, casual sex and hating on traditions is good, meanwhile striving for moral excellence is the path of the self-righteous asshole. I know that hooking up with random sluts is probably not being exceptional, but rather now, the norm. A girl I used to be friends with has a photo up of her deep throating a beer bottle and giving the middle finger as her profile photo. I want to tell her to get some class, uphold some level of civility, but coming from someone like me is just hypocritical. The result of all of this degradation of standards and behavior is pretty evident in my own life, no path, no direction and no goals.

Will my generation achieve anything of wonder for the ages?

Will I?

The Pyramids are still standing, the constitution of the United States still holds its ink. The Taj Mahal, the Great Wall of China, the Colosseum of Rome, Apollo 8. I grew up watching Star Trek and being captivated by the future, it now looks more like the movie Idiocracy. Animalistic humans cobbled together united only the laws of the nation-state. Savage instincts guiding them toward gratification in the moment with lust to tear down anything that doesn't appeal to all. Whatever, maybe it's not what I think, but what I actually do. Maybe my purpose is to keep myself, and those who I care about, from becoming like that.

A heavy sigh and X gets clicked to put some brakes on the bad news express.

Enough with the world hating, I'm going to get some pussy.

6 Boost

I'm going to miss this car. The steering wheel is soft leather and oh-so precise in its feel. BMW makes a wonderful automobile and farting into the
leather is satisfying on its own. High intensity lights chase away the night
as twin turbos carry me from green lights in a whispered whoosh of spool.
The stereo booms with the sunroof open to the moon, hand-winging the
air, some magical moments of car ownership. All the way up Main Street
is where she works, our meeting spot just off a quiet side street. Pulling
over the car to park and I notice she's not here yet. Buttons on the steering
wheel help me to conveniently turn on the radio which quickly floods
my ears with carefully engineered bullshit.

Heavily auto tuned music thuds and jives about love in a night club,
drilling the funk into my ears with the subtly of a jackhammer.

"Baby you're fiiii-iinnnnee and I waaaaant to take you ho-oh-omm-
mmme."

Heavy bass follows with several "Yeah!" from Lil Jon punctuating
the beat.

During these moments, bashing my head against the steering wheel
seems like a good idea. Why doesn't he sing the truth?

"Baby I find you highly attractive and I want to have sex with you
tonight for no other reason than you're attractive and available."

Fuck.

More head nodding, less thinking about the lyrics.

Streetlights bathing pavement in pale creamsicle orange, every car
looks black or grey in this light. A couple walking their dog gives me shifty
glances as they stroll by. They probably think I'm picking up drugs. She
gets me high, costs nothing, and her loving is a natural health product. If

only my love was as organic as hers. A lone shadow skulks up the sidewalk at the end of the street, short with boobs, it's her. She has a little happy bob when she walks, full of life and carrying kisses to me.

At halfway up the block I see her face, she's smiling as usual. Stepping out of my car, she walks into my arms for a big hug. Her hair carries scents of juniper and sandalwood, her cold little hands slip into my coat and tickle for a moment. I leave her embrace and open her door. She says she's so tired and her eyes wait only a few seconds before closing, her petite head resting so peacefully in the optional BMW sport seats. A precise click follows a press of the seat heating button, the warmth from the car as my surrogate for love.

These streets teem with freaks. From Main to Broadway, Broadway onto Commercial, through the lively night rolls four wheels of dead animal and alloys, driving a little slower when the redhead nods off. Turbo purring underhood, engine noise a masculine appetizer for sex, the underpass of the SkyTrain station works to amplify the six cylinder and four stroke concert. Wafting pot smoke fills the car, probably from the group of hackey-sackers loitering in a small park.

You have to be high to kick a ball around this late.

Xenon lights make the shirtless and screaming guy that just sprinted across my path look pale, while further down a group of longboarders rips it across 1st Avenue. She's asleep peacefully and I drive slow not to disturb her, my foot gets a little heavy on Hastings and the car rockets deeper into foreign east side territory. Just as I get ready to make a left onto her block, a fist fight breaks out at the 7-11 on Hastings. The teenage homey kid inside me still cheers for the skater kid to win over the skid, despite the number of fights I got in as a kid against skaters. Pulling up to her house and I have to gently wake her, the heart can't help but feel a precious tingle smiling at the little drool she left on the leather.

A short yawn-filled walk to her apartment's outside foyer, she fumbles with her keys and takes three tries to open the door.

Cheap rent usually means buzzing fluorescent lights in ceilings above brass mailboxes.

Refusing to reminisce and dragging myself down her hallway, my nose bathes in stale cigarettes and dog fur. Harking back to my own days of poverty, living on under a thousand per month for everything. After paying rent, canned foods joined yellow packs of bologna and Wonderbread as staples of my life. Before the Internet, I never learned to live better. Her little hands have woken up and we get into her place on the first try. Closing the door behind me, she's almost in her bedroom already. Trying to navigate her cluttered apartment in the dark proves as difficult as having savings in Vancouver. Blind steps and wide shoulders collide to tag-team a painting to the floor. I trust the direction my cock leads me, a vagina positioning instinct leading to her room without any-more impromptu interior design. She's mostly dressed and already fully asleep. Bedroom window curtains casting streetlight shadows to give her skin a chalky tone. Her lips a moist, pale grey. Climbing in next to her, the comforter lacks any comfort other than warmth. Even though I'm next to her, I still feel so alone.

7 Empty Is the New Full

The world is such a noisy place when your eyes first stir in the morning. Two slits twitch a few times before shutting again. Pipes rattling, a glass of water filled, maybe. The rapid buzz of a ten-speed being back pedaled throws an unwelcome wave in my tranquil pond of slumber. Some green asshole is recycling, a few bottles clank together, the shitty, cheap scratching of blue bin plastic dragged on asphalt. Right now my sleep takes priority over the earth. A bird chirps a happy little tune to remind me of what a prick I am.

The scent of coffee mixed with the pillow, pretty hair with mocha, almost. Weight shifts on the bed and I can feel a hand gently peel back the blanket covering my face. Sunlight tears in through the window and proceeds to bounce off the walls before finding a home in my retinas. Slamming shut my eyes as hard as I can, but to no use. Daisy yellow tones burst through tired eyelids, morning needs to only wait for my surrender.

The red haired girl has her hand on my side and brings a steaming cup close to my face. Precious caffeine filled brew wafts aggressively to chase off the scent of pillow sweat. A mumble of thanks, my body curls up slowly to tuck the pillow into my armpit. Leaning onto my side, she passes me the broken-handled mug and beams a 'good morning!' Ignoring her wasn't my plan, but etiquette and thoughtful behavior are best found in the reflection at the bottom of the first empty mug.

A few large mouthfuls and I'm spotting my has-been face blurry on wet ceramic, my tongue burnt and palate unsatisfied. Her smile makes up for the cheap, syrupy chocolate aftertaste. That same 7-11 ghetto gourmet from my truck driving days. Being 19 was a lifetime ago now, sucks how the coffee hasn't improved much in my life. She comments on how fast

I drink, I smile and put my right arm around her and pull her close for a quick peck.

"Eww, Coffee AND morning breath, gross!" she squeals, jumping off the bed.

"Come on, I have things to do today!" She says, turning around to walk out the bedroom door.

She's maybe 5'4, with a spunky demeanor, red hair just under her shoulders, a wide set of hips, small waist accented by a pierced belly button; and some nice legs. Two giant perfectly perky breasts, spotted pink and peach nipples any man would love to suck on. She is really shy in bed, unless she's on M. A bad man introduced her to it. I may have felt guilty the next day if her body and sex weren't so mind blowing.

Naked and not intending to dress soon, but there is no way she's coming back in here as long as my breath still reeks. I stumble out of bed, knocking over a glass of water and muttering 'shat' half comically. One step and already some shit got fucked up, this wouldn't bode well if I still cared about being good, but she won't notice the carpet lake anyways. Out of her bedroom, I hop over a pile of shoes spilling from her closet spaced between her room and the bathroom. It looks like a volcano of dirty flats, hiking shoes, and loafers. My curiosity bends over and places a pair of red high heels down the side of the round pile. Lava, I snicker as I credit myself with the first artistic vision of the day.

A gleeful hop into her tiny bathroom, scanning the counter for the green toothbrush she bought for me. Nice girl. I pearl up my whites and check my breath, a human mojito, or laundry detergent, something in between those. A smell wafting off me, a faint odour of her bed lingers on my body. That mild sweet female scent, no doubt there are pheromones that I can't perceive influencing my mind. The immediate reaction of getting turned on tossing my train of thought into a flaming wreck at the bottom of a sharp, steep curve. The pipes rattle as I brush and rinse, I'm sure she can hear it. Rinsing my mouth out a final time, a breath check once before giving a stupid grin in the mirror.

Stepping out of her bathroom, her striking figure catches my attention. She's smoking a cigarette on her balcony, a hint of underbreast peeking out from under her tank top. She has her back against the side of the sliding glass door frame, her side profile makes her breasts look huge. Thin white legs with toned muscle are propping her up, my eyes catching shadows under her slightly stiff nipples. Her striking crimson hair blows in a light breeze, my imagination sums up life as an x-rated Aerosmith video from the 90s. The sun is already high in the air and casts a glow on top of her head, shadows play on her face. She must have felt my gaze and turns her head to look me in the eyes. Smling, she asks if I still believe in pants. With a giggle I smile back and say nothing, dart into her bedroom, and jump into her bed. I'm laying naked under the covers, the excitement of exhibitionism stirs in me and the anticipation is very arousing. I know what I'm going to do when she walks in here.

Just as I'm ready to ask if she's chain-smoking the whole pack, she steps into her room. Squish.

She looks down at her now-wet sock with a horrified look on her face. Sitting up in bed, my hand reaches out to grab her. She's scowling at the carpet in a pose of frantic dismay. Stretching forward with the blanket over me, a tug on her shirt gently pulls her into bed. She laughs landing on her back next to me, knees up to her belly, her wet-socked leg high in the air.

"Uhnn! Ahh! Take it off!"

One of our first conversations we agreed how much wet socks feel nasty when worn. Grabbing her other leg with a grin, and off comes the non-wet sock. She turns her head and frowns. I pull up her shirt to reveal her beautiful natural breasts, fingers tracing lazy circles down smooth belly skin in search of jean shorts and a way inside. Her hand finds mine to pull it away from her pants and she pulls down her shirt.

An errant few hairs fall from her bangs into her face. She blows it back up with mildly frustrated gusto followed by a smirk.

"Really? REALLY?" she says, "I bring you coffee in bed and you spill my water. I step in it and instead of pulling off my wet sock you try and undress me!"

I was only undressing her in alphabetical order.

She laughs. "Tank top comes after shorts." she snorts, as she takes a pillow and puts it under her head.

My excuse becomes, on pretty girls, anything worn as a top becomes a blouse.

"You're such an idiot!"

She smiles.

Grinning, I lean in for a kiss, her tongue finds mine and my body reacts fast. My left arm slides under her pillow and half on top of her, kissing her while my right arm finds her chest. My index finger and thumb start to slowly pinch and twist her left nipple and our face sucking ramps up passionately. A bite of her upper lip and she exhales hard. She tilts her head back and sticks her lower lip out. My teeth grab onto it briefly, the nicer side of me choosing to give it a suck instead of a bite. I like to keep her guessing.

Letting go of her nipple, my hand reaches up to brush hair from her face. Tucking it behind her ear causes her to sigh, her face relaxing while my fingers caress the nape of her neck. Her head turns towards me slowly and her lips beckon me closer. Slow kisses and soft bites of her ear, working down to her shoulders I feel her back rise and fall on the bed, writhing with desire. My right hand kneads her breasts and she lets out another small gasp. My mouth meanders down towards her right mound, the beautiful pink and peach nipple standing up for some needed attention. Horny lips find it, my tongue rolling over to tease her before grinding it lightly with my back teeth.

Alternating the sucking with a gentle biting, an excited beast's paw rips open the button on her shorts. They quickly open and my finger crawls down and makes a tunnel into her panties. She grabs my hair and gives an 'ooh' as my mouth works her nipple faster and faster. A probing hand fully enters her panties, my middle finger finds her sweet spot already drenched with excitement. Exploring digits find the hood and peel it back between my index and ring finger, my middle puts on the pressure and I rub in sync with the biting and playing on her nipple.

"Oh, oh my ... I have to leave for work.. Soo ... soon..." Her voice trails off those last few words.

I stop playing with her clit and slowly start penetrating her with my middle finger. She arches her back again, bashing her breasts into my face. Moving up a little to run my mouth down her chest, I dot kisses from her breasts to her panty line. My finger is halfway inside giving a come-hither motion. She pushes her knees together while her feet splay out to the sides, her eyes closed, with her mouth open and breathing hard. My left arm pulls on her shorts and she uses both of her arms, arching her back to pull off her pants and panties with one move, then off with her top. She falls back onto the bed to spread her legs wide, my finger finding its way back inside. Both of her hands clench the sheets. Her face is turning red while fingers wiggle inside, sliding in and out of her as far as they can. I speed up and she turns her head towards me and opens her eyes, her expression one of an erotic agony.

Warm juices are flowing down my finger and onto the back of my hand. I feel her lips and muscles tighten and loosen in rhythm. Her pussy tightens at quicker intervals, matching the speed and depth at which I penetrate her. The odour of her wetness, the sight of her tight body dancing with pleasure; the sound of her moans hit me on a primal level. The hairs on the back of my neck are standing as I am fully in the moment. An animal. Fucking.

"Right there, that's it ... Don't stop," she purrs, her eyes widen as she tilts her head up. Her body goes tense as she lets out another gasp.

"I ... Have to work, you ... Come fuck me now or ... Or I will be late" she stammers in between breaths.

I had been too caught up pleasuring her to notice my pre-cum all over her blanket. She is shaking with pleasure as she reaches out with her feet to my hips, pulling me in.

"Come here, come," she whispers.

I nearly fall on top of her and the head of my cock rests against her, pointing up towards her belly button.

"If you want to cum you need to do it now, I have work in 30 minutes." She smiles and wiggles her hips up, trying to get me inside her.

As her red pubic hair tickles the bottom half of my shaft, my hips twitch uncontrollably away from her. The tip of my penis lands right on her clit and her face shows delight. Tingling with excitement and pulling back just a little more, the soaking opening of her blooming bubble-gum pussy moistens my better head. Wasting no time, I push it halfway in, and with simultaneous moans and shudders, our bodies come together to ram it inside. Squeezing her legs on me tight, she tenses up and grinds our pubic bones together.

"Hurry, I'm not used to getting it... like this..."

With her legs on my shoulders, watching myself slide in and out at a fast pace. Her girl parts are moist and delicious looking. Very stimulated, her nearly-fuschia toned lips are wreathed in milky white skin, an orangey tuft of prickly hair neatly trimmed above it. Her legs are so soft, holding onto them I appreciate their supple, shammy feel. Working to thrust hard and fast, in minutes I'm breathing heavy and dripping sweat onto her. She is holding her headboard, shaking it with every moan.

"I'll be late, finish ... Last chance!" she yells, I think she's serious.

I pull out and push on her leg to roll her over.

"Finish like this, inside me, you have two minutes."

She positions her wide hips in the air, grabs the headboard with both hands, and rests her head down on its side.

She's presenting herself in a completely submissive position with her head down and her genitals exposed right to my face. Her tiny blushing asshole and pussy are both soaked in our combined sex wax. Her gorgeous, round ass soon receives a light smack, to which she demands I put it in. Moving to stand up on my knees and grabbing a hand full of my cock to line up the head, locked on target. My penis slides in gently and I lean back to watch the lips of her body bring me into orgasm. Her wide, bountiful hips charm my mind and I soon feel a pulsing sensation in my scrotum. It begins to fill my body with electrical sensations and a slap lands on her ass once more. She feels the early pulses of my orgasm about to arrive, her demands that I finish growing louder.

"Yes, yes, fucking do it, fill me!" The redheaded trollop screams.

Trying to grant her frantic wish, I fuck her as hard and as deep as I can. Sliding inside her and pulling all the way back, stabbing forward to split her inner goddess in half. Just as the pain from my pubic bone ramming hers grows to a near intolerable level, I erupt inside her with one last push to the hilt. Gifting her a little bit of me with each throb, after a dozen the sex feels complete. She quietly gasps, her own body squeezing down on me almost to help receive the sticky gift. Feeling the last of our mutual spasms, I crash down next to her in bed, sweat and sex fluids soak into the sheets for her to remember me by.

Moments later, she's up and my clothing is thrown onto me. I put it on without wiping myself off and I soon regret the feeling of wearing a giant wet sock for a shirt. She frantically gets dressed and we power walk to my car. The conversation on the ride there is upbeat and light hearted, save for one comment. She smiles and flicks smoke ash out of the passenger window.

"I don't think I've ever been used for sex before." She casually rolls it off her tongue while we're at a light.

I didn't say anything, never having really thought of what she was to me. I guess if you don't think of what a girl means to you, she can't mean much. Ruminating over this after dropping her off, it's hard to shake the feeling that we're just using each other. It sort of hits me in the Starbucks drive-thru line up. Of course I'm using her for sex, as much as she uses me. I live in a city where it would take me ten years to afford a down payment on a house, and that's if I cut back my lifestyle so I live in poverty while saving. Housing prices will probably go up faster than my savings can grow. What can I possibly fucking offer a girl besides my dick?

8 Something For Nothing

My mind wanders over whether or not my fluid transaction of the morning was full of purpose or just temporary pleasure. Yeah, I do find her eloquent in speech, perky, satisfying, and with a touch of class. Her dad probably spends time with her and shows he cares about her. The car jerks forward and spits out a ca-chunk of a less than elegant mechanical diarrhea. I stalled the car. The left foot gets lazy on the clutch when I'm drive dreaming.

I push the start button. A pleasant, subtle vroom alerts me to the engine running. You used to have to actually turn a key, push the gas pedal in, and wait for the engine to fire. Now getting a car started mirrors dating; one poke and we're ready to move on. Ease up on the clutch, inch the car forward, stop. I'm now giving a purple rectangle paper to a yellow haired girl for a white cup of brown fluid and a few silver circles of beaver, boats, and moose. Her smile through the drive thru window is perfect and my customer experience is magical. If I could stretch out our ten seconds of bliss into a relationship that would be equally as happy, I'd have it made. Maybe my eyes would learn to not even notice her chipped tooth or imperfect left eyebrow. Who knows, someone in love could even grow to adore those flaws. A steaming cup from her hand to mine, and then it goes in the optional hundred and forty five dollar BMW sport holder. Pulling back into traffic is accomplished by spinning expensive tires for giggles. Foam shoots out of the traveler lid and joins the residue from the last coffee on the console below.

The Starbucks is soon a blur in my rearview, the last outpost of consumerism on the outskirts of a valley of poverty and shit. My art studio loft is on the long other end of this street of reuptake inhibited smiles.

Mad Max didn't have heated leather or a non-fat, no whip, half sweet venti mocha, but fuck me if Oppenheimer Park doesn't remind me of Thunderdome. The streets are lined with beaten down looking people. Their faces echo the stained, once clean storefronts. The small neon "OPEN" signs mimicking the faint glimmer of hope left in the eyes of people who end up down here. Sometimes I stare while picturing every one of their heads as a hand with middle finger extended. I frantically laugh and speed up when I think of how close I've been to becoming one of the fuck you zombies. As if doing thirty kilometers-per-hour faster could outrun debt or addiction.

Shadows cling to everything a little more down here, even at noon on a sunny day. Unmarked crosswalks are everywhere and people zigzag through traffic. The view from above reminds one of scattering roaches when a light comes on in a low rent apartment. Up ahead a grimy yellow signals some bullshit delaying my drive. Caught contemplating running it for a moment too long, and I end up needing to use more brakes than normal. The tires give off a chirp as anti-lock brakes dig in to stop. I grab my almost-tipping coffee in my right hand and nothing spills out. Yes. The image of the internet meme success kid pops to mind while stopped at a red in the heart of Sketchville. Do these people even know what The Internet is?

I glance around with undeserved haughty disgust, mixed with curiosity and sprinkled with fear. My eyes meet with those of a native guy sitting on the sidewalk with his back against a building. The whole block might remind someone of a gutter as trash is strewn about everywhere. He's wearing a Canucks hat, green t-shirt, blue jeans, and tennis shoes that were probably once white. I wonder what he's thinking while looking at me. He has no idea how delicious this fucking coffee is. I bet he probably thinks I had everything handed to me, much like I think he probably has never held a job. A few generations ago, his family and people were free to roam and live how they've always lived. Now he's obsolete, his community and spiritualism given the token treatment. Here, bang this drum and smile for the camera.

I'm lost in thought and a double tapped horn from behind brings me out of it. I have no idea how long the light was green for. Throwing it in first gear, my impatient feet give it enough clutch slip and gas to open a new conflict on the Niger delta, or some other shithole I could care less about. The next block is a blur and my red BMW blows through a late yellow that marks the line between feces and fancy. The road turns to cobblestone about a half block ahead, a few tourists are out. I stop to let a group cross the street. My eyes glaze over as my mind returns to the native guy. If he had seen so many of his friends and family getting high, maybe he couldn't build another vision for anything else in life. Looking to my own relationships, maybe my nonchalance stems from how inevitable divorce seems to be. If I don't play your game, I can't lose. On the flip side, my dick can be friends with a million pussies, but if my heart doesn't play nice with others, what then?

My right hand leaves the wheel to find the play button on the stereo. Back to a default Gastown frown and muttering "Fuck" to myself whenever life's gloom gets too much. I'll take this opportunity to put some heavy metal on to drown out the narrative of self-doubt. Driving my aluminum chariot around the block, into the urinal smelling alley, swipe, click, and the gate opens its mouth to swallow me. I whip the agile car inside and watch it close, preventing any windows from being broken in the urban hunt for loose change. Parking and taking the elevator up to the studio, the lift sounds like it's about to completely disintegrate. Old sushi welcomes me home. There's a shit-ton of emails I have to sort, a post-it reminds me of an event, and piles of laundry equal only in height to the mountains of dirty dishes. I pour vodka with cranberry, 50/50 mix. I smile and imagine myself relaxing against the side of a building, watching busy assholes sipping overpriced coffee.

9 Cold Trickle

The rain battered down in waves, fall's wind cutting it into the shape of sails, with each gust a new form. It appears as a clear blue whip chastising streets of red brick, light spilling into puddles machine-gunned by a mad sky. It's late afternoon, my furrowed face matches the tension of fabric at the back of my neck. A huge fucking drop had already ran down my spine once, that cold trickle can ruin an eggnog latte, even one poured by Natalee. She's always wearing a smile, but girls at work sort of have to. Her intricate leaf drawn into foam has distinctively turned more yonic. A pack of cars jostle up the nearly flooded street, and my cab pulls up with the groan and stink of budget brakes.

Hunched over to protect my coffee, a free hand reaches out and the cab's door opens a moment too soon. Crack, knuckles meet stamped steel. My left middle finger crunched into the door when Habib or what's-his-fuck tried some good ol' fashioned door courtesy. On the road to hell rolls yellow cabs with thoughtful drivers. The pleather stretches as I squeeze into the back of a Prius cab. Pointing with a non-bleeding hand, I inform the driver to take me to Commercial Drive.

Tick tock, patter patter patter. Beep! Patter patter. Distant spinning tires shriek. The street is filled with the busy cacophony of steel, glass and rubber beasts everywhere while rain drums away on the cab's roof. The hypnotizing rhythm of the wiper blades swiping back and forth lazily, the lonely turn signal ticks while begging for an opening to get inside of. Fond recollections of my similar desires post beer and blow. My knuckle stings in pain. The cab gets moving briefly and slams to a halt. A delivery truck screams by, the horn held down. It's hard not to think of a herd of snorting bovines jostling and pushing towards an abattoir, the solipsist in me demands my eyes close off their world. A successful pull back into traffic and we're on our way.

My Starbucks cup is smeared with blood, a perfect occupy ad. Probably get at least a dozen likes on Facebook with this, maybe a few retweets. The coffee is warm still and spice of the nog nudges a small grin across my rain greased face. Reaching into my pocket and pulling out my phone, 21 minutes until 4 PM. I have 21 minutes to get across town to deposit cheques before the bank closes. This morning my landlord took my call about the rent being a week late. He wants an email transfer, tonight, so I have to bring coloured slips to the bank. I'm not even *that* broke, just lazy and irresponsible. A tip of the coffee cup back a final time, only foam left. Down goes the window, and with my best poker face, the cup begins its adventure in the free world. Maybe I'd care more if anyone else in this neighborhood did. The driver yabbers away on his bluetooth in whatever language, stopping behind another line of cars. Brake lights and turn signals daub together in raindrops, the wipers clear the glass canvas.

There is a smell in a warm, wet taxi. Faint tobacco and new car cherry scent are the hallmarks of a downtown cab. Picturing massive amounts of coke that were in the pockets of all those people sitting back here makes my sinus tickle. Drunks, horny johns, little old ladies who need help getting groceries, but really need it for some company. It would suck to be old without kids or grandkids. The tragedy of outliving your friends as the world forgets you. The descent into irrelevancy while waiting to die. Watching Seinfeld followed by M.A.S.H.

I sigh and sulk back into the seat. The cab driver continues to babble on while we remain motionless, tension from this traffic raising my blood pressure. Tilting my head to the side, a tired forehead rests on the window. The glass is cold, and makes a sandwich of rainwater, oil, glass, and skin. Residue and steam makes it hard to even see a reflection of my face in the window, eyelids half closed from boredom. In the humid heat of the cab, green irises and bloodshot whites serve up what resemble Mexican colours in half-moons. The whirring sound of a tire spinning on pavement, a driver to the left cuts off my cab and forces us to stop. Like a reed in a flooding creek, head sliding on window grease without care, resigned to moving however the current wills it. We're stuck at the same light, but only one car back from the light. Thinking about the next dozen or so intersections I need to cross, a frown tries curling across my lips. Someone call housekeeping, my day just shit the bed.

Grey blobs shuffle beyond the steamed up window. The umbrellas look like each person holds their own personal black cloud above them. Looking down at my bloodied finger, sanguine has my hand sticky and ugly. The way blood seeps into every fold of your skin, it looks diseased. I don't really have anyone to show this to. Times like these I feel what the idea of love is.

I wish I knew if she still bites her fingernails. It's been months since we talked. She scolded me for driving fast around my neighborhood, later on I figured it was only because she cared. I think she was embarrassed that she chewed her nails. I didn't care because I bite mine when I'm bored too. Once we timed her to see how fast she could put her hair back into a french braid. Something like four seconds. I remember it was impressive to watch her do it, with all the motion of a sweatshop factory, but completely silent.

The cab pulls forward for a few hopeful moments before stopping. Broken glass litters the road and a BMW roundel lies shattered among the remains of some asshole's shitty afternoon. Somewhere inside my head Russel Peters cracks off an Asian driver joke. A break in traffic and we rocket down Powell Street, sending spray towards a group of people smoking outside the Sally Ann. I laugh when I shouldn't. I laugh at that too.

Passing the police station in the heart of the ghetto; so Vancouver. Cruising by huddled bus stop figures and my eyes catch a glimpse of a couple holding hands. I don't like to think about love. Every social contract, every belief system, everything I have been taught to believe growing up is a lie. From Santa to Jesus, all lies. The wars on drugs and terror seem like some macabre theatre of death with no story, no point, and no chance at victory. It is as futile as a war on sex would be. Politics, gender roles, right and wrong, good and bad, all seemed so easy to know when growing up, now living in a world as ambiguous as my beliefs.

The last bastion of my faith is my foolish belief in quasi-meaningful love. Another empty institution built up by idealists, not realists. I'm quickly seeing the concept of love being just as flawed as a belief that prayer can help. Cupid shoots heart-shaped hollow points that do no good for anyone. I wanted to hold on to some ideals, traditions, and the idea of romance. They all seem like part of a dying system and forgotten virtues. Now I think that love is the only thing that can cure me of this cancer of apathy. I used to feel that conservatism was the wiser choice, now I realize it's a lost cause.

My values are nearly nonexistent, as are my allegiances to any group or community. I'm the perfect globalist individual, I know my rights in the charter. I'd be completely free if it weren't for the shallow faith that I will find love as intense as the last time. My back grows heavy with such a pack of monkeys on it; love, liquor, money, drugs and pussy. That haunting thought that I might not have to settle is sometimes the only thing that this engine runs on anymore. I think of the world and all of its problems, the grim outlook on debt, austerity, social ills and skyrocketing costs of living.

A never ending blanket of soot-black cloud swirls around the earth. The planet looks like a nightmare. I grab the moon in one godlike palm. Cold

58

burns my skin, popping and sizzling the way a doctor freezes off a wart. Squeezing it hard and pulverizing it, it pops and crumbles in my clasped hands. A fine crystalline powder slips through my fingers, white dust lazily swirls around the night side of earth. Now reaching out and cupping both hands around the sun to extinguish the flames. The sun refuses to die easily, flames shoot and spit with fury from between my fingers. Embers and jets of smoke rush into my face, only deepening my resolve to smother it. An eddy of dying fire twists and curls around my wrist, the inferno bleeding itself out. I feel the life of the sun fade, the fire and smoke sputters and only a dull orange glow leaks between my tightly held hands. I release it from my death grip, the ashen ball almost looks sad. It cracks and begins to shudder, collapsing in on itself and becoming a tiny black hole. I look back at the lonely darkened sphere of dirt and water, the only place we all call home. One single point of light on the west coast glows as my mind's eye zooms in towards the dim beacon. Closer, closer and even closer still as the picture becomes clearer from the eternal midnight that engulfs the rest of the planet. I see the amber light of a bedside table glow from a bedroom window. I see myself in bed, smiling, kissing a woman who radiates happiness. I guess the romantic soul left in me really still believes. The world could end and I would think everything was OK, because we had each other.

I daydreamed most of the drive again. It's 3:55 when I make it to the bank. The cost of the cab fare ends the pregnancy of my wallet as the cash vagina births a wrinkled twenty, curling to return to straw shape. My change is a whole two dollars back, which is then given as a tip while stepping onto the street. The world greets me with an ankle deep puddle for my right foot, and a drop of rain served cold down the back of my neck.

Eight people. Eight fucken' people with nothing better to do, than to stand in front of me. Rain rushes to hug the floor and the back of my neck feels even colder. The bank is warm, stuffy, and full of sniffling noses. A child swings the line rope back and forth while his mom is lost on her iPhone. An old man leans over her shoulder and watches her play Angry Birds, fascinated. A fat guy in a blue parka is staring at a young girl, popping her bubble gum. Her friend looks a bit older, has a green streak in her hair, a hoodie, and she's playing with her tongue bar on her lips. It intrigues me to imagine what she's thinking about, or if she's thinking at all. An Indian guy in a Grizzlies jacket stands in front of me. He smells like smoked cigarettes. A brunette politely waves and says 'Next please' and an old Chinese man shuffles up to the wicket.

The bank is like a relaxed hive, worker drones slowly go about their business with smiles painted on. Polite talk is the norm and laughter is rarely heard. One fun thing about this place is making it a point to be a jackass. Bank happiness is beaming a big happy smile into one of the cameras, and taking the opportunity to stick my tongue out at the kid who shakes the rope furiously and laughs. The food channel is on the bank TV screens. Some overly medicated chef is making some overly flavoured food, the juices from the pork ribs in high def. Perfect and falling off the bone, my stomach growls. The faces she makes after tasting her own food mirror those of a girl receiving oral sex in an adult film. Eyes almost ready to roll back, brow relaxed, head lifts up and to one side. You think she just squirted all over a couple other girls while getting fucked by a strap on, rather than having a bite of ribs.

"Next."

An Asian bank teller sits with a poker face.

"Next."

The Asian bank teller remarks in monotone, again.

The girls are texting on their phones. Neither have said a word to each other in the bank, I figure they're probably texting each other about the creepy fat fuck in the blue jacket. The old man smiles and taps the girl on the shoulder. She turns around with a raised eyebrow before giggling out an 'Oops!' as she skips over to the teller. I turn back to the TV. They're making my favorite, kettle corn. Basically it's a salty and sugary mess of popcorn that pimp slaps you across the face with a handful of yum. In my mood right now, I just want to sit on my couch smoking joints, watching bullshit on Netflix while eating kettle corn and casually jerking off.

The bank door opens and a car horn fills my ears. The spray of wet car tires mixes with the noise of a closing umbrella. The door takes its sweet time to close, but I enjoy the cold, fresh air brushing my face. There's a bulletin board near the door I hadn't seen before. The words 'Day of action on bullying!' are sprawled across the top in large blue letters. Various slogans headline other smaller groups of text too blurry to read from here. One of them is 'Everyone is worth it', the other 'Never judge someone else'. As an adult, I wish I could believe in these, but it's highly unrealistic. One other catch phrase falls prey to my condescending eye. 'Love yourself for who you are!'

What if you're the bully?

My eyes squint and I'm having a hard time reading some of the notes. A greyish haze covers the letters and they mesh together to look like Egyptian glyphs. Fuck, I think I'm starting to get a migraine. The familiar blind spots start out as a piece of vision just missing, expanding into jagged lines of scintillating lights in my vision; like rips in space and time, a TV channel on rabbit ears. My eyes close and a deep breath fills my lungs to bring some peace. Meditative thought on clear air and blue skies. I breathe out and envision the pain taking the form of black smoke pouring from my nose. In with the good and out with the bad. Stuffy oppressive heat in here, while the rain and sweat soaking my neck and back makes for a sticky, gross chill. Shit feels like me today, I suppose this just tops off my karma cup. Dizzy eyes wander and try to find something to distract me from the incoming headache. Tax free savings accounts, RRSPs, mortgage brochures, these things are useless to me. What am I going to do, give up on living downtown and moving out to a 600 square feet dive in the suburbs of Surrey so I can own a box in the sky? RSPs? Do I think civilization is still going to last long enough for anything to retire to? If I'm not dead by 60 I'll make Leaving Las Vegas look like a toddler's tea party. Jagged lines and ridges of oblivion cut into my vision, the line moves forward and my stomach turns sideways. Breathe in. Breathe out.

The epitome of depression is not caring, shrugging and resigning yourself to your perceived fate. Looking at the cost of housing and everything in this city makes me want to give up, smoke joints, do my daily work, bust a nut and repeat. No wonder so many people just live the way they do, if I can see things this hopeless to build upon anything here, I'm wondering what someone unemployed and uneducated must think. Sell those drugs, pimp that ass, work those streets, hustle all you can for whatever you can get. My mind is a swirling maelstrom of pain and defeat. If I just had a joint, strong coffee and some darkness I could relax.

"Next," the Asian teller calls out.

I've always told myself there is a point to all of this, it's the journey, not the destination. Life was a scenic trip for a few years before the internet. Now I know how the other side lives, their money invested in outrageously priced housing, silver spoons sitting sideways up asses, just profiting off the underclasses paying their mortgages. Foreign investors use the city of my birth as a piggy bank, divorce wiping out so many people's normally inherited legacies. I won't ever own any land, I won't have a backyard to show my future children earthworms and daddy long legs.

I'll be a slave to the dollar forever.

A tick of pain shoots through my brain.

"Next," says a chubby blonde teller. The line gets shorter and my feet shuffle ahead with mummy styles. I need to stop thinking like this, writing my own future before it's even here. It's not too late to change, but doing what I do, I could do this forever. Laughing quietly to myself and then laughing again louder when the fat guy in the blue jacket looks at me. I have all the freedom in the world, but the men who I envy, envy me. I'm the one getting laid from beautiful, tight bodied girls. No anchors and no responsibilities. The world is open and women are willing for my taking. I'm healthy and if migraine headaches every blue moon are my worst malady, I think I'm doing pretty good. I have to remember to tell myself that nothing is written in stone and that a man with balls can do anything. I used to think that being a man meant I had to be able to bench press the most, be able to kick anyone's ass if I had to, to be able to fuck the hottest women and have others waiting for my attention. All bullshit sold to me, to keep men insecure little consumers, easily controlled. Craving a bigger car, flashier shirts, Jagerbombs, and easy nameless sluts with big tits isn't the manhood that I believe in anymore. Ok, maybe I still like fast cars. If I had an idea that the RRSP ads would make me think like this, I would've used the machine to deposit these payments.

"Next," drifts in my ear, barely audible over my own thoughts. Just what the fuck am I doing in this rat race? Working for little scraps of paper to take to a bank, to deposit it for more scraps of paper, back to my lair where I arrange the next night of drugs, alcohol, and socializing so I can put my fluids in another female. What purpose does this serve other than my own self-aggrandizing, I don't know. I guess it can be fun when you're numb enough to not think about it. "Sir," Here I am, languishing in bullshit self-pity when other people think I have it so good. Sometimes I-

"Hey buddy!" rings in my ear as a poke dents my shoulder.

There's nobody in front of me and it's my turn. I thank the guy behind me for letting me know, philosophizing in lineups is the broth to a bad mood soup. Willpower drags me slowly up to the wicket followed by putting my meal tickets down on the counter. Stacks of over three thousand bucks in dirty porn dollars and only three hundred in art sales. Shows what priorities we have these days.

The teller's fingers zip over the keypad and he asks how my day is.

"I'm chipper!" I say, giving him a coffee breath smile.

I request $500 in cash back, after a few minutes of leaning on the counter he returns with my cash all in fifties. I'm soon clutching some fresh salmon pink bills that flow downstream and into my pocket, signing off on my transaction; I'm done. My head is pounding and I walk out of the bank looking like a refugee from life, shoulders down, eyes in a squint, ungainly faced in depreciation of my own existence. How's my day? Fucked.

10 Men on Strike

My fridge is empty again. Dirty white walls provide such contrast to the solitary deep red and dried stiff slice of turkey bacon. Rancid tzatziki is sitting above veggie drawers that contain some sort of failed experiment. There's an old, foggy tumbler of booze left uncovered. Smells like white rum, and I hate white rum. A pre-drink would be great before my pre-drinking tonight, so here goes I guess. Lifting it up and shooting the several-day old rum back, it tastes like old turkey, rum, and flat cola. If desperation had a taste, it's thickly coating my tongue and is about to start stabbing my guts. My dumb ass somehow happened to totally forget that I had a bottle of Jack on the kitchen counter, sitting in the bag still. Old Man Rum angrily stomps around inside me as I open the bottle to swig back a big cleansing mouthful. Refreshing. I send another mouthful of Jack down to deal with his shitty neighbor.

Venturing out into the open world simulator that lies beyond my front door requires preparation. I slip my feet into some shoes, a warm coat, sunglasses, and take my wallet. With the basics out of the way, now comes the most important part: to get stoned enough to handle other people's bullshit. I have to choose my weapon wisely. There's a little nimble glass pipe, cleaned regularly and great for quick, small hits. The metal pipe bong gets backed up more often than truck stop shitters next to chinese take-outs. In my poor bong's defense, if you take the time to put some cleaning, love, and ice into it; believe me, it's smooth as silk. Perhaps I'll bust out the big glass cannon, the barrel happens to be a detachable cylinder that you can put in your freezer. It tokes so smooth I'd fall on my couch and daydream the next two hours away. I'm feeling like I want to remain on earth, so choosing the small glass pipe seems appropriate. Packing a small bowl and soon toking away, I enjoy a cough free smoke. A wave of relaxation washes over me, and for a few minutes I won't think so much.

With my head aloft in the clouds, I'm finally out of it enough to go into the world. I pause for a moment to double check that I didn't forget anything before leaving the house, looks like I'm ready. The door locks with a groan. The frame is a little crooked so I have to lift up on the handle to align the deadbolt with the hole. What a pain, I could ask the landlord to fix it, but I don't care *that* much. Down the hallway to a shoddy elevator ride, moments later I strut out of the lobby. The cool air jolts me awake and my hands find my pockets fast. I don't really keep track of days, it's the middle of winter and this coat can't fight off the cold. Another few dozen steps and I'm at the portal to the side show neighborhood I live in.

I smell fresh shit right outside the gate. Swinging the steel barred door open and immediately it's necessary to dodge several piles of stinking brown decay. I should be in the Russian Circus the way I step to the right, hop from the right leg onto my left leg, missing a smear to my 2 o'clock and a couple of errant log bogeys to my left. A lunge onto my right foot now avoids a fresh puddle of urine trickling off the streetlight to my left. Another hop and a diagonal dodge to my right and I check my shoe for Gastown pie. Nada. I tilt my head back a bit and smile, fuck yeah.

My brief moment of solitary success is rudely interrupted by the sound of a man retching across the street. I turn my head and watch him throw up on the middle of the opposite sidewalk. Now I frown with the realization that there's no witty name for puddles of vomit. Public lunch? Meals on heels? Cold demands my hands to bury themselves deeper, closing the jacket in the front.

Finally at the end of the first block, those first fifty steps are a real doozy. I have a red light and the cars anxiously stop-and-go through their green. Little THC gremlins sketch all of the cars transparent for me, high strung tap-dancing feet on gas and brake pedals with sewing machine rhythm. A ghostly white skinned androgynous person crosses the street against the signal. Angry faces of drivers honking, their displays of frustration only slow down the addict's pace. A few people screech their tires and go around the pale zombie. It passes me while staring at the ground, chin on chest. They say these people spend hours and hours searching the ground for anything someone dropped, money, drugs and half-burnt cigarettes to throw into the hole they call a life. A couple of scummy looking guys are crossing with the signal, the sounds of a sick chest gurgling as one of them spits a giant gob of phlegm on the sidewalk. Sickly green lung gel lets off a loud slap as it finds a home on concrete littered with old gum, cigarette butts, and trash. I overhear the words fuck, shitty, and Luongo several times in between both of them laughing. The light turns and I have the walk sign.

Across the street and a quarter ways down the block, a few normals are spotted. Guys with normal haircuts, regular belts, fitted pants. They pass me and no one makes eye contact. Faces in this section of town are drab and only a little bit more welcoming; IT workers, accountants and pretentious fucking bloggers. A Chinese family climbs out of a minivan. Halfway down the block and I'm catching up on a short, waddling granny. She unexpectedly jumps to her right and puts her back to a storefront's window as a BMX rider is barreling down the middle of the sidewalk. He's coming right for me and doesn't look like he's moving, I start feeling pissed off. He's some shitty runt of a man, small features and a blue bandana over his face, a black hoodie reveals mad slits for eyes which I proceed to stare down.

I instantly know I can't let him win by moving. He's 50 feet from me. I'm already close to the right hand side of the sidewalk. If he hits me he is going to do it on purpose. He's at 40 feet, now 30 feet. I keep up the same pace. 20 feet and he's still heading right for me. Just put more weight in the front of my feet. Ten feet and he hasn't swerved. A fraction of a second before impact, the BMX tool turns to go around me a bit too late. My hands are in my pockets while arms are tense, my bodyweight braced for the impact. My elbow catches him in the shoulder and, by the sounds of it, he crashed hard. I smile. A few more steps and that old lady grins at me. In a thick European accent she stammers "He crazy, fucking bike. He asshole!" I smile, nod, and keep on walking.

Tattoo parlors, a media facility, and smoke shops are the main businesses on this stretch of Cordova Street. Looks like an urban hippy's dream. The old lady was probably on her way bong shopping, maybe getting a butterfly on her lower back.

At the next light, a woman in a wheelchair is begging for change. If she wanted my advice, she should learn to sell porn. A scrawny white kid in pants ten sizes too big turns the corner, spits, and rips loose a barrage of swearing into his phone. While waiting at the light, my eyes wander to a blonde girl driving a Mazda. She notices me looking at her, and looks back at the traffic of people crossing the road. Her light turns yellow and she begins to turn. Her eyes find mine again, she smiles, and my cheeks peel up into a genuine smile back. Just like that she drives down the road and disappears. The kid with the baggy pants uses fuck four times in the next sentence. The next thing is "Ok mom, love you too!"

I couldn't have left that curb quicker.

Feeling pretty agitated now and I realize why; I forgot to put my sunglasses on. Overcast skies, not really a sunglasses day. Could be the weed, but this adventurous feeling might keep me from going into my own world of sunglasses and headphones for a little bit longer. The only person I've seen smile was the blonde in her car. She smiled as she was leaving. A half block down and I must have looked at 40 people, no smiles. I imagine all the people as Welsh corgis, frolicking and running around playfully. I once went to a corgi meet, as a corgi groupie. My friend had one of those ridiculous midgets, part goofy, part furry, the rest love and biscuit toots. All of the dogs and the owners got along save for one particularly skinny corgi, which dug a hole on the beach, growled and didn't want any dogs coming near it. Maybe that's the corgi version of sunglasses and headphones.

At the end of the next block, my route turns left to head to Yaletown. I'm across the street and soon far beyond shady characters outside of The Cambie. Passing a couple of hipster food joints, Apple laptops almost out-number people. At Hastings and Cambie the crowd gets really fucked up. You'll see anything here. Wandering tourists, Asian packs, loud Brazilian students, hipsters in berets, the occasional gorgeous woman. I notice a few more grins, but still only a few people smiling. A native guy eating a burrito, he's so happy I wonder if he's on something, or if those burritos are just that damn good.

The light turns and my pace picks back up, eyes look ahead to spot a man holding the hand of a child. The woman he's walking with is holding the kid's other hand and they stand out on Hastings. The child is a little blonde girl with a few missing baby teeth and a huge smile, she swings and takes big moon-gravity steps as the couple radiate happiness in such a bleak part of town. Laugh lines are always a dead giveaway of a genuine smile. The child giggles as they walk passed me, the man says 'whee!' as he holds her tiny hand. Something inside my head envies that. Quick feet fly up and over the next curb while the fresh memories of that happy family sear themselves into skull meat.

The next couple blocks are a wasteland of working professionals. Drones shuffle by with cubicle faces on, Dockers pants pressed to keener levels of corporate dress code. It is not for another couple blocks before I start spotting a few dolls walking around, fingers or ears on Blackberries. Glad RIM encodes BBM, least Shela or Kim get spied on about what d-lister they hooked up with last night or who has the best M in town right now. Come to think about it, I would definitely like to know who has the best M in town.

Walking into Yaletown feels like another planet. The women all carry length of legs, high cheeks, and good botox jobs. Tanning salons and shops line the streets among the boutique restaurants; no bodily fluids around to appreciate. The air is surprisingly fresh and I almost miss the toilet-hood that surrounds my loft. A brunette in front of me has a perfume that tickles my nose, smells like an ex. Her bottom looks like a couple of melons, the yoga pants stretched out wide to cover her ample ass. My penis stirs in my pants, so I stare at a bus stop ad long enough to settle down.

I step into an upscale bar known as Section 3. It's hard to tell sometimes who works here and who doesn't as almost everyone is dressed in black. Maybe they're here for the funeral of my liver. I'm here to meet a friend. Glancing around quick, Doug's spotted drinking a beer at a back booth.

Sliding onto the bench across from him, "Doug-ie" grumbles off my lips, with emphasis on the syllables.

He laughs and asks how I'm doing. I'm doing pretty good I tell him, a bit confused sometimes. He asks if I'm still going with a girl, three girls ago. While filling him in with the gritty deets, his response is a series of laughs and sighs broken up with drinking breaks. When it's his turn to talk, it's discovered that he has fucked almost as many girls as I have this year! Last year he was clearly in the lead, as I had a girlfriend most of the time.

We laugh and share stories of raw dogging sluts. He had a girl throw up in his bed last week. While laughing, my next story is a reminder of how my ex threw up in his room during a party. The laughter stops for a moment as he tries to be serious, then maniacal laughter follows. The waitress comes, I'll have an order of a double JD and coke; he orders a pitcher of beer. Upping the ante and ordering tequila shots seems like a good idea. The waitress is all cutesy, and sweet as peach. She has a smile from ear to ear. The moment she turns away from us her face loses all emotion. In my head I imagine her as a total bitch in her personal life, what a reflection of self.

Doug sighs and says "Ah shit man."

He takes a big drink of his beer. Quickly glancing at my phone reveals two new messages.

Dougie puts his glass down, leans back in the booth and asks "Do you ever feel like this is all for nothing?"

I stare.

"You ever think we are playing a losing game?"

Alcohol was meant for conversations like this.

"Which game are we talking about? There's not just one," I say with a crooked smile.

"Life man, life" Dougie sneers. "Like I just had to replace the transmission on my truck, why do I need a truck? It's to get away from this fucken city."

Dougie points down at the table.

"This city is just a rat race within a rat race within a rat race. We're just all competing for our own little chunk of cheese. Every man for himself and to the victor goes the spoils."

My head nods before I can even nod it consciously.

"Remember that shithead, Todd? We got him into clubs and we hang out with him a bunch of times and what happens? He tries to fuck my girlfriend." Frustration twists Dougie's voice into a nasal snarl. "Our buddy

71

Shane breaks up with his girlfriend, loses everything he has and goes into debt. The only reason that hasn't happened to either of us is because we keep women at dick length."

A chorus of furious nodding happens on my side of the table. The waitress walked up in time to hear about women and dick length. "Charming conversation fellas!" the waitress lets slip cheerfully, "it's not the size that counts, it's the-"

"-The motion of the ocean!" escapes my lips to interrupt her before slamming a tequila shot right off of her tray.

She chuckles as she puts the pitcher down, then the shot for Dougie. My next cold drink doesn't even have time to hit the table before she puts it in my hands for a long pull.

"Go on," I say.

The first warm wave of liquor hitting my system hugs me on the inside.

He continues, "Like what do we have to look forward to, or do? I can't keep myself entertained forever on pussy, booze, drugs, and partying. Then again, look at the family guys we know who are always bitching about their lives. My married friends talk about their wives like they're annoying bitches. Steve has to work, cook, *AND* clean!"

We both laugh. That guy is such a chump. Spineless Steve is the perfect beta male. He's a friend of Doug's I've met a few times. It's the classic beta white guy dating a stern Chinese girl. Is he happy? Being on such a short leash and still feeling good as a man would be tough.

"Dylen, remember that blonde chick you were tagging last year, the one with the beautiful brunette friend?" Dougie says, "Those chicks are a great example of what we have to deal with. They are Monica Lewinskis."

My eyebrow raises here, maybe. I'm not sure as I take a big pull of my drink, the jack was all on top and the fumes cause my eye to flutter.

"Chicks these days want the permanent alpha. They want a man who just fucks them and doesn't care. Want to know why?"

Mentally I can see where this is going, I live it.

"Why?" I casually toss out.

"Because caring about something other than yourself means you will have to change your behavior." Doug chugs back the last half of his beer.

In the dance of drinking, I take the lead here. Shooting back my entire whiskey and coke in one gulp followed by pouring another round of beers. I like the alternating sweet tones of hard bar and beer, but it doesn't do anything good for the breath. I fuck the pouring up and give him head in the least gay way possible. My beer somehow ends up poured perfectly. Doug takes a sip of foam with a look of disdain on his face. He clears his throat and gives his speech.

"Think about it Dylen. Remember all the times you did not give a single fuck about anything other than getting a nut? How much did you succeed?"

I smile. I want to interrupt him and remind him of the parade of young plenty of fish poon tang he had a few years back when I met him. The guy was an amateur gynecologist.

"Yeah, you see that the alpha behavior is all that matters. There is no worrying about your values or what you believe in, or who you are. It comes down to what you do and your social weight." Doug and I both take a drink. Before I can get a word in, he continues:

"My last real girlfriend practically tricked me into loving her. We were casually fucking and having fun. She knew I was seeing other people and she said it bothered her and she wanted to be with me. Up until that point everything between us was great. She would show up late at my place and just crawl into bed with me, give me back rubs, and all that sort of cuddling. We started to have sex over just fucking, ya know? I would just lay there in bed with her, playing with her hair, watching movies. It was just where I wanted to be and it felt like it was starting to go somewhere."

Nods toss him some acknowledgment, and another long drink of my beer rebuilds my smiling state.

"As soon as she knew I wasn't seeing anyone else, she dropped a bomb on me. She was seeing someone else. I was fucking crushed, dude."

"She's an alpha too, man." I say what I believe.

Doug looks puzzled.

"Look, we can't pretend things are the same as we want them to be anymore. The genders are fucked. Men are heartless Lotharios, beta males, Warcraft nerds, feminine limp wrist non-sexuals, or homos. Ok, the lines aren't that clear, but you get the point. Maybe she was just holding out for better? Women are taking on masculine traits and they see submission to them as weakness."

Doug looks pissed. He probably understands that I wasn't insulting him. Doug takes a couple of drinks. The rest of my beer is thrown into my throat.

"Well" Doug says, followed by a long pause. Doug is topping up his beer and filling my glass, perfect pours.

"Then I guess you do get it, it's just another fucking rat race."

"Only if you participate in it" I reply.

Dougie laughs. "What, just not date? Then what, keep picking up sluts for one nighters?"

Shaking my head followed by another long drink of my beer, I reply.

"No Doug. Here's my theory. Think of people as people, not as men and women anymore. 50 years ago it was white and black, now its shades of grey. Any hot woman knows her value in the sexual economy and she can use it to find the best mate."

Doug cuts in "-gold diggers."

My outstretched hand palm down gives a see-saw motion.

"Not quite, but similar. They're looking for someone to play the game with. Someone to follow the rules with, but they have the option put his balls in a jar under the new laws of modern relationships."

Dougie doesn't react. He just takes a sip of his beer.

"I get it though, it worked before where the man ran the show and the woman was passive and expected to breed. This was when religion and duty to family and community was hammered into people from a young age. The social contract was simple. The man brings home the money and he has autonomy, the woman has a role tied to the children and the home. There was very little autonomy outside of those walls. Now men no longer need to support women, while women no longer need to fall into the role of being mothers. Socially the stigma of being an unmarried mother is pretty close to nil."

Dougie scoffs, "Oh man, yeah, single moms are such easy lays."

"Hold on, I'm not finished. It's good that women have their freedom and rights, but men need to adapt to this. Maybe if we change how we approach dating, we can guide the modern girl into wanting to assume that motherly, good wife role?"

"What the fuck are you talking about Dylen?"

"Modern life has changed everything and the woman is no longer expected to do anything, while the man is still expected to fill his role. I'm just saying that if a man takes the lead on showing her happiness, while clearly expressing his expectations of her, maybe our relationships will improve."

Dougie nods.

"I'm glad women don't have to be shelved and expected to breed, cook, and clean anymore. I'm not so sure that we, as men, have been able to adjust to this. We're lead around by our dicks more than anything else now.

I have no sense of duty to anything other than my own self-pleasuring. I'm not a leader or a real man, I'm just a dude who fucks a lot."

I don't know if I feel good or bad about that.

Dougie slaps the table. "You're damn right Dylen. I've been thinking the same thing. What the fuck do I do anything for these days? If I try and find a woman I have the thought that everything is bullshit, man. If she finds someone that entertains her more or has more, she can leave me in financial ruin and just fuck off with him. If I don't get married and I stick to how I live now, I'll be 50 and getting dick zits fucking girls from the Roxy." Dougie says with a tone of disgust.

"To dick zits!" I say, as I raise my glass.

"To dick zits now and forever." *Clink.*

We chug back our drinks and pour another round of beers.

"You know my folks, they hint that I need to grow up. Grow into what? My mom is on her third husband and she's miserable. My dad still works and lives in a basement suite. He lost the house in the fucken' divorce, then his business went tits up due to taking six fucken months off to deal with it." Dougie says, shaking his head slowly.

In my mind I know just how out of touch boomers are.

"I know for a fucking fact I ain't ending up like either of them. Fuck that." Dougie sighs, furious nodding on my part.

Another drink and an obsessive compulsive check of my phone. A couple messages but nobody that can't wait.

"What's the next step?" Dougie asks, not knowing if he expects me to reply. Apathy numbs, I'm unable to even shake my head.

"I think the only thing we've got left to try, is to just be honest with women in what we want." I say in my most serious tone.

Dougie stares at me for longer than a few moments, and then sort of chuckles. "You're kidding, right Dyl? You mean, come right out and tell a girl you're looking for loyalty and eternal love? You go ahead and try that and you can text me when you want to do drinks when you utterly fail."

"Dougie, I don't think it's-"

"You of all people" Dougie interrupts "Oh please, all of a sudden you're so fucking wise and noble Dyl. First you have Claire, remember? She loved the shit out of you and you dumped her because you liked bigger tits."

That rat fuck scumbag feeling hits me and my head tilts down a little.

"Oh then you just think shit is a big party for a couple of years, fuck her for a while and then what? She put so much time and effort into loving you and what I witnessed was you living the same old way you've always lived. You've spent so much time looking for something better, looking for your next big conquest to satisfy your selfish fucking ego."

I stare at my beer.

"Dude-"

"Yeah there is no dude, Dyl, you try and flip this into some new age bullshit when all you've done is play shit to your advantage. You fall in love with a couple of girls, wig the fuck out on both of them, and I'm supposed to think you have the answers?"

"Naw."

He shakes his head with a look of disgust.

"Naw."

Dougie's eyes stare through mine as he finishes his drink. Dougie lifts up the empty pitcher and waves it at the waitress. I can't help but think I've done to girls what his last girlfriend did to him.

"Dougie, I know man, I know I've been doing it wrong. I'm trying to say we, as men who know what we want, we need to come up with an alternative. What we've been conditioned to do is to act like there's no tomorrow."

Dougie laughs. "Have you seen housing prices? You really think there is a tomorrow here? Come on man, I've known you for how many years?" Dougie raises his voice. "Now, all of a sudden, you change your tune to this pseudo-good guy fucking white knight who believes in love and being open and honest? Sounds like you've lost your balls along with your fucking mind bruh."

I can't dispute the mind part.

The waitress shows up with another pitcher, the look on her face indicates she's heard our conversation heat up. She leaves the pitcher without pouring any drinks. Grabbing it out of alcoholic instinct, a shaky buzzed dickhead pours two horribly foamy drinks that spill all over the table.

"Fuck" Dougie lifts his cup in time for beer to run down his arm.

"Shit, sorry!"

"I'm drunk too, I wouldn't pour any better," Dougie says through a laugh.

"Doug, I'm trying to say we need a new model for the modern alpha male. Not the drunk asshole that fucks the most tail, but the man we can all respect. He who upholds society, someone with the wife he actually wants, the job he isn't a slave to, and the respect the head of a family once had."

Dougie's bellowing laughter blows foam from his glass.

"Uh huh, haha, you're so fucked in the head. Those days are long gone man, long fucking gone."

I tilt my glass back and get a mouth full of foam.

"Yeah, they're gone, but it's not to say we can't evolve into a healthier alternative. Would you want women to have to go back to being barefoot in the kitchen? I don't. I like seeing a chick have her interests, career, and a well-rounded personality. I don't want them thinking their only value is between their legs to us. What we're liv-"

"Living in a time of extremes where you find either one or the other, yeah, heard it before man." Dougie's voice peters off at the end, his beer is half gone.

I nod.

"But what are we, Dougie? Think two women haven't gone drinking together and asked each other what's wrong with men?"

"Yeah, sure they have, but do you think for a second they have any idea of tradition or values these days? They want the kid for status and their own happiness, no deeper sense of purpose. Men, Dyl, men need to keep that deeper purpose alive."

"I thought you said traditional love was dead?"

"It is for guys like us, Dyl." Dougie nods slowly, "It is for guys like us."

Leaning back, the plush leather seats cushion the hard blow to my psyche. Maybe he's right that the time of the modern nuclear family is over. Lacking any savings, I have no culture, no traditions. I have faith in nothing. I spend my time just eeking out a living in this city and onto the next girl, next drink and next joint. Sure it's fun, but it hardly feels like being a man.

"Doug, I don't know man-" I spin my beer glass on the table. "I think we can still have it all. Men like us need to assert ourselves the way our grandparents did. We see a problem, solve it. If guys like us want a deeper connection to a woman, stop doing the same old, same old. I'm trying. I really am."

I'm not lying to him. I hope I'm not lying to myself. Dougie pours another beer for himself, glassy eyed and wet lipped, we must be getting drunk.

Well, I'm just done thinking about this for tonight. Pfft." Dougie grumbles.

We bump glasses and raise a drink in silence.

Dougie and I split the bill. We're silent for a while and certainly mulling over our statements. He's right. A lot of why I have had sex with so many women is for the perceived status of it. Remembering my first threesome, the girls came out to party with my friends a few weeks later. They got drunk, obviously, then bragged about how much fun it was. Being in my early 20s, my friends treated me like they were genuinely impressed. The girls were just out of high school, so slutty, and so horny. Being young, recalling how my dick just wanted to fuck any cute chick it could to prove that I was an attractive, successful man. What a bad joke. The people I knew who had the most sex back then, nearly all of them had kids and fell into poverty and dating raunchier women. Never did they end up dating some of the caliber of women that graced my life in years gone by. Dougie's right, I think I fucked myself into this, and the only way to get unfucked might be to not fuck as much or as fast. Is it even possible to base a relationship on mutual adoration, values, traditions, and not just the fucking, status, or money? Whatever, if I think about it, I won't have fun tonight. Dougie's back from the shitter and we're off to a Thursday night at the Roxy, the one bar where you can always count on younger women looking for older men.

11 Getting Friday on a Down

The sweet and shitty smell of the Roxy wafts out onto the street. If a creature was made of Tang and could take a dump, the smell in this bar would be its rotting feces. Self-important doormen hold the chump line waiting while the much shorter VIP line moves fluidly. A guy in the shiniest shirt ever seen is standing outside bumping fists with a bouncer, a smoke behind each ear.

"Why are we going here again, Dougie?" My commentary as we walk up to the VIP line.

Dougie barks back "Just shut up and enjoy the ride dude."

Shrugging and smiling, I spot a few cute young chicks walking out of the bar. A petite girl stumbles and falls onto the sidewalk, making a pile of hot mess as her skirt flips up. A round of 'Oooohs' comes from the crowd lined up. She picks herself up, chin glowing with a little concrete rash and turns around to go back inside.

"No, get her out of here." The doorman demands, grabbing her other friend.

"Fuck you! I need my coat! Tiny dick fucker!" the wasted girl replies, not even looking towards the club.

"Hey!" A voice shouts into my ear.

"Hey!" I turn around.

A bum with a long beard is standing facing the lineup.

"Anyone want to see how many pushups I can do?" Zero takers.

Dougie laughs, the wasted girl fell down on her ass as her friend is trying to put her in a cab.

The bum turns to Dougie, the biggest built guy in the whole lineup. "Buddy! How about a pushup race?"

"No thanks man." Dougie replies without looking at him.

"Hey dude, come here, I'll light your beard on fire for a dollar." I hear called out from behind me.

"Sure!" The bum replies with a smile, stepping over to the lineup, leaning his face over the railing.

The punks behind us snicker, half the crowd has their smartphones out to record the upcoming show.

A flick of a bic, once, twice, a third time and a flame erupts from the metal cap. The bum closes his eyes and a barely-drinking age kid in gold chains and an affliction shirt lights his beard on fire. With a small spark, the matted hair belches out a stinking cloud of smoke as the rest of it catches ablaze. Coughing and slapping at the flames with the fire still burning, the bum saving himself by using his jacket to pat out the inferno raging on his face.

The doorman yells over "Get the fuck out of here! Now!"

A charred bum holds his hand out for the dollar.

The young guy and his friends howl with laughter, Dougie stares with a scowl at everyone in the lineup, and I shake my head in disbelief. The bum's face is clearly burnt and his beard mangled, blackened and nearly all burnt off. The baby-faced tool throws a loonie on the ground.

"Fucking sick," Dougie says under his breath.

"Wait- here dude," My fingers fumble in front pockets for some cash.

The doorman steps over "I thought I told you ..." as a $20 slips from my fingers to the bum.

"Thanks man!" He says, snatching the money and high tailing it away from the bouncer.

"Don't fucking do that shit again!" My hollering drunk voice makes a surprise guest appearance on Granville Street.

Who knows if he heard it, he's probably going to blow that money on something worse for him than a little bit of a charcoal mug. Whatever.

Dougie smirks at me, "Did you really just give that guy twenty fucking bucks for that?"

I nod.

"Haha, first you're talking about traditional love, and now you're paying bums to stop letting people light their beards on fire for a dollar, what's gotten into you?" He snickers.

My face explodes in goofy laugh.

The VIP line moves fast. With a check of my ID, and a shitty $10 cover, it's time to engage the Roxy. A quick scan and it's easily a casting call for d-bags and slutty Jersey Shore rejects. I shouldn't be so arrogant, I'm no better than anyone here, drinking and looking for something warm and wet to bring home. Dougie squeezes in to get a couple of Jagerbombs and comes back with four.

"Might as well load up, you don't want to get caught in that fucking line up," as he nudges his head in the direction of the packed back bar.

We wander over to the dance floor and find a rare open table.

"Our lucky day!" I say loud enough that the girls next to us hear.

Dougie moves his chair and bumps into a girl's chair on purpose.

"Oops." He speaks through a smile at the chubbiest of the three. I've seen this tactic so many times before.

The music is all cheesedick, Bon Jovi streams through the speakers, followed by Journey. Young girls bump and grind strangers on the dance floor, trying to one up each other for attention. Dougie and I shoot back our Jagerbombs, he pushes the glasses to the side and moves over to say something to the chubby girl at the table beside us. She turns around and hands him her drink, he sips it, and pretends to choke on it, before laughing and saying its pretty good. The girl giggles and Dougie introduces himself. She says her name is Regina. That must have gone over well in school.

Dougie turns to me, "Bro, say hi to Regina and friends, I'll be right back with drinks." With that he gets up on a drink run.

Sliding off my stool and walking over to the table of girls, I make eye contact with each one.

"Yeah, you guys shouldn't be talking to my friend."

Regina squints, "Uhh, why? He's funny!"

"Yeah, I know, but he has some really messed up ideas of funny. He thinks two girls one cup is a romantic comedy."

One of the brunette girls coughs and smiles.

"Did you just say, two girls, one cup?!"

I nod.

"My brother sent that to me last week, it's so fucking gross!"

I smile.

"Do you hate your brother for it?" I ask, she pauses and replies. "Uhm, no, he's my brother, of course not."

I grin.

"What about ... if a lover sent you that?"

She frowns, "He'd have to be a pretty amazing lover."

I think I can set Dougie up with this spinner.

"Well, you've just met my friend, if you're lucky you'll know by the end of tonight."

Regina covers her mouth and laughs, the other two remain poker faced.

"I'm Dylen, good to meet you ... Regina right?" I offer my hand, Regina shakes it.

"I'm Shelby. Yes, named after the car." She's the skinny blonde who doesn't like two girls, one cup.

"I'm Ash," Spoken by the dirty blonde with the turquoise V-neck.

After the introductions, I manage to squeeze out the basics from the girls. Shelby has a family of car nuts, Ash is in Vancouver for the year, visiting family and working as a personal trainer. Regina knew these two since elementary school and loves Bon Jovi. Dougie comes up with a huge tray of shooters and drinks, when you need something to help you carry your liquor, you mean business. Little happy yellow shots litter the tray and are soon relieved of their fluid burdens. The night swirls and mashes together in music, lights, sounds, fluids, and bumping shoulders.

Soon I'm dancing with Ash and her arms are around me. Dougie's tongue is in Shelby's mouth right behind us, my eyes catch Regina at the table; looking at her phone. Finding balance getting tougher and my back growing sweaty, Ash and I retreat to the table. Her bag gets spilled on the floor, as I lean up from grabbing it, she kisses me. We make out right there and then. Dougie's back at the table, he says something and taps me on the shoulder. Ash's tongue in my mouth. More shots. Ash grabs my hard cock under the table, and rubs it until it's down my pant leg, clearly feeling its size.

Lights.

Everyone squints and 10s drop to 7s. Anything below a 6 and you have to get out of the bar, fast, before your dick loses its courage. In a swirl of sound and light, stumbling, we nearly get into a fight outside the bar. Dougie grabs my arm and tells me to shut the fuck up. Cops. We walk halfway up the block, Regina trailing behind us two couples.

"Are you guys going to be ok?" Regina pleads.

"Yeah sweetie, we're fine! Look!" Shelby says, doing a ballet move of sorts.

I guess she's trying to prove she's not roofied.

Ash shivers. "I just want to get home," she whispers to me. Without hesitation I take her by the hand and lead her gently to a cab.

"You guys going now?" Shelby calls to Ash.

"Yeah," she replies, acting tired but looking lusty.

Regina runs over and hugs Ash. She looks me in the eyes and says "And you better behave!" I wink.

Starts and stops, green lights, red lights. The West End. Her low rise apartment smells of old cigarettes and anal lube. Ashley's little place with nice hardwood, classy furniture. My drunken ass knocked over a plant while trying to take off my shoes. In bed before I know it, fucking, she's on top, maybe going to puke. The bathroom was nice while blowing chunks and trying to keep my boner. Brush my teeth using some crest and my finger, back into the bedroom. Fucking her missionary, it feels amazing. The flash of my iPhone, maybe I just took a few trophy photos. Squeaky bed and the headboard pounding the wall. Rolling her on her side and spoon fuck her, moans fill the tiny apartment. Stumbling while standing on her bed and knock over a lamp, managing to pile drive her pussy for a few minutes until falling over again. Finally her on all fours and slamming in doggystyle, cum on her ass, and it all goes black.

I hate waking up like this. My phone beeps with an alarm at 7:30 AM. My head is pounding and my tongue tastes puke. Ash is still passed out, but grunts in disapproval that I'm getting up. Her room is a fucking mess, clothes everywhere. Where the fuck is my underwear, pants and shirt? Digging around in the mess of her room reveals my ginch under her bra. Throwing one leg through the briefs I notice specks of dried blood on my dick, looks like my middle finger that I used to probe her is coated as well. Fuck. There's throw up mixed with cat fur crusting up my socks. While sneaking out of her room quietly to grab my shoes, putting them on I notice one is full of dirt. Fuck. Keys? Check. iPhone? Check. Wallet? Wallet? I look around for my wallet. Opening Ash's bedroom door, light floods in and my wallet is sitting half buried under a bra. Snatching it fast to check for taxi funds. I have $30 in cash left, and an ATM slip of a $200 withdraw last night. Fuck. Closing her bedroom door this time without even trying to be quiet, then seeing myself out. It's cold and it feels good on my fucking pounding skull. Nausea washes over me on my hustle towards Davie Street. Eight AM, shit, maybe I had booked an artist today for some studio time, yeah I'm pretty sure I did. Made it to Davie Street and then accidentally hailed a cab with my bloody period hand. A smiling brown man stops, my tired body hopping in the back and then commanding him to Gastown. My life, the way I've lived lately, is a kamikaze mission that never ends.

12 Lessons in 1080p

The door cracks open, smells of dirty dishes greet me as smoke spirits barely linger. Feet of lead, step after another step, turning the corner to my right. The studio space is basking in rich warm sunlight. On perfect, cloudless winter days like this, the sun ricochets off the cream coloured building across from mine. I wonder why I feel so at home in a space that's so alone. The pre-drinking choice from last night, Jack, sits on the counter missing a neck's worth of fun.

What a night. My hungry stomach forces me to drop my phone on the couch, kick off my shoes, and pull some leftover stir fry from the fridge. After dealing with heating my meal, something glossy reflects on my couch. Current events and keeping up to date on the world is important, sad that my subscription to this magazine seems to only fuel my shitty moods. The cover reads "Death of the middle class", it doesn't register in my head yet. Glazed eyes and pages skipped through, the pictures are what I'd expect. My wiferowave and her pleasant beeps lure me away from The Atlantic, briefly skimmed through. The Jack scowls at me.

Leaning up against the counter, this is my dining room table. My head is throbbing. The steam tickles my nose. Cheery sunny day fills my studio, only making me feel cold. The handyman doing repairs inside my head needs to put down the chainsaw. My dick is sore again, totally sexually spent. Everything that I thought when I was younger has turned out to be a lie. Here I am, having had great sex the night before with a tight bodied girl, and yet I'm dissatisfied. A baby corn crunches between molars. Sometimes I give these girls what I think they want, and not what I want. Jack winks at me from the counter.

I love baby corn and black bean sauce. Sitting down in a flowery chair, the bowl of concentrated life sustaining yum gets placed on the coffee table. My iPhone is about to tell me what happened last night. The photo wall that pops up is full of colour. Photos taken of last night reveal busy streets, blurred lights, blonde and brunette girls. Spoonman on Granville makes for such a novel photograph. Glaring neon lights streaked by a slow exposure, a row of shots ringed by unfamiliar hands. Flipping through the photos and I'm greeted by another row of shots, and another. In the future the iPhone will record your blood alcohol level as meta data in each photo. A shot of of my mouth on a breast is sure to have been when wasted. Tough to believe I went home with a girl I don't know again, photos of her body on my phone proof of a successful urban safari trip. A quick video of her legs spread, and I'm inside her. Objectively, I could use to lose a few pounds. My newly forming gut casts a shadow on the good parts. The bottle of Jack laughs.

A laundry load of thoughts whirl around inside my head. Am I living in a mad world, or am I the mad one? By what metric can one measure his own dysfunctional behavior? A flick of my finger scrolls up on my photos, far up and back in time. A few photos of her, the girl my heart actually still misses. Funny how it works, you pine and bitch over one woman, and yet make no effort into being with her or find another like her. Instead you're out doing shots with a girl you view as a piece of ass, drinking so you can get in the mood you need to be in so you can fuck her and have a fun night out. Jack is the hammer used to smash any purpose in life. Laughing to myself while I put my phone down, personal freedom and prosperity are my only goals. There was an election this weekend. I was more concerned with drinking and putting my dick in a female than voting. I feel like such a peasant.

Still, maybe it's possible to take this with a grain of salt as being a peasant is pretty fun these days. Without expectations of responsibility, I'm free. I jump to my feet and dance to a beat from memory. A hop, skip, and a jump to my desk, hands work my computer into blasting out an old Too Short track. Tonight I'm supposed to be going to the opening party of a new photography studio, douche buoys in an ocean of pretentiousness. First things first, I'm working on a piece of light art today. Shit, the girl I'm working with will be here soon.

I fumble around with making myself look semi-presentable. The artist that shows up is bubbly and young. We spend the morning trying to find the right heat level for the glue gun. We have this metal basket we're trying to glue cotton balls to, then attach a piece of yellow neon tubing to the bottom to create a white cloud with a yellow lightning bolt coming down from it. I'm trying to host this Stormy Nights themed art party in April and it doesn't seem like we're going to be ready for then. Fuck it. Hot glue turns out to burn my gloveless hands over and over leaving welts, at least she can laugh about it. Hours later, we finish the basket and it looks somewhat decent. I collaborate on art so naturally that these pieces seem to build themselves. If only lasting love was somewhat similar.

The girl signs the guestbook listing what was accomplished today and is gone. My place is a fucking mess and it takes a half hour to clean, how one girl can end up using five dishes for her own personal lunch and three cups for coffee, I'll never understand.

Might as well get this party started, it's already 6 PM. Reaching into the kitchen drawer to pull out a tumbler, it's soon begging for ice cubes and hard bar. Or just straight liquor, in this mood ice is just garnish and doesn't help me get to where I'm going any easier. Opening the fridge to grab some whiskey, I leave it open for a few seconds too long. Wasted vegetables and old chicken assault my senses. I can't remember the last time a home cooked meal was made here, or shared with anyone. Closing the door, my mouth opens and in goes a big gulp of whiskey. Down goes the glass, my eyes close, friendly winds escape nostrils.

Stepping away from the kitchen with a fading frown, if I wanted to ever be seen as a professional, I should learn to put my camera away properly after a shoot. It's risky and dumb to leave it on the couch with the lens cap off. Then again, that dirt on the lens actually makes some photos look a bit raw. I documented some of the work we did today, and the battery is nearly dead. I'll plug it in, copy the files off, and then charge it for tonight. The USB cable fits in the port and Windows pops up to greet the Canon 5D MK2. Looks like there are nearly 15 gigs of photos and video on here, so I copy them and lazily paste to desktop.

Windows isn't very subtle in letting me know the drive is full. Flashing drive lights are serenaded by the long grinding of my hard drive before the disk space manager pops up, followed by my frantic closing of that shit. Clicking the C: drive, and I anticipate having an early evening of being a digital monkey, swinging from folder to folder in search of waste to fling off my hard disk. Fat lesbians have been selling well lately, my job being to put small porno clips online with a banner ad under them. One folder reads 'chunky lesbo slutzzz' with 8 gigs of pie loving dykes inside it. Open wide recycle bin! A few trips to the kitchen for more Jack and its only freed up a few gigs. The thought crosses my mind to go get another drive, 1 TB these days is cheaper than a night out drinking.

About ten folders deep in my C: folder, a few long forgotten gems grace my monitor. It's been a long time since I've had to make room on my computer. A WMV thumbnail image hits my retina and I recognize it as a sex tape made with a girl named Tess. Long brown hair, a skinny body with small lemon shaped breasts and a large, round ass. My dick immediately swelled in response to her memory. Hormones cause thick saliva to form in my mouth while electric excited tingles flow down my spine. Her sex floods my mind and I'm instantly turned on at finding this fantasy flesh treasure on my drive. Our first meeting feels like it could've been yesterday; martinis, shit talk, laughing and banging our hands on the table. We were asked to leave, so we went to her place and fucked right in front of her windows.

My paranoid mind runs deep, so the front door needs to be locked to watch it. Detouring to the bathroom to pick up a hand towel on my way back, I think I'm going to need this. The intensity of the memories flood back once I double click the movie, her delightful body getting fucked by me slams my mind with stimulation. After a few minutes of intense self-pleasuring, I'm flat on my back on the couch, spent; the movie still playing on the screen silently. The audio is fucked and it just hums, I hate sound when I'm watching porn anyways. My eyes close and a smile runs across my face. She came by to hang out and do blow a couple times, and drank a twixer of pear vodka straight from the bottle. The first time she asked me to take photos of her nude, the second time it was if I would make video with her. Her long middle finger loved to slide in and out of herself on camera. That huge ass with those little legs, her moaning wasn't faked at all. She really loved to finger fuck herself while being watched.

It was all her idea, too. In my old apartment, she questioned me on how I felt about artistic nudes. Not being too much of an idiot, her not-so-subtle cues could be seen a mile away. Of course I told her I enjoyed the female form. With that, she smiled, pulled her tight pants down a little and pressed herself up against the wall. Snap.

"Don't get my face in these photos, ok?" She said, almost bashfully.

Of course not was translated into nods of reassurance. She brushed her hair back behind her ears, and pulled her pants down slowly. My eyes locked on her ass, and a little hint of a pink waxed slit peeked out from between her legs. My pulse was racing, fingers that were gripping the camera had turned white.

She threw her head beyond her shoulders and arched her back, the beautiful symmetry of her smoothly bent body matched the curves in her full, womanly ass and hips. Amateur eyes guided her to bend forward, she flowed her body into a downward dog yoga pose. No wonder she has such a nice body. With her pants at her ankles, she giggled as she stumbled to one side. Lending a hand to help pull them off, her musky erotic scent lingered in the air once the panties hit the floor. She was naked and bending over for me to take photos, and was very turned on.

The memories fly through my head, a buffet of erotic images. Back in time and I can still remember the cold AC giving her a few little goose bumps. A few more photos are taken, and she stops to walk to the kitchen. A residue of blow is on the counter, and an unopened flap finds its way into Tess's palm. Unfolding it, she dumps it, and cracks it with a Fitness World card. Two big lines for both of us, and we bang them back. I feel a shiver down my back as the sexual energy just consumes my mind. She shivers a little, picks her shirt up off the chair, and puts it on while walking to her jeans.

My back starts to get sore trying to get these photos, high elbows on the counter top just don't really support me enough. A tornado of cocaine in my nose shakes the shutters on my heart, I should find a stool to sit on and catch my breath. The animal in me can focus on nothing but her alluring body. She steps into the legs of her panties, her hair falling in her face after leaning forward to pull them up. Her eyes fall on the obvious bulge in the front of my pants. She smiles as she walks over, her hands find my knees and she leans into my ear.

"I want you to do something," She coos. "Come."

Her hand finds mine and I'm pulled into the bedroom, she hops on the mattress and gets into a doggystyle position.

"I don't want to fuck yet, I want this to last longer tonight." She pulls her panties just down to her ass crack.

On her knees, she backs her barely covered ass up to the end of the bed.

"Cum on my panties and ass, I want you to get off."

She's a petite girl, I remember last time, we had sex once and she was sore the rest of the night. Not sure if I had fucked her hard or just until we ran dry. I haven't had sex with her sober.

I take the camera off and drop it on the bed. This might be a new speed record for how fast my dick came out of my pants as I smack it across her ass cheeks. I'm surprised that I'm almost already hard, considering the blizzard going on in my sinuses. The soft skin on her ass feels silky and warm to the head of my cock, and I rub it at the top of her ass crack. Her panties rub on my balls.

She softly and slowly mumbles "That feels good" through gritted teeth.

My pants fall to my knees and I struggle to stand shoulder width apart. My belt buckle makes a clanking noise against itself. Electric shocks of pleasure ripple up my spine and a chill washes over me. The cocaine, liquor, and sex mix up a cocktail of deityhood inside my mind.

I am a god, and I will commune with my people. As your lord, in the form of a grey wolf. Her waist looks so small and narrow, while her wide hips and ass so full, a spring lamb for the taking by he who dares.

She lifts a hand to her face, spits, and reaches back between her legs and grabs my dick to stroke it. I see my penis disappear between her legs as the wet, soft hands glide up and down my shaft. She grips soft on the middle of the shaft, and squeezes harder as she pulls towards herself. Her soft palm slides off the head with a knee-weakening moist grip.

My heart is racing, silence washing over me for a moment, my eyes close with my head tilted back. With a deeply exhaled breath, I picture my bones standing, without flesh. I feel my nose is frozen, every hair on the back of my neck at attention. I know she is stroking me right now, but the world has stopped and I'm completely in my own psyche, enjoying chemical bliss. Every synapse in my brain is in tune with pleasure. I know I'm breathing, but I don't feel it. The body's heart pounding inside my chest with a mind afloat on sexual highs, the soul left to hitchhike.

All I feel is an intense warmth and pleasure inside of me, an energy that flows from dick to brain, and back down again. Car pooling my ecstasy down California highways of carnal pleasure ten-lanes wide, an extinction event of boredom, that pandemic flu of paradise. This is the opposite of a plague. Everything is glowing. I lose all concept of that which I have no concept for. I open my eyes. Looking down, she spits on her hand again and says "I'm getting tired, you need to take over," a horny tone in her voice. When I first opened my eyes I wasn't very hard, but the sight of her body gets me going again immediately.

I reach down and grab my dick out of her hand. The head glows an angry red, and I push it down to rub against her panties where her beckoning lips peek out.

She moans softly "Not yet, more teasing ..." I tell her I know and rub my cock up and down her damp panties.

The head just barely pokes the cloth inside of her, and she gasps. I pull it back out, her pussy being teased sends a shock-wave of chemically enhanced pleasure through her body, my knees shiver. I breathe out hard as she reaches back and pulls her panties to one side, and rubs my manhood against her dripping wet folds. Her hand finds the end of my cock is covered in precum and she moans a little.

I jerk my dick hard and fast and put the head into the top of her ass crack. My other hand grabs her hip as I ask her how bad she wants to feel me cum all over her ass and pussy. She leans forward and re-positions her bottom in the air so that her pussy is practically staring me in the face. That beautiful, soaking wet looking tight rosebud sits under a perfect little asshole, marking a couple of bullseyes. My breathing continues to rise while contractions shoot through my iron-hard shaft, calling out to her through a new plateau of sheer pleasure as she is rubbing her clit. My right leg swings up onto the bed. My right hand has a firm hold of her hip and I'm rubbing myself with my left hand. She has her face buried in the bed with her back arched up as high as possible. Her finger darts across her clit and her pussy is a bright moist pink. A trail of wetness leaks out of her and her lips glisten in the bedroom light. Both of us are breathing hard in the moment that seems to go on and on.

In her most demanding tone she growls, "Put it in… now…"

The bed is rocking against the wall as a chorus to gasps and moans, pleasured claws are dragging the blanket half off the bed as she screams that she's cumming. Her body shakes and spasms, a warm blast hits my leg as she squirts and shakes all over. Savage hands are holding tight on her hips when a tortured roar slips out of me. The surprised intensity of my orgasm pulses when I pull out to cum, a shot hitting her halfway up her back, the next I aim perfectly for her asshole. The third and fourth hit home, a fifth crowns the hot mess I just made between her legs.

Her body stops shaking as my right leg gives up. Falling onto my right knee, it's barely supported by the edge of the bed. A mixture of our cum flows down her ass crack, onto her well-exercised, engorged woman parts, and on both sides of her inner thighs. Her face is red and makeup smeared, hair matted wet. Laying onto my side, I notice my body is sweat sheen'ed. We stare into each other's eyes briefly while breathing hard.

With twitchy motions aspiring to addiction, I shout "More cocaine!" and slap her ass, leaving a stain with my cum-soaked hand.

After that, we both put a patchwork of random floor clothes on, and headed back to the kitchen for more blow. She could barely walk in my PJ bottoms.

Fuck that night was so hot. She passed out for 24 hours, crashing hard once all the liquor and drugs had been sifted through our souls. After finally waking up, she cooked me Chinese food before heading home. Today you'd never guess she loved to get high and fuck, her profession strictly white collar, her friends and family all upper crust.

She's such a good person, I still don't know who used who more.

I sometimes want to give her a call and catch up, but I leave what we had in the past.

We have no connection now other than the time machine I call a hard drive.

Laying down, drunk and spent; having jerked off to my own amateur porn. Doubt my attendance to any art show would happen even if they paid me to go tonight. Don't even have the drive to be getting up off this couch. A half-hearted effort to clean myself up is made and it's time to grab a blanket and pillow. It's like 7:30 PM on a Thursday night and I'm ready to pack it in, lame. Whatever, it's hard to go out and socialize once my sexual needs are taken care of.

13 Huggles

Another Friday's here and I don't care. Lacking serotonin puts me in that purgatory headspace where resting won't satisfy me and the idea of partying is just a drag. Anxiety to produce something fills my mind, morning throws open the gate and waits for me to charge out of it. Life is a long Monday. Somehow the energy to get out of bed comes to me, teeth get brushed but a shower fails to manifest. I pick the least wrinkled shirt to wear as the coffee machine makes fun of me. Each sputter from Hamilton Beach a reminder that at least it has a purpose.

Morning at 9 AM is too early. My day kick-started as artists trickle through the door, lighting up the studio with productivity. Painting, songs, talking, and one artist's home baked cheese bread. She's getting better at this, still too much salt. I find my Zen and manage to get a canvas piece of my own started. Last night's reminiscing fuels today's flurry of activity. Friday's work hours fly by in a daze and soon I'm in the middle of a few joints being passed around during the end-of-week meeting, smiles all around. The studio clears out of the artists I've been working with, my staff goes home, I'm all alone and it's 6 PM again. Sighing as I look for a place to sit, fucking finally with some time to myself.

The couch beckons me to take a deserved break, I sit down and the first shoe comes off easily, the other refuses to kick off. My frustration level ramps up, the back of my heel finds the edge of the couch frame to pry the other one off. One arm extends behind the couch grabbing at a fleece blanket stashed there. Laying down and wrapping myself with it, soon cocooned and peacefully relaxing, alone. A friendly reminder goes off on my phone, shit. Guess those cocktails Misha wanted this Friday night aren't happening. Misha will take the hint without needing to call her. A rock bottom libido makes masturbation seem boring. I couldn't even be bothered to use Misha as a human fleshlight tonight, and certainly not while having to leave my house to entertain her first. I doubt she's waiting for me anyways. My mind clears and my world goes quiet.

Blue grey steel, the crush of stale air, it's my turn on duty, and I get up off my bunk. Cramped spaces, metal pipes, dials and gauges are telling me about the world outside. Diesel engines roar and clatter from some unseen source. It's impossible to tell which direction all this noise is coming from. Aesthetics don't matter, utility and function do. Everything is lit in red. A maze of corridors and passageways lead to the bridge of this empty vessel. The periscope is ice cold on my face, and its pitch black outside. I'm all alone. Solitary, I'm underwater hunting for something, even in my dreams. An alarm goes off.

My phone is ringing. I sit up and fumble around for my coat on the ottoman. The ring continues screaming in my tired ears, someone must really want to talk. Maybe it's a bill collector.

"Hello," the word a grumble from my throat.

Her warm familiar voice on the line, she's off work, bored, and looking for a friend. She sounds unhappy in the way happy flowers can remind you of funerals. Karen invites herself over before my offer to hang out leaves my lips. She'll be here in 10. Hanging up the phone, a whiff of stench hits me. A quick sniff of my armpits reminds me of garbage. I smell of stale farts, sweat and trash.

Peeling my ass off the couch wasn't easy. Frustrated, minutes wasted finding my razor, slayer of neckbeards. After a quick shower and being meadow-fresh, some new grey hair makes me feel old. I'm glad all the younger women around keep me feeling youthful. Its dark out, the solitary bathroom light throws shadows around the loft. Crypts and closed coffins have less isolation and better lighting at night, maybe a couple of switches flipped on will fix the atmosphere. Some bums are yelling in my alley. Usually it's "Fuck-something" or something indecipherable mixed in with the crashing sound of shopping cart metal, not this time. Today it's "Charlie, you know you're gonna get it!" Whoever Charlie is, or what he's going to get, doesn't sound good. Being glad I'm not Charlie causes my skull to break out in smile hives. My phone cuts through Charlie's bullshit problems and alerts me to my friend's arrival. It's been awhile since I've seen Karen, my curiosity bites on how she's been doing.

Pressing 9 to buzz her up, a minute or so later my door beeps to greet a visitor. Her steps down the hallway are silent, she must be dressed down. Karen turns the corner of my foyer hallway and isn't smiling.

"Hey," I say. Not exactly my best at an enthusiastic greeting.

I did miss her, even though I'm poor at maintaining friendships. I have a hard time showing people I care, or knowing when someone cares about me.

"Hey," she whimpers.

She puts down a liquor store bag and her purse on my couch.

"I need a smoke," she mumbles.

"Why so glum, chum?" My voice, so keen.

A nonchalant elbow rests on my desk, Digital Photo Professional up on the screen. She normally checks out my latest photos when she visits, this time she's agitated and ignoring them.

"I'm DONE with men, done."

Her hands find her smokes and she walks past me towards the window. She probably needs me to be an ear.

Anxiety is laying down, back unnaturally twisted and arched, finding her fingernails in wood.

While listening to other people's problems, nerves dart my eyes around the room. Daymares spawned by broken emotions, lamenting my own torments that might someday unlock their own cell doors.

Fresh dirt patted down with a shovel, hidden rocks clang on metal. A thunderclap follows the crescendo of rain and the finality of burying your past. Cliché.

I don't want these memories sitting around in a sunny park sipping wine, I want them to know exactly where they belong.

I pick up my pipe, baggie, and lighter and join her by the window.

The cherry burns a pumpkin orange, a dot of fire reflecting in her wet eyes. She turns her head and exhales out the window. "I am not kidding, I wish I were a lesbian," she says, her voice jagged with sadness.

Her modest clothes fit a little tight on her, a red sweater, blue jeans. The instinct to hug her hits me, but I don't.

"Do you have any idea how many guys have lied to me about what they want? I'll be in someone's arms for an hour, cuddling, and if I stop them from getting any, I'm the bitch, really?" Another drag of my pipe, I can only nod.

I know exactly what she's talking about, as a teenager my hormones raged, emptying me of my ball juice and tact. It took me a decade to awaken to the idea that sex could mean anything. I don't even remember if I lost that principal, or if any belief in it existed in the first place.

This is Karen's latest visit, and I'm her best male friend. That seems odd to say, considering I haven't been that great of a friend to her. We used to have sex and talk music, a relationship based on convenience for me. I lived blocks from her workplace and she saved an hour and a half worth of commute by staying over. I guess at the time she was more into hookup sex, and I was certainly happy to oblige. Now she's been explaining her empty love life after watching her younger sister have a kid before her. I try and remind her that her sister's relationship is rocky and probably not going to last. So what if she's had a child, her sister will be worse off when the guy eventually fucks off, but it doesn't make a difference to her. She sees herself as unattractive to men for anything other than fucking.

"Dylen do you know what it's like to be told one thing and consistently witness completely different actions?"

I want to tell her I have, but I'm usually so caught up in my own bullshit that I forget.

"I had a guy that took me out for drinks a few times. He works on the floor above me. He was a real genuine guy who even remembered my birthday when *YOU* didn't."

My small glass pipe is packed with some dank, fresh bud. She smokes her skinny menthols.

"I knew about his dog and how it had cancer, his mom's business and how it got robbed. He drove me to get a battery for my car. Do you know how this made me feel? Wanted. Respected. Valued."

She flicks her ash out of my window.

Sparkling lights of the Vancouver waterfront burn deep yellow. In the distance a port crane is lifting a container, no doubt full of cheap Chinese shit.

"What do you think happened next Dylen?" She says my name almost with a sigh.

Her eyes drop to her burning smoke. Flick.

"Nothing good," my sardonic reply lingers in my mind, what a downer.

Getting high isn't to feel a buzz anymore, but instead to forget her problems. Caring hurts.

"I get a text from his wife, asking me who the fuck I am. Yes, his wife. THEN you know what happens Dylen? He ignores me. He won't even acknowledge I exist. I've passed him at work and he won't even make eye contact with me. Do you know what this has done to my heart Dylen? Do you?"

My nose tingles as empathy takes its toll to weigh down my eyelids. I put the glass pipe to my lips, light, toke, and exhale. Numbed reality in bite sized pieces is easier to forget.

In a time gone by, showing up at her work and busting his fucking head would be a good idea. I'd take the time to beat a man until he's bloodied, then kicking him when he's down. Laughing as his head flops around and hearing that guttural breathing when someone is unconscious, then stomping him in the balls until his testicles are full of hemorrhage gravy.

World-Star! World-Star!

Teach him a real lesson for insulting her honor and hurting my pride. Maybe he just gamed her for a little action on the side. Maybe somewhere on a PUA forum he's explaining how he first gained her trust at work, in the elevator. Whatever, she's not my sister, no skin off my back. I've probably done similarly heartless things that I've forgotten about.

Karen crosses her arms on the window sill and puts her chin down. She flutters her eyes and swallows while her head drops to rest on her forearms.

"I've been raised to believe that men are inherently good and that I'll someday be wanted, and I've refused to believe you're all fucking like this Dylen." The anger in her voice cuts into my tranquility.

She briefly lifts her head for a drag, and rests it again on crossed arms.

"I just don't know anymore, not anymore."

Her eyes close, blue smoke curls from her nose and into little vortices before drifting away. I move a little closer to her and put my arm around her. A wannabe caring hand rubs along her shoulder and pulls her in, I wish I could tell her to hold on to hope, but I can't. Lies are lies, even when told to make someone smile. Many words can describe the type of dickhead I am, but a liar isn't one of them.

Her sweater is warm to the touch. The soft fabric feels very gentle and feminine in my palm. Menthol and perfume surf the breeze and this smell will be forever burned into my mind as a sad one.

"Whatever," she says, her arms uncrossing.

She flicks her smoke into the alley below.

"Do you want a beer? I brought a cold six!"

She stands up and steps over some of the pillows that lay scattered by the window. Last year I built a thickly carpeted wood platform, about a foot off the ground, triangle shaped and pushed into the corner. It serves as a relaxation area that keeps turning into a confessional.

"Yeah," I reply.

My place is in a warehouse converted to a loft with 20 foot ceilings, the fifth floor is higher than a normal five-story height. Directly under the window is an alley, a two-story warehouse across from it. I can see the next street over and a trendy club sits facing my building along that street. Bad bitches in near painted-on dresses, loud, drunk men puff up their chests. Tonight, like every Saturday night, there are fights and bullshit spilling into the night air.

Karen returns with a Corona. It's ice cold, what a good girl.

"Come on, I have some new music to show you," she smiles, turns, and walks over to my computer.

It's at a stand station behind a curtain that currently separates the photo studio from the art gallery and business portion of the studio. A

THC filled haze floats through the air from another relaxing glass pipe toke, the showoff in me blows a smoke ring out the window for style. A blonde girl outside of the nightclub screams and wraps her arms around a fat brunette. Thirsty lips command a long drink of my Corona, my subdued attention leading me to my computer. Karen's a little short with a Brazilian like body. Plump, round bottom, thick legs, and a large double d-cup chest. Her figure is very well proportioned and her face is Adele pretty, if a little girl-next-door plain. In make-up she's a fox, but it's about as much of her style as a four door Mercedes would be in yellow. Her arms barely reach over the top of the desk, which is designed not for sitting at, but for standing. Feels good to see her relaxed and smiling, she's able to let down her guard and just be herself around me.

"Ok Dylen, this is an old track but I just discovered it, and I think you'll like the video!"

A heavy guitar riff pumps out of the speakers and my eyes look at the clock. Its midnight, should be good for another hour at this volume.

Karen and I alternate our musical choices and lose track of who's Corona is who's, multiple times. Several cigarettes and bong tokes over the next hour, light hearted conversation, and dancing lift the spirit. It could be the booze, but my heart warms knowing she is happy, even if any of this sexual tension won't go anywhere. We sit by the window and watch people file out of the nightclub at closing, people falling down like dominoes. The club's bouncer gets between two guys scrapping. A stretch Hummer limo pulls up with pink hoverlights.

"Oh Dylen, look!" Karen says with excitement "It's like the automotive version of The Jersey Shore!"

I laugh, "Does it have truck nuts?" I question out loud, she probably doesn't even know what truck nuts are.

Karen finishes the last sip of our last Corona.

"Wait, I take that back, it's white and has pink lights, that's kind of cool. It looks like ice cream floating on bubble gum, or a vanilla ice cream float over cream soda!"

Being so stoned, my tongue flickers in excitement with what that would taste like right now.

"Mmmmm," I almost drool on the desk.

Karen looks at me funny.

"Dylen, you're the only guy who makes porn noises when you think about food."

Three AM. The nightclub is finally silent and the window entertainment is no more. Karen and I love to people watch. We collapse together on my couch and I cover her in a blanket, spooning until she falls asleep in my arms. Laid down next to her, I get pretty hard out of instinct, but I don't try anything. Besides, I've already filled her up many times in the past, and fucking her would feel like I'm going backwards. I hate the idea that she would think I'm just another guy who hangs out with her to get my dick inside her. Don't ask why it bothers me so much. My only thought about that is she reminds me of what a traditional woman was like. Demure, submissive, kind.

When I first met her, she was always smiling, wanting to talk about happy things, how she loved her family and how much she admired her mom. A product of divorce like I am, she instead decided to try and love more instead of letting the rage from being abandoned get to her. Look where that's lead her to now.

Here she is, a bit older, a bit more beaten down in life. It hurts me to see someone without a bad-bone in her body getting used as she does. I look at her face and begin to imagine all of the girls who get into the porn business, used, grinded up like meat, fucked and facialed for the men of the world to jerk off to. Maybe porn whores are people too, like Karen, trying to eke out an existence for themselves. Maybe missing fathers made them crave male attention and receive it in the easiest route possible, Karen's lucky to have a mother who put so much effort into teaching her good values. Without them, she could be just another internet meat hole, used by inconsiderate people for their own profit or pleasure. I carefully move off the couch, open my fridge, and pour a stiff whiskey on rocks.

As chilled spirits touch my lips, the clanking of ice cubes around the cup fill my ears. It's surprising how loud the little details are at 3:30 AM. The gate of my building rattles open as if the alley wanted to say good morning while popping ice cubes says good bye to sobriety. Sometimes it surprises me how fast I can drink a near full glass of whiskey, these three ice cubes don't take up much room in this glass. Karen deserves to be with someone better, which is how I felt about the first girl I fell in love with. I couldn't date someone who couldn't be proud of who she was with.

Tall, young, educated, and classy with perfect teeth, I couldn't help but feel that I would ruin that chick. Karen deserves better than someone who would use her, and that other girl certainly deserved someone better than me. I loved how she would turn down any of my music with swearing and aggressive lyrics, the fact she had sensibilities to offend gave me a rush. I actually had to behave. The more I got to know her and her pure essence, the more I realized I couldn't ever be with her. Why? I'd hate myself. I was sure I would bring her down to my level, rather than being able to pull myself up to hers. Maybe that was tradition thinking for me.

A few years have gone by, wisdom now showing we would have met somewhere in the middle. Traditionalism can kill something before it's even allowed to grow. Maybe that same social idealism prevents otherwise compatible people from ever believing in their love. So modern to feel that we'd be incompatible in the long term due to family reasons and status. Anything but by how we'd treat each other. My own family drowning in divorce and apathy. Uncles and aunts of mine fight like children, inventing spiteful nicknames for one another. So much so, my story to strangers and lovers became that I was orphaned. Her family is so close-knit and loving, I had thought there's no way they'd accept me. I saw photos of them on Facebook and I pictured us together, gathered around her family dinner. Concerned parent faces wondering where they went wrong with their daughter. Then again, usually the raunchiest of chicks hide in plain sight. I laugh to myself and picture her on a mattress on the floor nude, doing lines of coke off the dick of some random hookup; unaware of her class.

There's a muffled noise from behind, looking behind me I see Karen rolling over on the couch. She's all bundled up under the covers and looking so peaceful. I'm learning to appreciate the quiet moments as much as the ones full of bang pow boom.

14 Thought Zombie

Contemplating the universe with my dick in my hand, how it ever comes to this is anyone's guess, but I know how it makes me feel. This warm tube appendage holds so much power and strength to keep one going, and to chart a course in life. My penis is the compass needle that should point in the direction of a friendly home port, carrying me across an ocean of possibilities. Instead, I wander and float, taking needed supplies from passing ships. Ancient sea faring people used the constellations to guide them, a sky full of beautiful heavenly lights. On a clear night in the middle of a calm ocean, I can only imagine the peace and simplicity of that moment; the opposite of my life.

Blackbeard, my dick is Blackbeard. A poor choice of name, my pubic hair is a light brown, when it's allowed to grow. The opening at the tip is a cannon port, firing rounds into or onto a girl to complete the fluid transaction. My second favorite position is when the girl is on top, leaning forward, her back arched for extra tension in her vagina. Memories of countless perky young tits float on my thought stream. Beautiful breasts bouncing against my face, my hands holding onto faceless hips while pushing it in deep. Finishing inside her, I always feel like I've accomplished something, a lack of that feeling when I waste cum on a stomach, tits, ass, back, or face. Visions of gold coins, parrot on my cock. I crack a smile. Little eye-patched sperm bandits, so eager to board another ship and wage war in wombs. My penis, the skull and crossbones on my underwear, pussy juice is as intoxicating to me as rum, a lust for plunder on the open seas of dating.

If I had children by this point in my life, they'd be completely fucked up. I could have some out there and I wouldn't even know.

Rhythmic rain faintly pops and snaps, just me myself and I in the dark. A record that has reached its end, the needle as it marauds across the surface mimics the sound of cloudburst on my windows. I turn over onto my back and old springs under me groan and squeak. I can't sleep. I'm kind of horny and my mind is racing, the slide show of ideas and thoughts turn to sexual memories, evoking exes and flings, their voices, their bodies. I was really popular among local nightclub girls in my early 20s, and all of the attention got to my head a few times. I hung out with my girlfriend and her friend all day at the beach, having fun and being flirty with both of them. Later in the day I was supposed to give the friend a ride home, a detour to my house for lusty, wordless, cheating sex. She was a petite and very sexy Asian girl, tiny ass and perky tits, her vagina's labia was much darker than the rest of her skin, a deep brown. I came inside her and drove her home. I would go back a few times and get blowjobs in my car, my Mustang being so obnoxiously loud, she would have to sneak out and meet me blocks from her parent's house.

Rain. It's simple. I relax and clear my mind. Rain. I still recall the way steam rises from the surface of outdoor pools. Years back I rented a house with a hot tub and pool in the backyard, used many nights for impromptu parties with liberated females. Bikini tops are as unnecessary as phone calls back after fucking. Underwater lights and chlorine laced kissing at 2 AM. My dick conjures up the image of another Asian girl, this one was deaf. I remember she couldn't speak very well but she was very cute. She also would do my dishes whenever she visited, for free. I would pay other girls to clean my house after sex back then, fifty bucks to do all the dishes, wash the floors, and take out the garbage. Her way of showing that she was horny was to say 'love cock' while giggling and holding her hand across her mouth. It was more like 'luv kok' but nothing was lost in translation. I feel my penis stirring, asking what's up. That deaf Asian girl had a really odd vagina, the lips were a purplish grey, and swelled up during sex. I never liked her much, I almost feel guilty.

Is this what other guys do? Is this wanton behavior towards women and what's between their legs the average behavior and thoughts of men? If so, how do I keep any daughter of mine away from men like me? My mind jumps back a decade, all the girls I was with, they wanted to do it. I remember how they would meet up with me knowing full well that we would have sex and that I was seeing other women. Why would I feel bad, unless I believed in gender roles and women to be the less promiscuous, delicate flowers I grew up believing in? No, no, that's antiquated.

Think back to how many women have flat out told you that sex is the only way we connect. I struggle with a traditional mindset and a life that is nothing remotely close to traditional. So much casual sex, I've forgotten more than I can remember. Maybe I'd feel worse about it if I had written it down, the ultimate testimonial to sociopathic dating for sex. My mind wanders through so many scenes of carnal lust. A warm summer's evening, meeting a blonde girl from Coquitlam with giant breasts. She turned into an escort a few years later, I remember she didn't call me back for a month after we had sex the first time because I shot my cum into her hair. I remember it wasn't on purpose, it was doggystyle pullout and the orgasm was particularly strong.

Black and white mirages mingle with skin and shadow, flickering imagery of my first shocking experiences years ago come back to haunt me. I had dated some pretty conservative women before I had my first car. Having a vehicle turns cannon fodder into an officer. The power you have to move people about, take them places, keep them warm, comfortable, and music to carry an upbeat and flirty mood. These two trouble maker teen girls, both 17, met a 19 year old me.

JASON BRYAN

I had a Mustang, the chrome 5.0 on the side a virtual badge of a wanna-be bad boy. I picked these two girls up after talking to them on a local chat line. You could go to a phone booth and get a free hour for a single quarter, as long as nobody else used it. I talked to them for ten minutes before they asked for my phone number. I picked them up in Langley, drove back across the city to my place while they supplied the booze taken from one of their moms. Glacier berry mixes with Russian prince vodka for a 50/50 mix, the trend of strong drinks cemented at a young age. The shorter one, Courtney, gave me a CD to put on and explained her dad gives her liquor to party with on the weekends. It was a Wednesday, but they have a presentation at school they wanted to skip, and I seemed like a cool guy on the phone. I remember the taller one, Hillary, a sharp featured brunette with a beautiful pair of lips. We share laughs about the alternative schools we all fucked up at, our stories are pretty similar.

Later that night we would listen to music, download music from Napster, get blindingly drunk and fuck. No condoms, of course. The girls would be awkwardly making out, but having fun doing it. I fucked Hillary from behind as she straddled Courtney, then lowered my body down and fucked Courtney, she squealed. Hillary passed out and Courtney and I listened to music, drank, and talked. The next morning they Skytrained back to Surrey and I didn't hear from them for months. My dick is pretty hard remembering Hillary's swollen teen tits, and Courtney's big bubble ass on her tiny 5'0 frame. Both had ample amounts of pubic hair, their excited pussies both glowed a pinkish red between pale white thighs. I remember nothing else about them.

I'm pretty hard, but I don't move my hand. I squeeze my dick and more memories play on the back of my eyelids. Living at the time in Coquitlam, there were several periods of life without a steady address.

112

Of all the places I lived as a fucked up youth, this was the most fun. A basement suite with one bedroom and two horny and cocksure young men; liquor, girls, shift work, and Nintendo wrestling games filled my life. I had a shitty job involving three and five ton trucks on a graveyard shift, the head office not even paying attention to the wakefulness or sobriety of their drivers.

Everyone I worked with hated themselves and each other. Get in, do the job, get out. I never socialized beyond 'hey' and 'see ya' with the longer term employees, only the younger guys got along with each other. Everyone else was too concerned with who's getting more hours and the easier route, a stew of union politics and uppity blue collar drones. The only thing that kept me going to that fucking job was the promise of some cold booze and hot pussy on the weekend.

My friend, Chris, had a reputation for pulling in women with his looks and silence. He had a quiet presence that women found alluring, and riding the bus to and from work he would meet high school seniors on a daily basis. He had invited me to crash at his place after a messy, very messy, separation with his young girlfriend. She was 16, cousins with my friend Amanda. Both families equally as fucked up, Amanda to later OD and die as a hooker on Kingsway, while Chris's ex ended up having several children with one night stands. He had a ton of porn magazines from as long back as I knew him, when we were 14. He seemed to know how to seduce women much better than I did at the time, maybe it had to do with how he also started drinking at a much earlier age. I can't even remember how many girls him and I traded back and forth, a couple of 19 year old Lotharios offering bad girls a place to drink and crash.

Life was just a day to day existence at the time, very little thought originating from my head. Days spent seeking out vice, income, pleasure, and laughter. Where did that kid come from, and how did I end up here?

Two particular groups of girls came into our lives, one were volleyball players who followed Chris off the bus. He bought some coolers and a cheap large pizza. The girls came by as I was just awakening from my graveyard shift slumber. Five PM, it was already dark out, and the girls hopped onto the pull out bed and shook me awake. I remember being surprised at how outgoing they were, but then Chris told me they were drinking shots on the bus ride home. Blackstreet, Dr Dre, and Tupac sound like they're rapping underwater, our ghetto blaster long ago blew out its speakers.

The basement suite was more like a poorly converted garage than a proper living space; the walls were paper thin and the construction visibly shoddy. It was perfect for a couple of low life guys with no direction. The tile floors, while cold to the bare foot, helped amplify the tunes and we partied into the night. Chris and a skinny brunette disappear into his room, the door opened a crack and the skinny girl coos the slightly chubby brown girl's name. I was stuck in the main room with a pretty cute but plainly dressed blonde girl. She says "sexual" at nearly anything that turned her on or that she enjoyed. Seeing her friends disappear into the other room together elicited a drawn out "sexual" from her mouth, emphasis on the x. We were drinking and chatting about bullshit, but I wanted some play too. I asked her how experienced she was, she had said her parents never let her date.

She was so shy until she had a few drinks to work up the courage to bluntly ask to see my dick. Being shy and worried her friends would catch her, she put the blankets over her head, covered my body with it, and took my pants off. She rubbed my hard cock over her face and curiously played with it. It was pretty enjoyable and I had a drink in my hand, feeling pretty boss. This went on for some time, the blonde girl rubbing my dick across her soft cheeks, nose, and lips. She put both hands on it and squeezed it too hard, spilling my drink on the blanket. We both laughed. Almost caught with her head under the blanket, the bedroom door opened and the brown girl stumbled out, sobbing, in only her panties.

"What's wrong?" The blonde girl asked, hastily trying to hide the fact that she's straddling me.

The brown girl sits on the couch and quietly sobs. "So ... so embarrassed," she mumbles.

I pat her on the back with a booze-soaked hand. "There's nothing to be embarrassed about here!" I remember telling her, clueless to what just happened.

She explained that she was trying to lose her virginity, her friend and Chris didn't want to stop long enough to get Chris's penis in her. The whole night of drinking was supposed to be about her losing her virginity and not her friend cheating on her boyfriend. Being the gentleman that I was, I offered to take her virginity. She smiled and was shocked that I would want to. She had no hesitation in getting under the blanket and taking her panties off, the blonde girl under the blankets beside her.

I got on top of her, my half-hard penis dropping down to her opening. She was wet but I wasn't going in, her eyes closing as she opens her hips up wider.

"Ohh.." she quietly moaned.

Slowly I began to enter her, getting harder from the moist massage of her tight inner lips.

"Ow... ow, ahh," she groaned. I pulled back out a little, and as I did, she clutched me in her legs and whispered "Don't stop." In one push I had thrust in her all the way, she shrieked for a second and let out a gasp. "Oh the sensations," she whispered, the blonde girl parrots, "Sexual!"

I fucked her slowly for a few minutes and asked her if she wanted to try it doggystyle. She said sure and I rolled her over. Our non-passion had ran down her crack, her brown asshole, a few black hairs creeping up from her vagina, glistened with her juices and blood. A wide set of hips and a bountiful ass, each thrust sent a shockwave through her cheeks, up onto her back. The blonde girl had her hands under the blanket and she sat there, watching intently. The sounds of the bed bouncing could be heard through the walls, the stamped steel legs of the fold out couch tapping out a rhythm on tile.

This period of my life was a time of major growth. I had started to become aware that there were no standards, or rules, for men and women. This newfound clarity hit me hardest immediately after sex.

I finished on her back and she collapsed onto her stomach with a sigh. She was smiling and breathing hard. I fell onto my back between the two girls, and pulled the blanket up over my quickly going flaccid self. The brown girl was so happy to have had sex finally, she high fived the blonde girl first, and then me. I remember it was after 1 AM when Chris and the skinny brunette came out of the bedroom, those wild girls gathered their stuff, put on innocent faces, and headed home.

I booted up the Nintendo 64 and gave Chris a thorough ass kicking at one of the wrestling games we used to play. These were some of my favorite times with him. Our matches would extend into the hours sometimes, but this one didn't. A Kevin Nash big boot busts his face open in red only :50 seconds in, I let up on the beating for a minute or two. He's getting frustrated and I don't want him to rage. He begins to put me into cheap little choke holds over and over, I respond with three pile drivers in a row, 1, 2, 3. Only four minutes into the match, too. Chris threw down the controller, walked into his room, and slammed the door. The shitty drywall cracked along the ceiling. I shut the machine off and got ready for bed, virgin blood marinating my sheets.

Dreamland awaits me.

A person in the suite above me peeing. A faint stream of urine in a toilet, a softening plinking of piss-beam into drops; the flush. Living there, I really began to experience how gritty life can be. People move through their routine looking for stimulus while oblivious to seeking higher purpose. Painted little lottery balls in a tumbling golden cylinder, life revolving the ball-cage around crashing people into each other, leaving their marks and smudges. Some colours never run, others change greatly over time, others go blank. Maybe if I had been raised differently, I would have never been in the position to see life like this. Meetings are much less random when you're goal driven and have faith in a culture or way of life, rather than seeking stimulus to quell boredom and piss yet another meaningless day away.

It's funny to recall how important it was to me as a teenager that my girlfriend was a virgin. I lost my virginity at 15 and then dated a 13 year old for six months, taking her virginity due to little supervision, total boredom, and raging hormones. When I wasn't in school, I was invisible to my divorced parents, their single lives taking precedence. Was that the start of seeking so much sex for pleasure, the fact that we could have such pleasurable fucking with no worries or consequence, freeing me from boredom? I think of what the Church said about contraceptives over the years and wonder if they were right to a degree. Does it take the love out of it? No, it frees us from the limits of our bodies. We can fuck and enjoy more of life because of contraceptives.

Right?

I shouldn't blame drugs for my own promiscuity, and being promiscuous isn't bad. You're only a boring prude if you don't fuck as many hot bodies as possible. Maybe being a swinger is the ultimate goal; to have a mate that allows you sex with anyone you choose, safely.

I don't want to ruminate on this, when I turn ideas over in my head this much, I feel like that shit smelling homeless guy screaming about the end of the world. To what point does this thinking lead to? It never does anything better for my life. My youthful-self had such idealistic views to what sex was supposed to be like, special, loving. I'm 35 now and sex is the last thing I care about when it comes to a *girlfriend*. I picture the type of woman who I want to date, and it's someone who needs me, and wants to be needed by me. Free, yet together.

I squeeze the flesh in my hands, and I'm soft. The sensation brings back more memories. The married Russian girl I fell for, her style, love, and dreams were all so European and all very lady like. She surprised me with food, gave me hour long massages, and would love to lay in bed and kiss for hours. She looked strikingly similar to one of the girls I ended up with at Chris's den of debauchery. Crocodile girl.

I shiver as I recall how Chris dumped a bucket full of snow on me while I was sleeping, what a fuckhead. I woke up gasping for air as powder filled my nose and caused me to inhale, choking on it and falling out of bed in my underwear to laughter. My first instincts kicked in for flight or fight, and I growled in startled anger. Chris had a whooping, high pitched laugh when he was feeling mischievous, and it followed him into the yard as I sprinted out after him in my ginch. A couple meters outside my door and I realize this might look bad to the neighbors, but I have to toss a few snowballs first. A hard packed iceball slams into Chris's side on my second throw, the cold air and snow up to my knee pushes me back indoors. I watched from the open doorway as snowballs were crisscrossing the driveway while I could hear girls laughing. He must have picked some up on the way home, again.

Throwing on pants meant the battle of a lifetime, artillery sized snowballs and body checks into huge drifts of snow that stuck into clothing.

The girls were completely soaked when we went back inside, but not in the good way, yet. We offered them shirts to change into while their clothes dried, after we drank paralyzers and put on some music. There were four girls, one of them a cute brunette named Deanna. We ended up hanging out for a few days, sometimes making out when drunk, a lot of petting, a group of horny girls with nothing better to do and a couple of 19 year old guys with access to liquor. I remember Deanna asking me to go get her nachos from 7-11, which I did. After I got back and she finished eating, I remember her telling me I get my reward now. She brought me into Chris's room, away from the other girls, pulled off her pants and panties, and spread her legs on the bed. Instantly excited, I got on her, fucked her for a whole total of five minutes, and came on her stomach. She wiped it off with my shirt, pulled up her pants, said "I hope you enjoyed that," and walked out of the room.

I would later find out that she was a 17 year old runaway; her father had molested her and threatened to feed her to crocodiles if she told anyone. Chris and I had been contacted by the mother who found the number on her call display. Deanna usually goes missing for a few days at a time, but this time, it was a week. We gave genuine sympathy to the mother and felt bad for a few minutes. This is where Chris started the nickname Crocodile Girl. I met up with Deanna years later off a local dating website, she came over and we had sex on my toilet during a party. Her violently riding me caused the back of the toilet to crack and the subsequent leak and repairs cost me a few hundred dollars. I never saw or heard from her again, but she lingers on in my mind.

My dick is half hard. I don't want to think about her. Deanna at 17 and her again at 20 were very similar looking, the 20 year old her had full breasts and a waxed pussy, she showed up to my party in jean shorts and no underwear. She sucked on a popsicle, sitting on the kitchen counter, staring people down. She was aggressive and sure of herself, perhaps the best way she had of hiding her fucked up past. The crotch of the jean shorts weren't very good at covering her, soft labia peeked out on one side and a few people at the party would whisper to each other to look. I squeeze my penis in hopes the memories of that fucked up chick would go away.

Waves of dim coloured lights scatter across the backs of my eyelids, the blanket smells of sweat, body odour, heat and lingering girl. I want something else. If fitting into the mold has lead me here, where I'm in bed and recalling so many nameless women I've had sex with, then the mold must be broken. This is a sicklove for the bottle, the pill, the line, the pink slit, the high moments of life with none of the downsides and none of the responsibility of having to care about temporary partners. None of the respect or dignity of feeling wanted. A disjointed flashback to a recent fling, we drank at a bar, talked about life. We later ended up fucking on my couch. Vivid images of her pale little ass slide through my mind, my hands on her hips as a spider's web of blonde hair erupts over her face, neck, and shoulders. Her moaning while I finish on her, she wipes cum off her with a towel while I step to the kitchen and pour myself a glass of water. She flicks on a light switch to find her panties. I walk back to the couch and slide my hand across it to find cold leather, and take a seat.

I feel relaxed, she just found her panties. She pulls them on one leg at a time, and with a snap of the elastic, she bursts into tears. "I know you don't want me here now," she chokes out through a whisper. Her lithe wrist finds bangles on my desk, clinking together while she slides them up her forearm. I walk over to her and put my arms around her, "Don't say that, you know I like your company". She's right in a sense, I like her as a person, but after sex I just wanted her to leave.

Emotions battle nitric oxide inside my confused appendage, images of past sex still pleasantly churning inside my head. My purple couch, the night before the morning I fell in love with her. The girl I call Dark Heart, I can't drive over the Lions Gate Bridge without her face, her touch, her essence coming to mind. She probably thought I was just another notch on her belt, her having chased me for two months. She had been wasted, had coke given to her by my friend's ex in the Roxy bathroom. We made out in a 7-11 and knocked a bunch of shit over before we were kicked out. Here she was, on my couch, wasted.

Her eyes could barely open, she pulled off her pants and panties to spread her legs wide for me, a little bit of hair growth around her juicy and wet slit. I didn't want to fuck her like the rest. I didn't want it to be this way, just another fluid swap, a girl that I feel from the inside a few hot times before she becomes memory. I touched her delicate parts and lost interest in her body, her being completely wasted made me feel like I could be anyone. She would fuck anyone right now. I fell asleep next to her naked, and woke up stewing in her piss.

She pissed the couch.

We woke up at roughly the same time, her face a grimace of hang-over and headache. She asked me for a ride home, I grunted no. I was laid down in her piss and didn't feel like fucking driving. She got dressed and saw herself out, I stood up and the smell hit me. Body heat warmed urine over leather, if I marketed a cologne, this would have to be it. The couch took hours to clean. I'll never forget as I was showering off her golden juice, how much I actually liked her. I didn't fuck her like the ones before her, I wanted it to mean something. What a pussy, I felt like a total faggot for not nailing that hot slut right then and there. What weakness I showed by not giving her what she wanted, a good hard drunk fuck. At least then she would have remembered me, what I felt like inside her. So many women I only remember because of sex. If I had just fucked her, maybe she'd remember me. I sigh. She once told me unhealthy people love in unhealthy ways; I'm beginning to think she was right. My hand kneads my penis; completely limp.

15 Phoning It In

Seagulls and brake squeal don't get me out of bed, but having to pee does. I usually leave my phone beside my bed when I sleep, in case anyone needs to reach me in the middle of the night. I always had the idea that a real friend is someone you could call at any hour, if your car had a flat, or if you're feeling shitty. My friends now mostly don't have cars, and we drink away our feelings together. Stumbling to the toilet and my aim is spray and pray, I don't think I hit the water at all. I flush my deep orange away as a darkened toilet nags me to drink more water.

Sleeping bones need a few stretches while my brain is a sluggish mess until coffee. I feel reborn. Last night I must have spent hours holding onto my cock and pondering life, it's already noon. The smell of diesel exhaust hits my nose as beeps from a backing up truck puts me in an urban trance. Dazed, I sit down on the couch while the coffee priest begins to dribble a commune with his people. What conclusion did I come to last night? I don't remember if there was one. My phone is beautiful. The icons greet me with cheer and usability maximized by pleasant colours and developer conferences. A few texts from friends, one interests me for more than a passing moment. Misha wanted to come by at 10 with some banana bread, her next message is a reminder for this evening.

I don't remember what day it is. A few taps and I know it's another Friday, my mind floods with prediction of enjoyment tonight. Kiki and Misha are always fun, I love to rub upper class elbows. Little crackers with jelly, cheese, crab meat. Tangy cocktails of lemon juice paired with pome-granate juice, a hint of mint and enough sparkling white to give it some fizz. They'll call it something like lounge/garden fusion, proper speak for getting your lean on. Having lived in fucking poverty I can appreciate getting robo'd up while worrying about rent. You just have to remember to pick the right bottle for the DXM trip, keep an eye on those aspirin levels because those ambulance rides aren't cheap. The crowds at the fashion shows never have had to live in a roach-filled bachelor suite, their smiles and gaits are groomed. Shiny, new, so perfect are these luxurious apes.

My grey sport coat will work with my tight black pants. I call them the ball crushers, after discovering that sitting without supportive underwear will turn my grapes into wine. The black CK's need a wash, I was out with some chick last week and make-out fueled precum left a stain in them that vaguely looks like Russia. Vodka for predrinks if the girls meet me here first, if not, I still have an unopened twixer here I was saving for myself.

My mind wanders, opening Facebook on my phone. Wish the coffee maker would hurry the fuck up. Mindless status updates, political links, pictures of people's snotty kids, a Rhianna video with her ass and titties hanging out. Phil Corgiman, a Facebook dog I added months ago, wrote a message that resonates within me.

'Hello my facebook friends! Woof! My owner and his girlfriend aren't getting along anymore. :`(Sometimes people aren't sure of what they want or who they are and people do change! I don't think I'll be around to be friends with all of you for much longer. I want you all to know that I will miss you so much and that over the last year you all made me really really really really REALLY! HAPPY!. Maybe if mom and dad can work things out I'll be back but right now it doesn't look good mom won't be around to update this page anymore after this so take care all!!! I will miss you, Bye! –Phil n mom'

Breaking up for me has mostly been easy, losing interest after a brief period or a couple years at most, just repeatedly finding it was time to move on. I miss having those uneasy flutters inside of deep attraction and adoration, rather than the lust in my dick that drives me now. My mind floats an image of a butterfly, black and digesting inside me. Yellow majestic wings which once brought me love carried on the winds of pleasant rewarding anxiety, caring. These once brilliant monarch masts are now torn and folded, bubbling in a pool of acidic stomach bile. The happy little cartoon butterfly face blackens as it liquefies and becomes a caved in, blistered nothing, dead and putrefied. Losing the butterflies is numbing, losing a dog would be heartbreaking.

Coffee's ready.

My afternoon is a smear of caffeine and work. A client buys three paintings, new art gets hung up, and I upload some porn movies to advertise the hot seller of the month; black lesbians. If art sales is connecting people with manifestations of emotions, thoughts, and perspectives, porn sales is about getting people into lust. I exploit the brain's inability to see beyond sex organs and wide open holes, feed them what they crave in the moment and move that product. The people in the videos are inanimate objects, props. I post porn to YouJizz the same way someone puts up a piece of their art on my gallery wall.

You put the paint in the right places on canvas to illicit thoughts, a price tag next to it. The porn has men and women who are just products, animated dolls without any mind connection to me, just holes and holefillers arranged like marionettes dancing for a crowd of men sitting in the dark, the backgrounds of most porn sites are white. Monitor glow always reminded me of indoor moonlight. I can block these thoughts out long enough to sell it online, the extra cash put towards liquor and party favours. The bodies of beautiful women used for masturbatory purposes, the complete amputation of intimacy. I learned how to cum on a girl's face from porn, but I never liked the girl much after I did that. This bout of afternoon depression is chased away with a lighter and a fat joint, thinking this way can't be healthy. Not thinking at all is my preferred state.

Misha calls me, her and Kiki are driving through Kits blasting music. The raw excitement of her voice yanks my face into a grin. Misha laughs and tells me Kiki had a shot of tequila with dinner and is driving drunk, Kiki protests on speaker phone, but her crackling laugh only makes her sound wasted. I laugh. I want to tell her to pay more attention to the road, but relax and put some faith in my friends being responsible enough not to drive when shitfaced. I hope. Misha barks that they're on their way and I need to be ready. There's no way the parking meter is going to steal money from Misha's 'Gettin' Juiced' fund. My mind dreams of biting and sucking on Misha's tits. I could block it out, but I just took off the cap of a 26'er of JD and embrace it wholly. Come to think about it, I need some new tits to suck on.

A few sips of that brew and I'm rip roaring ready to go out. I throw on some angry black people music to put me in the mood to party, and even comb my hair. A fresh razor obliterates my neckbeard and I pop a zit on my ear, the fucker bleeds a lot. Another swig of the bottle and I'm putting on my shoes, my fancy jacket's sleeves are too short when I bend over, need to remember that so I don't look like a tool. Hunter instinct guides me to grab tools of the trade; my phone, wallet and keys, finally ready to go. Lock the door, down the hall, elevator, and I'm on the street. Kiki and Misha spot me before I see them, and several blasts on the horn and my eye finds them flashing high beams from down the block. "Get the fuck over here!" Misha yells through the sunroof.

"Coming Mish, hold on," I mutter. A trip crossing the street and my shoe squishes a big pile of shit on the other curb. Fuck. Walking up to Misha's car, I show them the shit and Kiki hands me a water bottle with a spray nozzle top. "Dylen your neighborhood is so fucking gross. You probably have bedbugs, too." Misha frowns. I spray the shit off as best I can, as a single corn husk is stuck in the tread of my shoe. I begin to wonder how many dogs eat food with corn in it, and try to block out the thought as I hop in the back of Kiki's ride.

Kiki floors it. The car rockets up the street and Misha nearly drops the drink she hands me in a plastic bottle. "All I had, white rum, your favorite!" Misha cackles, obviously she hit the sauce already. Taking a swig and the lukewarm white rum makes me gag.

"Oh fuck you Dyl!" Kiki yells as she pulls over 3 lanes of traffic to stop.

"No, keep going, I'm not going to puke dummy," I reply, choking back bile.

I take another swig and my stomach contents go back down my throat. Kiki pulls back into traffic and I hand Misha the nearly empty bottle.

"We are going to have so much fun tonight guys!" Kiki bubbles as she blows a yellow. "Seriously, this show is going to be amazing. There's light art, beautiful fashion, some incredible jewelry, and the DJ has opened for Tiesto!" Misha fast forwards a shitty track into a kicking party anthem, my head nodding back and forth to the tunes while Jack and rum fight it out in my system.

Three near collisions and several yellow lights dashed through, we arrive in the Olympic village, near the venue for the fashion show. Kiki pulls out a white security card and pulls into an underground parking ramp. With a swipe the gate opens up to reveal an almost empty lot.

"My boss lets me park here if I wash his car for him. He's got two spots and never uses the other one, and I never wash his car!" Kiki says through a laugh.

I smile. Kiki would wash the car if he really asked her to, kind of why I like her in some fucked up way. I know her word means something, I really admire that. She guns it into the underground, whips the car around a corner, and pulls into a spot. I catch myself meeting eyes with her in the rearview and squint at her. She smiles and turns her rearview away.

Exiting the car, Misha and Kiki look sexy, both in high heels and some of their nicest clothes. Kiki is a little top heavy for modeling, but Misha fits the bill. I remember why we've fucked so much as we leave the underground, her switching walk shows off her gorgeous curves. The converted warehouse used for the fashion show is across the street and looks busy. Misha hands me a VIP card and says "If anyone asks, you're with ZOM Photo, got it?" I nod and put the pass in my pocket. Kiki looks at me, "Remember Dyl, be professional. These aren't your normal party people." Misha adjusts hers perfectly sideways, wedged between her breasts. Kiki sighs. I laugh. Kiki coughs and pulls the card out from Misha's breasts. We step through the front doors, trade our passes for stamps on the wrist, and mingle with the haughty crowd.

Bejeweled giraffe necks in gossamer stand next to penguins, or I'm just really ripped. Glasses clink together and my half-moon eyes wander for hors d'oeuvres, Kiki's breasts push into my back and I glide through the crowd. 'Pardon me,' and 'excuse me;' everyone is so perfect, I don't want to bump them. A silver platter ahead, a petite thumb and four piano fingers hold it aloft, a bounty of grape intoxicant on top traps my gaze. I have to remember not to say 'Give the liquor,' but rather, 'May I?' and 'Thank you'. The glass is of such high quality, bubbly pale gold seems to hang in the air rather than in the flute.

"What are you doing Dylen?" Kiki laughs, "Cheers!" Misha, Kiki, and I clink our glasses together. Kiki bounces a little and a ripple runs across her tits, still natural. "Oh hey, look who it is!" Misha says with excitement.

Then, I see her. Blue eyes set in a face of slight pink cheeks and golden skin. Those teeth are perfect, brilliant snow white chiclets. Raven hair pulled back tight into a bun, a purple metallic dress contours to her hourglass, my eyes spending time taking in all of her curves. Vertigo hits as gravity loses the strength to keep me centered, her essence draws me into orbit as my mind flounders in euphoria. A hairy, chubby hand slides around her waist. My heart ordered a filet mignon and what I got was bird shit between two stale loaves.

Kiki gives an awkward "Uhhm" followed by a pause, "Dyl, this is Eric, Devon, Miles, and Crissy."

Devon's eyes linger on mine and I've seen that look before. Eric's fat paws drip with gold, his suit a midnight black and without a crease, a picture perfect embodiment of cash and excess. My shirt is wrinkled and I can feel a piece of my dinner stuck between my front teeth. My mind wanders and I remember I only have $20 left to spend responsibly tonight.

Eric's hand extends out, an eyebrow raised and a smirk on his face.

"Pleasure meeting you," Eric says.

"Hey."

I shake his moist, doughy hand.

His watch is gleaming gold, moving Swiss and studded with diamonds.

My watch needs its battery replaced.

"Hey," I reply, not sure if that was more roar or whimper.

No one else offers a greeting but Devon, who gives me a smile and cheerful "Hello!"

Misha walks over with a "Heeeeeey!" her hands nearly juggling what looks like six or seven champagne flutes. "Dyl grab one!" she barks, and soon I'm double fisting dainty booze vessels. Devon even holds her drink like a lady, with poise, elegant and creating her own glow. She doesn't seem too interested in Eric, but he certainly keeps touching her elbows and lower back.

Kiki clip clops around the group giving hugs and catching up, the soundtrack of the night is some trendy house music that mixes hypnotic with crowd murmurs.

Eric takes a flute of champagne and holds it aloft. "A toast to Devon's first collection, the first of many." Expensive glass comes together and there are smiles all around, Devon blushes, her hand holding her drink is wearing a black velvet glove with pearls wrapped around it.

Kiki bounces up and down with excitement as she will take any opportunity to get men to look at her chest. Eric's eyes bloom and focus on her, Devon looks at me with a smile and turns away almost playfully, Misha elbows me in the ribs.

"Hey Dyl, didn't you get two of your protégé artists features in local galleries? Eric does the same with jewelry designers!"

I feel sick. I look at Devon and can't imagine her fucking Eric for a chance at getting her style in front of a crowd. I already could tell by how he always had his hand somewhere on her body. I hate being compared to someone who blatantly gets into a business to trade favors for sex, even though I've slept with a number of the girls that I've worked with over the years. That was different, I never helped or ignored a girl based on the priorities of my cock, and wouldn't escort them around like a show pony.

"Yeah, a couple of them are getting popular," I barely make my rent sometimes. Eric's watch is worth more than my life.

"I own several Vincent Gauthier originals, including his much heralded Gogh Stereo piece," Eric quips with a smirk. I know the piece, a print of it hangs on my studio's wall. Devon laughs, "Eric do you remember when we picked it up?" she squints while holding her stomach, her laugh half shriek, half belly laugh. "Oh Mish, we were in the Ferrari coming out of Kelowna with the top down, the piece was sticking waaaaay up past the windshield and we were trying to hold onto it. Then SOMEONE thinks it's a brilliant idea to stop for slurpees." Eric chuckles.

I try and not smile, but Devon warms my heart.

"*THEN!*" Devon holds her drink in one hand and puts her other arm out on an invisible steering wheel. With ballerina grace, she extends her arm and uncurls her hand, such elegance puts her upper class roots in centerfold. "Eric is driving like this and we take turns holding the canvas in the car, neither of us can see each other. I'm trying to drink my slurpee and hold onto this huge ... Square THING that's like a big sharks fin!" She reaches up with her hand and makes a fin, cutely wiggling like a fish between Misha and Kiki.

Eric squints and grins, waving his hand in the air while he talks. "To be fair, my plan would have worked if she didn't need vodka to survive hanging out with me." Devon puts her arms around Kiki and Misha's shoulders, taking care not to spill her beverage.

"Oh like I have a choice when you're putting mickeys of grey goose in my purse!" Devon retorts. Eric laughs nervously.

"So yeah, I put my slurpee down between my legs and open my purse to pour in a drink, and whoosh! Gogh Stereo is gone!" She throws her free hand up in the air and leans her upper body back with a grin from ear to ear. Kiki laughs while Misha finishes her third flute of bubbly.

Eric's friend's mouth drops open "Oh, my, GAWD!" in the most flamingly stereotypical gay voice possible.

"Gogh Stereo, It just fell out of your Ferrari!"

Eric rolls back on his heels and puts his free hand in his pocket. "Yep!" Devon kisses Kiki on the cheek and looks right at me.

"If you have the original still, it survived hitting the pavement at highway speeds?" the other friend asks.

Eric's smirk grows into a monstrously large Cheshire cat grin, a sneering smile. "We turned around and drove back to get it. The frame was cracked and it had been driven over a few times, but I have the number to a specialist in ancient art maintenance and repair. I sent it to Europe and had them get the tire tracks off of Van Gogh's face. All of the local restoration specialists claimed it was ruined, but my guy was able to save it." Eric beams at Devon. "Yeah, and because it was so trashed, we put it in the trunk and I got to have my vodka slurpee without being some sort of cargo handler!" She finishes the last sip of her drink, gracefully turns, and steps a few feet to exchange the empty for another.

Eric doesn't take his eyes off her, neither do I.

16 Dbaggins Is Not a Hobbit

The place is packed. There's standing room only, almost shoulder to shoulder with only a few gaps to walk through. An announcement comes on over the P.A. "Attention ladies and gentlemen, the first show is set to begin in half an hour. Doors will be opening in 15, so get something to sip and we'll see you at the runway!" The gay friend flicks his golden mane back. "I have to go get ready to take care of business!" he turns to Devon, "Honey, you're going to have an amazing first show, I'll see you guys after the intermission, holla holla!" Eric turns to Misha and Kiki, "Ladies, I have a chilled bottle of Vueve in the car, and a treat for Misha if she can find it. Here." he hands Kiki a BMW fob. Kiki's eyes light up.

"Oh you got your new 5 series!" Eric shakes his head. "750i, Devon helped me pick it out. She fell in love with the silver and I just had to get it." Eric's chubby sausage-hands reach down to pat Devon on her bottom. "Let's go, we have priority seating." Devon loses her smile for a moment, "Ok guys! We'll be right at the stage, meet by the bar at the intermission!" she waves. Eric looks right at me and says, "Cya!" He has his hand on her lower back and guides her through the crowd, looking back at me once with a smirk.

"If I didn't know you better Dyl, I'd say you have the hots for her!" Misha just stares at me. "Pfft, I don't think you know me, she's such a gold digger." I reply, turning my head to sip sparkling white, which might actually be champagne. Devon's perfume leaves me wanting.

Misha smiles, "Yeah well, if she is a gold digger, you can't really compete with Eric. Just enjoy the bottle we're gonna get out of his car later." I nod and pretend to check out the scenery. Devon is one hell of a woman, pisses me off to think that money matters that much to her. The $20 in my wallet and the $18 champagne flutes remind me why money might matter to the urban female. A smiling young girl walks through the crowd with crackers, a crab pate it looks like. I snatch one off the tray and throw it in my mouth, quickly grabbing another before her stern look finds my eyes.

Penguins and pretty ponies line up gracefully and file into seating around the runway, Misha and Kiki are both double fisting drinks and throwing elbows to get good seats. The rustle of chairs continues for about five minutes, or however long it took me to finish another flute. Devon and her cash with legs take a seat right at the end of the runway while we're sitting in the middle. Her eyes glitter and call to me. Desire felt, teasing me the way sandy beach and sun billboard ads do while standing at a rainy bus stop. Envy has never squeezed my chest this tight before. "Dyl! I knew it!" Kiki whispers. I turn and she's got a huge grin. Misha is looking away. I can't help but smile.

"Heheheheh," I chuckle, caught.

"You know she's probably so fucken frustrated with limp dick over there," Kiki is drunk.

I love drunken Kiki, she starts being so real and so honest. I don't think it's the booze talking when I say that I am attracted to her more when she's drunk, she drops her persona and speaks her real mind.

"You should totally get her number!" Kiki's doing her best at staying hushed, but it isn't working, half the row heard that. Before I can answer, a bass note drops and the lights are dimmed. Red lights illuminate the stage and an announcement welcoming us to the show proclaims we're in for a delight of the senses. My eyes casually wander back to Devon and I think I just caught her looking at me.

The first few ensembles of fashion come out looking like ribbons of clothes stapled to an anorexic's frame. Kiki leans to Misha and asks where the boobs are. Another group of women strut down the runway in white dresses, various different exquisite necklaces and bracelets adorn their bodies. "Oh, these are Devon's jewelry models," Kiki whispers. One asian model strikes my fancy, she's wearing the sexiest looking choker made feathers and jade. Her face, symmetry perfected, with hips that jump out of the dress and a pair of perky breasts. A few more pieces come out, each carrying a hoolahoop. Four women each in different coloured clothes stand completely still, staggered a few meters from each other on the runway. The electronic music reaches a frantic pace and the girls bend down and pick up the hoolahoops. They gyrate and spin the hoops which light up in different colours, a few 'whoops!' from the delighted crowd. A woman on stilts walks out from behind the stage's curtain and slaloms through the performers. She reaches into a satchel she's holding and throws large handfuls of glitter everywhere. Half of a handful lands in Misha's drink, "Fuck!" sums up how she feels about it. Kiki has her hand over her drink as she cackles over the throbbing music.

Blue lights strobe over the crowd, flashes of Devon tease my eyes and hold me captive. I have to force myself to look away, her beauty so intense that my body cannot ignore such charisma easily. The dancers file off the stage in sync with men in black jumpsuits walking out from the curtains. Finding inspiration from soldiers on parade, a long black pole with a hook on the end over their shoulders, precise movements while stone faced. They walk to the sides of the stage and put the poles in the air, bundled fabric tied by rope gives way to the hook men in black. Two long, looped pieces of black fabric hang from the ceiling 30 feet above the crowd, and two women, body painted head to toe white, are aided by the men and climb into the loops. Spotlights shine on the women and the music fades into a captivating opera piece while the hanging women writhe and tangle themselves up in the cloth. The body paint rubs off on the black fabric and creates a marbled swirl of light and dark tones, the fabric itself must have had some black paint on it as zebra stripes form on the women during their routine. The set ends to applause with vigor normally reserved for politicians and sporting events.

"Ladies and gentlemen, there will be a 30 minute intermission between shows, please exit the seating area as we prepare for the next show. Thank you." Curtains part in such a way that the crowd filing through resembles a white vagina birthing wealth. A particularly hot and well-dressed woman holds the arm of a fat, balding older man, 'You pay for it in one way, or another' is a sentiment I don't tend to share, but tonight it certainly stings true. Funneling out from the curtains my eyes catch a flickering light across the wide open hall, overhead shine hitting a martini shaker and beckoning me to pay a visit. Kiki clipclops behind me, her hand touches my shoulder "Dyl, we're going to go get the booze from the car!" I nod. Feeling the effects of several drinks in my bladder, now is as good of a time as any to break the seal, I guess.

Walking through a crowd is an art for some, pinball for some others. I've always been good moving through one, picking up on cues and the movement of the whole. Little cliques of men and women are scattered throughout the hall, usually one person talking with all sorts of body language and gestures. Rounds of laugher, cheers and toasts abound. Repeat and substitute celebrity gossip or bragging for the subject matter. Silver platter girls wait while hands snatch off delicious appetizers. A waitress with crackers, cheese, and crab cakes spots me, but it's too late. I already have two crab cakes, one just jumped into my mouth. I exchange a wink for her scowl. I don't understand why she's pissed, she's still getting paid the same whether or not the crab cakes make it to other people, or to just feed me. Maybe she's scowling because I'm getting fat, and I'd look better if I lost a few pounds. Yeah. Maybe.

Down the first flight of stairs I walk, sliding down the banister of the second flight, the basement dark with moody blue lighting. Shadows and exposed piping make the low ceiling look ominous compared to the brightly lit hall above, two girls outside of the women's washroom give me stranger's glances. Piping and electrical boxes tucked into the various nooks and crannies of this basement-tomb come restrooms make me think of the building as a living object, I'd like to admire it's anatomy a bit more, but my bladder is pissed. Ducking inside the men's room and it's beautiful, the way a chain restaurant's bathroom should be. Chrome, mirrors, cocoa wood. A fresh urinal cake, pristine and deep blue, I blast it with piss. A giant crab cake fart exits me with a satisfying rip, I smile and dribble, dribble, shake shake shake! If you shake it more than once, you're playing with it. In my 30s, if I don't give it more than a few shakes, some piss dribbles back out and stains my pants. Nothing says sexy like groin stains.

Washing my hands and checking the mirror, it's tough not to notice I look particularly good tonight. I smile and nod at myself. Not bad Dylen, not bad. Stepping out of the restroom, a tall figure turns the corner from the women's restroom across from me. It's Devon. I stop and she's adjusting one of the earrings, she sniffles a little, her head is down and she can't see me. "Hey Devon" I say, drawing out her name, almost a growl.

She stops and smiles "Oh, hi! ... Damnit!" she says frustrated, trying to get an earring back in.

"Here, let me," I step to her side and look at her earring. Its gold, curved with hints of the feminine shape, a studded spiral of green and purple jewels. Standing so close to her I can smell her enticing perfume and natural pheromones, my nose fantasizes of being between her thighs and taking a whiff of her certainly warm and moist pussy.

Brushing back her hair I can see why it's not staying on, the backing is broken off. "Here, it's fucked, look," holding up the little gold trinket to her eye level. "Oh shit. This is so embarrassing." Devon folds an arm across her chest and holds her head with the other hand. "My first show and my signature jewelry piece broke."

Taking her by the arm gently, I'm not sure if I backed up into the shadows or they extended out knowing my immediate privacy needs.

"No, not broken, stolen," I grin as the earring finds my pocket. "Problem solved."

She laughs through a pout. Her eyes flutter and she's trying to keep her mascara from running. To me it's just a piece of jewelry, to her, it's the reputation of her craftsmanship.

"I'm going to need that piece back, of course. You're friends with Kiki?" Devon gets right back to business.

"I heard about you, she said you have a certain style to everything you do. So do I." She relaxes and puts a velvet-gloved hand to her hip.

"Yeah, and you're the property of that stuffed suit I met?" Way to bring a hot girl down a notch or four, Dylen.

"Hah!" she laughs to hide being so offended. "That's actually my boyfriend," Devon stares into me.

Her eyelids close and squint a little just over her irises, her mouth thins at the edges into a slight smile as her brow tries to remain mad, but relaxes. Tell tale signs I struck a nerve, lusty tension a sure sign a girl wants you to kiss her. I step forward and put my hands on her hips without hesitation, locked on her gaze. "Is that what they call that these days?"

She trembles for a moment. Those beautiful wet, big sapphires shoot cupid into me, her high caliber womanhood enough to leave a goatse-gaped exit wound.

"A girl has to survive in this city, and I'm not some whore." she replies, matter-of-fact.

"Far from," I whisper.

My eyes closing, lips touching hers, the dart of her tongue meeting mine lights up my senses. Time slows and all I can feel is her hands on my back, mine falling off her hips and grabbing a handful of large, bountiful ass. She breathes out and the warm air from her nose tickles my face. My left hand slides up her back and I grab a handful of the hair at the back of her head. I can't help but lose the passion at this point when I realize the irony of our bullshit conversation. Of course she's a whore, she just made out with a complete stranger while dating a man for his money, I just knew what to say and when. We're the same type of person.

Our lips come apart and we both look around to see if anyone noticed. Devon adjusts her dress and then opens her purse, a hand up to her nose to sniff back something. "You got a bullet?" I inquire. "Yeah, here," she hands me a little stainless steel tube, the size of a brazil nut. A bullet is a little bullet shaped device you can fit in your pocket. It has two chambers separated by a knob on the side or a disc on the bottom. It has a hole on one end to snort coke from a chamber that you load by plugging one end, turning it upside down, turning the knob fully once, and turning it right side up and snorting from it.

I prep it for a hit and snort it back. She sniffles.

"Here," she hands me a business card. "Text me after the show, I need my earring back." She smiles, steps out from the shadows and heads up the stairs. Backing up against the wall, I can feel my dick pulling my pants tight around it.

"Wow," I whisper to myself, noticing that I'm still breathing a little faster. I don't know if it's the coke or her kiss, but my soul feels like it's on fucking fire now. I take off my jacket and lean my back up against the cold stone wall for some relief. What a rush.

My phone is eager to interrupt the nice moment between relieving wall and hot back. Misha and Kiki have texted me six times looking for me. Just as I notice their messages, I hear the familiar clipclops of Kiki and the cackling laugher of Misha shuffling towards the ladies' room. "Hehehe! I can't believe I was one of those server girls back in the day, oh my!" Misha laughs. Kiki giggles. "Dyl is going to freak when he sees how much we drank, he'll end up paying for $18 watered down drinks here!" "Suckerrrrrrr!" Misha bellows back. They both laugh and holler as they enter the white light streaming out of the bathroom. I prefer shadows and silence for now.

Time crawls by while skulking. Devon's cocaine and kiss feel radioactively passionate, I'm a walking ghost. Here. Now. My hands feel around my pocket and I pull out her earring. I put both her card, and the earring, into my coat pocket to keep them safe. I want some more of that, and I doubt Eric can light her up like I could. My coat goes back on and I duck into the men's room. Cold water on, a handful of paper towels, patting my face dry. I don't even want to think about having to watch her sitting next to him for the rest of the show. Fuck. Especially not right after what just happened.

I breathe in clean, clear air. I breathe out, from each nostril roar flames and soot. With each passing moment, dirty black diesel smoke stains everything it touches. The bathroom is soon covered in carbon as a fine grey ash floats delicately, almost to apologize for the apocalypse. I look at myself in the mirror and my green eyes have turned red. Cracked bones glow through loose skin made of little worms stitched together. I can watch a rock-grey cancer cell working to destroying me, sent to provide an end to pointless people. It tunnels through me, chewing its way from organ to organ and spreading hungry little copies of evil grey mouths. Full of jagged spines, each tooth has even smaller mouths on them, snapping and gnashing with clockwork rhythm, cute razor lips nibble on guts. I can't breathe, inflating tumors push against my ribs on the inside. The bathroom mirror shatters and implodes, replaced with a tunnel of concentrated consciousness. The intersections of nirvana and oblivion, where understanding anything more than your mind can take would result in your instant death, the protection mechanism the universe uses to keep our souls from disengaging at will. My life hangs in the balance for now, but the cancer is always winning. Time is death for all regardless, only purpose keeps our experience from souring.

I steady myself on the counter. The blow she gave me is fucking intense. I'm going to need a few drinks. I straighten out my collar and check for any residue hanging out of my nose. I dry my hands, exit, and walk back up the stairs. The hall is nearly empty and I just manage to sneak back into the runway area for the second show to begin. I spot Kiki and Misha and step on a few toes to take my seat.

"Where the fuck were you?" Kiki says a bit too loud, feeling eyes all over me.

"Sorry," I whisper. Better to explain later. My eyes catch two empty chairs and I notice Devon and her date are gone.

17 Pressure

The second show begins and I let my eyes wander through the crowd. I'm bored and not in any way interested in the action on stage. Figures prance and spin, flashbulbs go off, coloured lights play on the walls and people applaud. Charlie Brown's teacher comes on the PA system, I understand nothing announced.

Kiki pokes me, "Dyl, what a show! ... Dyl?"

"Yeah, fucken sweet," I reply.

Misha is wasted, stepping in front of Kiki and pushing her way past me. She can turn into such a bitch when drunk. Kiki stands up and follows me out.

Out the front door of the hall and the midnight air feels good on my face. Misha is bent over for a good 30 seconds while trying to do up a little fancy buckle on her heels. Kiki looks around a bit nervously. "Well, I think I should take her home, we drank that whole 26'er Eric left for Misha, *and* the bottle of Vueve! Where were you?" Kiki looks like she's not having fun anymore. "I was just mingling, you know," and I flash the little gold earring from my pocket. Kiki's face brightens into a silly smile, "Oh Dyl you dog you!" and she playfully punches me in the arm.

We both laugh.

"Hehe, yeah," I sigh while chuckling. "What the fuck is so fucken' funny?" Misha barks, her butt pointing out at the lineup of taxis and cars, illuminated in a mix of German xenon and Japanese halogen. "Nothin' Mish!" I say, walking over and standing behind Misha, pretending to slap her ass with a stupid look on my face.

Kiki howls and claps her hands.

"What! You fuckers!" Misha groans. "Fuck it!" she shouts as she kicks her heel off, hitting some guy smoking in the back of his leg. "Sorry! You're handsome!" Misha stands up and smiles at the guy. She turns back towards us "Not really, ugh!" and balances on one leg to take her other shoe off.

"Dyl, let's go to your place, I'm going to call night flight for another bottle," Misha says, opening the nearest taxi door. Kiki looks at the people patiently waiting in lineup for taxis and freezes up. I grab Kiki's arm and drag her to the cab, put her in the back, and take the front seat. "Asshole," a girl is overheard saying as the door shuts.

Misha and Kiki tap away on their phones in relative silence. The only words spoken are, "Crown or vodka?" Misha wanted more vodka. Vodka and water to keep slim she says. The cab dumps us in front of a few 19 year olds puking outside of the local Irish bar. I buzz us into my place and Kiki falls on my couch with a sigh, Misha hits the bathroom. "Dyl put on some tunes," Kiki says just as I put on a random breakbeat iTunes radio station, "Way ahead of you Kiki," I say through a grin.

The tunes are pumping. Misha is drunk dancing, or flailing more like it, in front of the purple couch Kiki is sprawled across.

"Eek!" Misha screams as she falls onto the couch, Kiki's attempt at catching her results in a long, sharp nail puncturing one of Misha's breasts.

"Owch bitch! I'm bleeding!"

Kiki laughs.

"Ow!" Misha half pulls her left breast from its bra.

"Look! Look at what Kiki did to me!" Misha exclaims, as if it was Kiki's fault that she fell over.

A little crescent shaped red mark and a tiny bit of blood marks the scratch. Misha walks to the bathroom and spends 30 seconds eyeing up her grievous wound. I look at Kiki with a raised eyebrow, she returns the look with rolled eyes.

"If this scars I'm going to be so pissed! I can never wear another summer dress!" Misha stomps her feet.

"OH BOB SAGET!" I drunkenly scream, mimicking my YouTube hero Tourettes Guy.

Kiki laughs. "Mish, you'll be fine. Calm down silly goose!"

Kiki strains to get up off the couch, her breasts must weigh a ton. My phone goes off and the late night booze delivery is here. I press 9 to buzz him up and walk to the foyer to wait at the door. Kiki clip-clops around the apartment in the background and I can hear Misha change the internet radio to bass-thumping ghetto rap. I count how many times the rapper alternates between the words "what" and "nigga" in 30 seconds. Six whats, and ten variations of the word nigga, but the beat is really catchy and I tap my foot to the track.

Knock knock. I open the door and I'm greeted with a smile. $80 goes into the hand of the grinning chubby deliveryman and I get 40 ounces of vodka in return.

"Thanks!" I say, I've never meant that more.

The door thuds as it closes, my excitement has me skipping back to the kitchen. Kiki, always the homemaker, already has three glasses full of ice and half-filled with cranberry juice. I top up the drinks, put the bottle down, lift up a cup and cheers to a fun night. Misha looks upset. Deep creases betray to us emotions hidden behind a mask of triple ounce drinks.

"*Fuuuck!*" Misha moans, and tosses her phone into her purse.

Kiki's brow goes into a rare scrunch,

"What's wrong now Mish?!"

"Nothing, I'm fine."

I laugh.

"Shut up Dyl!, Mish …what?"

"I'm fine. It's nothing."

Misha pulls her hair back into a ponytail and sits in a red leather chair. She takes a huge mouthful of her drink.

"Okaaay," Kiki has a sip of her drink and checks her phone. "Oh there's a party at Tammy's tonight!"

Misha takes another big drink. I've seen this before on Intervention.

My first thought to cheer up Misha is to crank the music and dance around like a complete tool. I make sure to pelvic thrust at Misha. Nothing makes her smile. Kiki gets up and dances too, and does the funky chicken. It's pretty obvious that Misha is miserable about something.

My glass of vodka disappears on a trip to my liver, followed by quickly pouring myself another. Kiki joins me with Misha's empty glass and her own half empty cup.

Misha yells out "Dyl, your phone is ringing!" just as I pour the first glass.

Kiki walks over to my desk and brings me my phone, I don't recognize the number.

"Hello?"

"Hey, I had Kiki text me your number, I hope you don't mind."

It's Devon.

"What's up? Haha, that's awesome," I smile, I'm sure she can hear the music. Kiki says "I'll take that," as she grabs the bottle to pour more drinks.

"Am I interrupting something?"

"No, just a few friends having a few drinks, you?"

"I'm bored, I need my jewelry, and I have no booze. I could trade party favors for some? Hehe."

Devon thinks the quickest way to this man's heart is through his nose.

I step away from the counter and sit by the window.

"Yeah …yeah come down. 55 Cordova Street. Text me when you're here."

"Okay … going to catch a cab! Bye!"

I hang up and wonder why anyone would date in this city.

Misha's pissing again, or texting someone in the bathroom. Something's up with her and she doesn't want to talk about it at all.

"Kiki, I have Devon coming over in a bit. Do you guys mind if I get you two to go so I can have some, uhh …"

"Alone time?" Kiki laughs.

"Yeah."

"How did you swing that, getting her to ditch Daddy Warbucks for… you?!"

I don't know if Kiki meant to sound insulting, but really, it kind of was.

"Obviously she knows when he's pumping her that she's basically spreading her legs for a paycheque. I can't imagine that sex would feel very good. I know I've pumped a couple fatties when drunk and I know that immediately after I cum, I want to get the fuck out of there and forget it ever happened."

Kiki stares at me with a blank face.

"Okay then! T.M.I. Dyl, T.M.I.!"

Kiki was never one for the red pill. It's better to keep her in the dark about some things.

"I uh, I guess we could go to, Sam's? We'll see when Mish gets out of the can."

I run my hand through greasy spaghetti hair, my scalp sweating crisco. Grit in the back of my nose with an old shoe soaked in vodka for a mouth. I feel perfectly dirty for what is about to transpire. Kiki finishes her drink and I head to the kitchen to grab the bottle. I can't believe they already put such a dent in a forty. My second drink sits untouched on the counter and I have a long pull from it, top it up with vodka and cranberry, and head back with the bottles to pour Kiki another.

"What's up with Mish?" I ask, knowing it's probably to do with some douchebag she's seeing, somebody like me.

"Her boyfriend is in Vegas and hasn't texted her in days, I think she's just worried if he's ok. She just wants to know where he is."

"Yeah, balls deep in some broad he met poolside, no doubt."

"Dyl!" Kiki scowls.

A muffled scream comes from the bathroom. The door flies open and crashes into the wall behind it.

"Fuck you Dylen, go fuck yourself!" Misha half screams, half sobs.

She slams her phone down on the bathroom counter.

"Let's *go* Kayla."

"Misha, calm down," Kiki says, getting up off the couch and joining her at the bathroom sink.

My mind is on the pussy delivery service that's coming, and hoping the tear brigade leaves before she gets here. Misha fixes her makeup and walks to the purple couch to grab her jacket.

Kiki follows her, looking at me with a frown. "Are you happy? Thanks Dyl, way to ruin her night."

Just as she says that, my phone rings to signal someone at the front gate. I push 9 to buzz them in. Kiki pours another half and half for Misha, who slams it in two large unlady-like sips. I walk over and sit on a plush reclining leather chair usually reserved for meetings. It's behind a glass topped desk that has the green neon heart behind it, across from the purple couch. Styles of Tony Montana and The Joker mix together in my world of shit.

The girls continue to look for things they've left. Kiki's phone, Misha's bag, a hair tie, Misha's lighter. Three door beeps means Devon just walked into the studio. Hearing her heels echo down the short hallway, in moments turning the corner to see Misha and Kiki frantically looking to leave. Misha immediately smiles and puts on a perfect social face.

"Oh hi Devon! Your stuff was SUCH a hit at the show tonight! I love your jade pieces!" Misha sings before giving her a hug.

Kiki kisses her on both cheeks, "You have to let us know the next event! I need to see what you have in the way of ankle bracelets!"

Devon looks flattered. "I don't ... I don't actually have ankle bracelets yet. I never thought there was much of a market for that here!"

Kiki giggles and Misha beams a smile to her.

"Well, we're just on our way to a private party, message me on Facebook soon!"

Kiki and Misha wave and say "Bye!" in unison.

Kiki waves and says "Bye Dyl!" while Misha walks out without a word.

18 Aftertaste

Devon walks to the couch and puts her bag down, then takes off her coat.

My eyes meet hers. She's wearing a black, skin tight dress. Her dark locks are perfectly straight, two beautiful highways of black hair draped over her buxom breasts, nearly popping out of her top. Her smile, body, and dress scream fuck me, my nose whispers for the snort me. When she walks her hips rock back and forth, a switch speaking to the oldest parts of my mind; her heels strum a subtle and sexy slow beat on the concrete floor.

Devon prowls away from the couch to squat down in front of my desk. Her chin on the backs of her sandwiched hands, elbows on the glass. Green light from the heart behind me only serves to highlight the blue of her eyes more. She looks up at me with a foxy grin and asks, "Is this where you do your business?" Inner workings of my brain gears grind out whether or not she's *trying* to seduce me, or if she's just naturally irresistible.

I point to the desk, I already have a straw out and a business card to chop with. She stands up, walks to the couch and opens her purse. Her hands find the goodies and she dumps the little package onto the desk. Bedroom glances over her shoulder while walking to my kitchen, I can't take my eyes off her, staring at her ass the whole way. She comes back with the vodka bottle, sits on the corner of the desk, and takes a big swig. I unfold the flap, a porn magazine was butchered to make this convenient drug pouch, a lithe model wearing torn stockings, the innards of her vagina spread open like a predator mouth. Eyes as vacant as mine.

Dump. Crush. Scrape. Snort. My head falls back and I look to the ceiling. The green heart on the wall behind me washes everything in a sick hue, a euphoric rush spinning my soul around. Everything speeds up. Devon startles me by sitting on my lap, she dippy birds down twice, once for each nostril. The music on the stereo pumps in tune with our pulses, Devon leans in and kisses me. Bitten lips, hand in her hair, my other hand reaches up her silky smooth legs, fingers gliding up inner thigh to stoke the warmth of her panties.

"I can't stand a man who doesn't just get down to business," she coos.

Her lips lock with mine and I stand up, carry her to the couch, and throw her on it.

"Oh that's how you like it?"

Devon loses her lady like act, fast.

I unzip my pants and pull out my shrunken coke dick. She giggles, I grab a handful of her hair and she's a bit surprised. I tilt her head up at me and smile. She squints and licks her lips.

She's on her hands and knees, I'm standing and I push my cock into her face. Her mouth accepts it and I rock her head back and forth. She's sucking while twirling her tongue in her mouth, soft flesh caressing the first half of my shaft. Sucking harder and harder on the head, the feeling of my precum leaking out and down her throat. I start getting harder and I let go of her hair, she looks up at me with her beautiful blue eyes, illuminated under a single light above her. Slowly beginning to face fuck her, spit slides down my shaft and onto my balls. Her eyes tear up a little and her palms are on my thighs. 'Gukkk gukkk,' squish squish, 'Gakk!' she gags and I slide out of her mouth. She uses a hand to wipe off her chin and brush aside some of her hair. She gives herself a cowlick with some missed spit, losing her princess vogue.

"You giving up?" I taunt.

"No," she replies, and puts her mouth back on it.

She deepthroats me, choking at the base, pulling her mouth off me to spit up on the floor.

"Shit," she breathes hard, a little shocked at her mess on the floor. I stick myself back between her full lips, soaked in a mixture of spit and precum. She looks up at me, jewels for eyes sparkling as her tongue flicks on my cock tip. Flexing my nearly hard dick, feeling the carnal desire overcome drugs, slowly fucking her mouth again. A good half minute passes and I speed up, getting harder and harder, she steadies herself with her hands on my thighs. I'm holding her by the back of her head to get a better angle. It feels amazing to crank my dick so deep in this mouth that kisses Eric each night, she probably busts his balls and now I'm busting up her throat. She gags and a huge trail of spit drops off her chin, the front of my legs are feeling wet, her nails dig in to get a solid grip. My tempo speeds up and I unexpectedly cum deep in her mouth, she gags, still buried in her mouth, I pinch her nose shut.

"Swallow, now," I command.

She closes her eyes and chokes again and swallows.

"Good Devon, good work," I smile.

She opens her teary eyes and smiles, my penis falling back out of her mouth. I step back and admire my work, her dress soaked down the front, her hair completely messed up. Spit, a little vomit, and a tiny few drops of wasted cum decorate the floor.

She wipes her lips off and sits back on her ankles. "Wow, I uhh … ummm," she blushes and breathes heavy. "I've never had it like that." Saying nothing, I walk back to the desk and do a fat line of blow.

Smug and temporarily satiated, my feet find their way up onto the desk and I rock back in the chair, triumphant. I feel like a conquerer. My chest thumps and my sex organ pulsates with energy. Devon, Eric's little princess, met me and less than four hours later was swallowing the load that I pounded down her throat. Where is my drink, anyways? Devon gets up , grabs a towel and places it across her mess on the floor. She looks at me a little bashfully, and walks to the kitchen, coming back with a glass of ice. Without a word, she pours me a glass of hastily mixed cranberry vodka, lifts her own to cheers, and we drink. She takes a sip and brushes a couple hairs out of her mouth, I chug back a mouthful and then some. Her mascara has ran a little, blue orbs glowing from the centers of black flamed fires. Her pretty lips glisten. "I should get home and get this dress cleaned, haha," she says, a hint of nervous excitement in her voice.

"I'm not finished yet," I say, my voice stoic.

"Yeah?"

"Yeah."

Music blares from the stereo. It's some eurotrash electronic mix, again.

My feet fall off the desk and I stand up, my penis still semi-hard. I'm shaking a little from the drugs and the cool temperature of the studio. I take Devon by the hand and lead her to the couch, stripping the dress off her, her bra, and her fragrant panties.

Wordless, mechanically separating clothing from cheating flesh.

Her pussy has just enough hair on it, I don't think she waxes or trims regularly for Eric, I hardly have to wonder why. Devon shakes a little, could be from the cold, or from being bent over naked on a stranger's couch. Her head is down in a green pillow, her royal ass is pointing straight up. Without a touch, watching as her pink asshole pulsates and clenches up every few seconds from lustful anticipation.

I need an angle to work from.

Kneeling on the floor behind her I spread her pussy open with two fingers. Thick clear webs of her own excitement stick to the innermost lips of her tender folds, the contrast from her tanned body causing her to look even more aroused. A deep breath slips from Devon's lips, I look beyond her hips to see she is squeezing couch in fists. Sleazily sliding one finger inside, her groans encourage me to fuck her with it. My digit is quickly coated in her juices and she tightens up around it. She softly moans again and again before I slide in a second, and slap her ass hard.

"Oh yeah ..." she coos.

"I bet Eric never gives it to you like this," I state, switching to my thumb and standing up. "No ... no. Never. Like this. Oh like this!" muffled little groans escape her while I probe inside, making sure to push down and drag the bottom of my thumb on her G-spot.

I stand up and move to get on the couch beside her, pleasure moans end as my other hand's finger enters her mouth, her tongue rolls across it while sucking, leaving a thick coating of her spit. Her asshole beckons and shall receive, my thumb sliding easily inside of her ass as she screams "Oh you didn ... nnn...t!"

"Yeah you need it like this, you're such a whore."

"I am a *total* whore," She repeats.

"Who's whore are you?"

"Oh fuck, yours, fuck I'm your whore," she moans. I work her pussy and asshole the way an angry boxer would use a speedbag. Her wetness coats my thumb to the base and makes a sloshing sound as it grinds in and out.

"Give it to me, oh fuck!" she yells, pulling one hand back to spread open her ass cheeks more. I feel her asshole and pussy tense up and her whole body shakes into a powerful orgasm. Her hips pivot forward and my thumbs shoot out of both holes. She falls on one side, her tanned body convulses on the couch, a few little moans lighting up my ears.

My right thumb is soaked in pussy juice and my left thumb has a little streak of shit on the nail. I lean over and wipe it on the inside of her dress. At least, I think that was the inside. She opens her eyes and purrs "Come here!" I pull her back into doggystyle, line my cock up to her swollen and wet pussy, the first push to the hilt.

"Uhnngh!" she squeals, putting a hand back on my thigh, her other elbow on her coat. I begin to ramp up the speed that I fuck her, fast. Within seconds my stroke is deep and hard, a rhythmic drilling sending shock waves through her ass fat, a forceful fuck pushing her into the corner of the couch. She screams over and over.

"More!"

"Harder!"

I put both of my hands on her hips and give her all I have. My cock feels like a steel rod in a furnace of pleasure, a lightning rod of sensation, my brain lights up and I reach a high that washes over me in waves. Gasping, closed eyes spun back in my head, the suction of her silky hole milking my own fluids out of me. I continue to fuck her and pound her until I feel my balls wet with her juices. Time and pleasure intertwine to blur the line between both, drops of sweat and her cum littering the couch; they become the clock to tell us how long we've been fucking.

She moves forward and wrenches her hips out of my hands, flipping onto her back. Savage sex posture of kneeling one leg on the couch, her ass under her own coat, and one leg supporting myself off the cold concrete floor. Pushing myself inside her, she arches her back so I can reach under her and pull her body closer. Her writhing tanned body feels so good on me, my dick inside a soft, warm, wet world of magic. My thumb reaches down and flicks her little pink clit, she bites her lips and closes her eyes. Her immaculate hair defiled, spread out all over the back of the couch and across her full and tantalizing tits. Eric never gives it to her like this. I'm giving it all to her, slowly pushing inside her all the way, pulling it back out and watching her essence of lust give my penis a wet sheen. Each time the head slips from her pretty folds it drags moans from her heavy breathing lungs, inspires scratches from her free hands on my hips and legs. Pushing my hips forward and looking down, watching my sex saber charging through swollen curtains into a sexual battlefield, emerging coated with passion. She takes a little initiative to grind her hips, and slowly riding up and down. Her hips spin in a vertical oval pattern, blasts of pleasure coursing through me, an unexpected groan rumbles deep from my chest. She uses her arms and elbows to support herself while grinding, and I moan a few more times helplessly as I almost pop completely out of her. An expert at teasing; her motions causing the head to be caressed by her skilled, flexing opening, she then welcomes it back into her deeply.

She rides me for another few seconds before I pull out, grab her by the hand, sit on the couch, and pull her on top of me. I can see her hot, wide hips and ass in the mirror across from me.

"Ride me and make me cum, now," speaking to her in a strict tone.

She bites my ear and neck hard, pulling my hair to the point of almost pissing me off. I use my hands to push her tits together, suck and bite her nipples, and pull her deeper. Her hair falls down across my face with the tips tickling my shoulders and chest. She reaches between her legs and lines my flesh spear up to her dripping wet slit. She sits back on her heels and the head slips in, sensations of heat and slippery pleasure tense up my entire body. She bounces slowly at first, speeding up once her fluids are coating me, and then gyrates her hips back and forth with the torque of her body weight. I move my hands down to her ass cheeks, pulling her down farther so her clit can rub against me. Just when I think she's hitting the right spot, she claws my neck and kisses me. Her tongue dips into my mouth briefly, her quick exhaling breath warm on my face. I feel the couch getting wetter under me, thudding and rocking with the fucking. My hands dig into her ass cheeks and spread them, while pulling her in rhythm and feeling my dick buried to the hilt in her, she shrieks and rides faster, I feel myself getting ready to explode.

"I want you to cum inside me," she whispers

"Keep riding like that, yeah like that."

She twists and thrusts her hips back and forth, and side to side. Losing my patience and grabbing her by the back of her head, my back arched to bury it as deep as possible. I fuck her with all of my might, pounding it in her and tensing up. Beginning to soak in both of our sweat, I push it in as deep as possible and feel the release inside of her. My cock pulses and dumps what feels like my entire load of semen inside her, her hair in my mouth, we kiss. Salty, numbing cranberry.

She falls forward on me, with me still inside. Both panting and sweating, I hold her for what must be minutes. There's still a half gram of coke on the desk, but I'm spent. We roll off her jacket onto the other side of the couch and spoon. She closes her eyes and sighs. I reach behind the couch and pull a blanket out and we lay there, tingling with pleasure. Usually at this point I'd turn the lights out as a hint of getting a taxi or sleeping over, but I'm too comfortable to move. My eyelids grow heavy and I soon join her, eyes closed, on the same pillow.

"Rinnnnggg!"

"Rrinnnnggg!"

"Rrrinnnnggg!"

"Rrrrinnnnggg!"

"Rrrrrinnnnggg!"

Silence.

"Rrrrrrinnnnggg!"

"Rrrrrrrinnnnggg!"

"Rrrrrrrrinnnnggg!"

"Rrrrrrrrrinnnnggg!"

"Rrrrrrrrrrinnnnggg!"

"Rrrrrrrrrrrinnnnggg!"

"Rrrrrrrrrrrrinnnnggg!"

Silence. One of my eyes opens. I shut it.

"Rrrrrrrrrrrrrinnnnggg!"

"Rrrrrrrrrrrrrrinnnnggg!"

Devon pushes off me and sits up. Eyes barely open, she reaches for her bag and digs through it.

"Rrrrrrrrrrrrrrrinnnnggg!"

"Rrrrrrrrrrrrrrrrinnnnggg!"

"Rrrrrrrrrrrrrrrrrinnnnggg!"

"Shit." She tosses her bag on the floor.

"Rrrrrrrrrrrrrrrrrrinnnnggg!"

Green oceans of Douglas Park's thick bladed grass extend into the horizon. Peck-peck. Fresh dew prevents picnics, but perfect for Sports Day during the spring of grade 6. Peck-peck-peck. I was probably about eleven when I saw a woodpecker wood pecking the shit out of a tree. Peck-peck-peck-peck. I still remember the booby-shaped tree I used to climb in that park. Peck-peck-peck-peck-peck.

"Rrrrrrrrrrrrrrrrrrrinnnnggg!"

She reaches over to her coat, it having fallen on the floor dangerously close to our towel soaked in cum. Her hand finds her phone and she answers the call. The sun's up, when did that happen?

"What ... what the *FUCK*, Devon!" I hear a man's voice clearly, Its Eric.

I didn't know Blackberries were as loud.

"What the *fuck* did you do last night?"

Devon grunts, "Wha ... what?" and scowls.

"I woke up this morning and saw you called at 4 am, then I had a voicemail from you, and it... it sounds like you... *fucking someone!*" Devon's face goes pale. She jumps to her feet. "Oh my gosh I am so..." Devon sobs.

I can't tell if she's rehearsed this. No! Whamarbl ..." Devon walks towards my kitchen naked and I can't hear what he's saying anymore.

"No, no, I need to explain, Eric, *please,*" Devon squeaks words out between sobs.

She grabs her head and then slams her fist onto my kitchen counter. My plates clatter together, a fork jumps to the floor.

"Eric, stay there, I'll be right over," Devon stammers. "No please, please ... ok, I'll be right there."

I sit up and watch Devon run to couch and throw on her clothing. Without even looking at me, she walks to the bathroom and fixes her hair. She comes back without a word and grabs her bag.

"What's up?" Even my smile is curious.

"Don't, just don't." she replies. "Don't even *try* to talk to me."

"Oh, it's like that? Ok." My smile turns into a smirk, a sarcastic chuckle puffs from my nose. I can't help but understand. I'm not going to pay her rent, shop with her at Marciano, keep her in hot yoga classes, spa appointments.

"Just forget me. Keep the earring," she barks while putting on her shoes. She picks up her bag, throws it over her shoulder, and walks towards the door.

"Tell me you had a good time!" I call after her, only her heels on the floor give any sort of reply. "Tell me you had fun with me!" I yell again.

My door opens, and closes with a soft click.

Just like that, she's gone.

I laugh.

19 Gone Goon

Friday begins with egg whites and turkey bacon. I sometimes forget to brew my morning joe before I cook. Hunched over my food, eyes half closed, the coffee maker gives off a few hollow sputters. It will be one of those days. A couple meetings, a bit of flirting, some paintings sold. One of the young artists working with me is starting to make steady sales of her prints. Seeing her smile brings me the first shred of sunshine today. I close the studio early and shut the world off at 4.

I wasn't always so eager to spend time away from people, but I'm enjoying it more and more. Going out and meeting the same archetypes over and over becomes dull. Meeting beautiful women I could love is rewarding, yet pointless. Over morning coffee, I read an article that sent me into a tailspin of negative emotion. The average home in this city is somewhere around 800k. What hot and intelligent woman would stick with someone who rents? Not much of a foundation to build a life on. Fuck it, might as well resign myself to porn and video games until I can afford true adulthood.

A few texts on my phone, seems like there are some fun events going on tonight. I hold down the power button and turn off the beeping mess. Nobody will notice if I'm not there anyways. What will I miss, meeting a girl whom I have nothing in common with? I'll watch her body language and pick up on her cues. In a heartbeat or three I can determine if she wants to get naked tonight. I double click the icon of a soldier walking out of flames and smoke. I think I've fucked myself into an emotional oblivion.

First person shooters are the new opiate, next to porn. Men finding purpose accomplishing tasks, shooting the enemy and being victorious. The endorphin highs I can reach when winning a match can get me jumping up and down with joy. I jump into a match with 64 players. The game just switched the battle arenas and the capture points, known as flags, are all neutral and grey. I don't bother setting up my microphone, as I play as how I live, a solitary hunter.

Other people chat away and form strategy, a barely pubescent voice speaks out "The plane is mine faggots!"

The match starts and I choose my favorite avatar, the engineer with C4 explosives and a shotgun. I run my soldier to a jeep and jump in as another player hops into the passenger seat. My left hand presses down on the W key and the jeep takes off.

The scenery is beautiful. Murder is on my mind while admiring rolling little grassy hills, dirt roads, mountains and the lust green forest in the distance. I can't help but think of Cultus Lake in the summertime. A voice cries out in a chain of swear words, someone took his plane.

"fuckin faggot jew niggers i called the fucking jet you gay homo ass fucks11!1~11!!!" rings out from my speakers. Someone older tells him to shut up, voice coms in games are worse than YouTube comment streams.

I drive my digital jeep over a hill and get some air. Whee. The suspension and bouncing effects are well done, only a few hundred thousand more points on my credit card and I could get an ATV in real life. Young entitled men continue to argue over the communal aircraft. My virtual soldier crashes his jeep through a fence and back onto a dirt road. The middle base between the two opposing sides is my target, if my team can hold onto this, victory is almost certain.

Pressing E, my soldier dives out of the moving vehicle which coasts to a stop behind a construction trailer. The walls are thin and destructible if hit by rockets or tank rounds, I don't plan to be seen though. I hide in a corner and wait, my jeep passenger runs off. The bitching about who gets to fly the jet continues and I can't hear the in game sound effects very well. Do I hear a tank coming? I wait. No. Someone with the username Sewerfart is spamming chat typing 'Justin Bieber is gay.' I hear a tank coming and check the minimap. It's not ours.

"Time to do this, hoorah!" Shit would fill my pants the first day of any real boot camp.

I release the X key and my avatar stands up from a crouch, side step with the D key and I'm peeking out of the trailer window.

The enemy T-60 tank is facing me directly, but the turret is pointed 90 degrees and shooting at someone with its machine gun. I duck and run out the side door of the trailer, and across the dirt road in front of the tank. Jump with Z and tapping SPACEBAR to go prone. Wait. No bullets came at me, go! I tap SPACEBAR and turn to look at the tank. Boom! It fires at a friendly jeep heading right for it, and it explodes. I'm almost completely behind where the turret is facing. A flash of movement to my left as an enemy solder runs from behind his cover, let's make this a fatal mistake. I deftly aim my shotgun and put two rounds into him, a happy chime sounds off and I get points for killing him.

Boom! The tank fires, and now the turret turns in my direction. I sprint my soldier towards the tank and go prone beside it, as this makes me invisible to the driver. The tank begins to back up. Shit, he knows I'm here. My finger finds the 3 key and I switch to C4 explosives, slamming the SPACEBAR, the screen shakes while jumping up and running along the side of his tank. Crack crack crack! He's spraying and hoping I'll make the mistake of trying to run away, rather than stick close. Just as I am throwing a brick of C4 at the tank, an enemy truck can be seen barreling down the dirt road towards me. The C4 somehow misses and lands on the ground. Shit! The tank continues to back up as I run along the side, and it crashes into a construction trailer ass-first.

I sprint past the tank and into the side door of the same trailer the tank hit. The enemy jeep whizzes by the doorway I just ran into, with the roof mounted machine gun peppering the trailer. Intuition tells me the tank is about to blow a hole in the side of this trailer in aboBOOM! The screen shakes and daylight floods in. My soldier barely survives the tank blasting open the trailer, I'm about halfway to the other end of the trailer and an RPG missile smashes into the opposite doorway, ripping it to shreds. Getting out of the trailer of death is my only option, and a tap on the SPACEBAR jumps me through the exit wound caused by the tank round. Boom! Where I was standing a few moments ago is now no more.

Another risky sprint away from the tank and my avatar manages to find refuge behind cover of a two story building. The tank is shooting at someone but it isn't me. Peeking out of cover and an enemy soldier is staring right at me, close range, with a rocket launcher. My soldier prepares for death with a digital prayer. The rat-ta-tat-tat of an M249 squad assault weapon becomes the chorus to a song about non-american deaths. I'm still alive and a smile beams across my face. God does exist, and he lives in Battlefield 3. The enemy soldier falls on his virtual face, having been shot in the back by some digital hero. I spot my savior. It's Sewerfart, and he's running across the road right in front of the tank. As the turret is turning towards him, I spring into action. Hold down SHIFT, pressing W. Hit 3, ran to the back of the tank. Left mouse CLICK, left mouse CLICK, turn, hold down SHIFT, press W. C4's stuck to the tank and I need to get into a range safe enough to blow it as I switch to the detonator. Left mouse CLICK. A massive explosion rips through the camp. I turn around in time to see bits of tank spread around, and the sad sight of Sewerfart's lifeless digital body in the middle of the road.

Good night, sweet prince.

Nearly 30 minutes of cat and mouse with tanks, soldiers, helicopters, and jets passes in a blur. Many acts of heroism are witnessed, and the battle is won. The score pops up on the screen, being first place on my team makes me smile, my waste tunnel dwelling flatulent friend is in a noble fourth place. With a strong sense of satisfaction filling my ego with pride, nimble fingers and excellent hand to eye owe my stomach a high carbohydrate tithe. Victorious and on a high, I exit the game and open up Google. What to eat? I feel like some MSG-laden cheap chinese.

I turn my phone on and surf on my computer to Ho's EZ Noodle. The Apple logo lights up and I wait. The phone boots to the main menu and a twitchy finger taps the phone icon, then the keypad. Before I can dial, the phone has a seizure as several texts come in at once. Bzzt, bzzzzzt, bzzt. Bzzt! Dougie never lights up my phone like this unless there is something going down. A curious read through several enthusiastic texts regarding liquor, drugs and babes, and I see an address. Depression squeezes chests and forces sighs from my loser gland, sitting in the dark and wasting my life in a video game. As if that isn't bad enough, soon I'll be eating food that will take years off my life while adding years to my decomposition. If I go to this party I will have fun, but it's the same old shit every time. I'm fucking 35, how much longer will I do this? I figure Dougie needs a wing man and on this basis I begrudgingly convince myself to go. I text him back and tell him I'm getting ready and I'll meet him at his place.

20 Tripping In

To get in the mood to party tonight, tunes are cranked as a fresh bottle of
JD gets cracked. A neck's worth in two gulps. I tidy up my rugged beard
and throw on blue jeans along with a black button up shirt. I comb my
hair and floss. I look great for a fat guy, but feel ragged. My coat gets put
on, closing the door behind me and off to the elevator. Soon I'm on the
street and swarmed by taxis looking for their first fare of a Friday night.
First stop is the liquor store, grabbing a bottle of cheap rye and some root
beer. I don't just share my Jack with any stranger. Second stop is Dougie's
place for a pre-drink, some time to shoot the shit and get a little buzz. He
updates me on these girls, all of Matt's friends but the hottest ones are
his customers. He gives a solid recommendation of them, Liz and Cara
being the hottest party girls Matt knows, apparently.

The party is at somewhere pretty posh, the Wall center. Dougie and
I are within walking distance and we decide to stroll up. We pack the
bottles in a plastic bag and head out. Friday night and Vancouver's streets
are packed, crowds of all sorts of stereotypes dot the sidewalks, Granville
street looks like a zoo. Drunks stagger up the street, yells of "Woo!" signal
a long night for suburbanites having a big day in the city. The din of young
drunks dies as we walk up to the swanky plaza on Burrard. It's an elegant
monstrosity of chrome and glass, trees with LED strings in them sway
back and forth like an urban glowing jellyfish. It's the type of place where
strangers only smile or shoot at each other.

Bellowing laughter fills the twilight air as a group of men exit the
building, pushing past the elderly doorman. "Watch it, cuz!" one of the
ruffians yells at the old fart in the red coat. His balls dried up a long time
ago, and defending a stranger is never worth getting jumped for. Dougie

and I don't say anything in objection as we file through the doorway. A hoodie wearing punk excreting from the building bumps into Dougie behind me. "Watch it fag!" the punk bleats out. Dougie turns and stares at him. "Oh you tough dawg?" the kid yells, wide-eyed and seeking blood. I don't think his friends can hear him, but there were at least a dozen of them. Dougie turns around and says "Not worth it," in a teeth-gritted growl. "You's a bitch! Faggot!" the kid yells in the lobby. People turn and stare but everyone is too afraid to do anything. I want to smash him. I want to hold him down and cut off his balls. I want to end his genes.

I picture myself in handcuffs, my studio replaced with three walls and bars.

I turn and head for the elevators, trying to stay calm. Dougie follows.

"Chickenshit faggots! That's what I thought! Bitch!"

I barely catch the word bitch as he steps out of earshot.

I feel bad for the doorman. Dougie laughs. The elevator doors open and we step inside a chamber of mirror, brass, and refined arrogance. If money could sneer. The buttons for the floors look like carved gold squares, the numbers recessed in green glass. 46 lights up and the doors close in perfect silence. The elevator accelerates rapidly and the rushing of air accompanies my ears popping. In seconds we're already slowing down and nearly at our floor. In heaven I imagine hallways this luxurious. The door to the suite looks fortified as a castle.

"That's a serious door," I remark.

"Like Fort Knox, to protect the hot pussy inside!" Dougie says as he chuckles.

I laugh while knocking.

In a second the door opens and a girl in a red dress greets us, electronic music pumps into the hallway. A beautiful woman treats my eyes to refined femininity, pounding bass stirs my soul, the beat matching the tempo of my inspired heart. "Oh hey, you guys must be Dylen and Doug!" I smile and introduce myself before walking in. She's Joellen and she has perfect teeth, chiseled features, a high 9. She's exactly who you'd expect to open the door at a place like this. Dougie introduces himself as I turn to look at the crowd. It's mostly women in dresses, hovering around their Blackberries and wine. Two guys sit on the couch, one with a pretty blonde on his lap. Both wear hoodies, jeans, and Yankees ball caps, probably DJs. Wait, I recognize one, that's Matt. A dealer I used to hang out with occasionally. I've been to his place a couple times, always so blitzed out of my mind I couldn't find my way back to his place if my life depended on it.

Joellen jumps gracefully in bare feet. She moves from the door with Dougie, spins gracefully, and opens the high end German sarcophagus of a fridge. "What do you guys want? We have aged whiskey, non-aged whiskey, vodka, *wodka* if you're Russian; and ... umm, everything else!" the fridge is loaded with take-out food, chilled liquers, and mixer of every type. Dougie's face lights up, and he asks for some 50 year old whiskey. He puts down the bag of cheap shit we brought on the counter, almost embarrassed by it.

Joellen laughs. "You don't keep old whiskey in a fridge, I thought you'd know that?"

She rolls her eyes and skips over to the kitchen island, her petite piano hands find a bottle I don't recognize and pours out a golden orange glass of whiskey. She bends over the island and reaches for a glass bowl with ice and tongs. Her thonged bottom peeks out under the short red dress, a perfect tight little pair of tanned pillows. Oh the luxuries that money can afford, my mind wanders to why I'm not at home, working.

Stainless tongs with "Zurich" in a laser-cut engraving deftly snatch a crisp, frosty berg of ice. The glacial rock drops into the glass with a loud plop, perfectly in sync with a heavy bass note that drops from the recessed speaker system. "Woo!!" a girl screams, Blackberry held high, fist pumping. The ice pops and cracks, she hands Dougie his drink. I request the same, and I get an even bigger glacier of ice. The tongs' jagged chrome teeth look viciously elegant. "Guys, did you know this ice is actually Fiji bottled water that was flash frozen? You have to wrap it in a towel and drop it on the floor to break it! Ice cubes what?" She laughs and her wine glass rises up in a toasting gesture.

I take my first sip of the whiskey, smoked candy rolls over my tongue. The buzz hits my empty stomach fast, I feel better, relaxed. Honesty translates out from my smile, brain translating the sensations into one of wearing a familiar coat or being held by my mother as an infant. Such deep flavour, my nose tickles with all of the rich tones playing inside me.

"Joellen, this is the finest whiskey I have ever had," Dougie says.

Each word with conviction and purpose.

A girl in a pink dress saunters over and puts her arm around Joellen, her left hand sports a geological alphabet worth of stones on several different rings. The right hand has a glass of piss-coloured liquid. I'm sure it's vodka redbull.

"Who are you boys?" pink-and-pale coos.

Dougie introduces himself and I. Cara is her name, everything about her screams out that she's acting. I give her a compliment on her purple and green spiral ring. "Amethyst and emerald, darling, costume crap," she shows me a plain silver ring with a large yellow stone.

"Yellow princess cut over platinum, Tiffany's of New York," she keeps her hand out while sipping her drink. "My fiancé picked it up last week."

Dougie takes her hand and looks at the ring closely. I can see he is phase transitioning already, his fingers touching hers, the tips of his finding her palm. I almost audibly pronounce "Brilliant."

Electronic southern hip hop beats blare over the speakers. Lil' John can be heard asking all of his niggas to put their hands in the air, and the girls wave Blackberries and booze to the track. Cara smiles and is still letting Dougie play with her hand while he gazes at the ring, she calls out "Waka Flocka next!" gruffly. One of the guys on the couch laughs.

I hear a whiny voice behind me "You guys got a light? Fucken' lost my purse." a girl in a blue dress and messed up hair has a smoke hanging off her bottom lip.

Cara says "Darling, my purse, dear," this time with a British accent. I watch as the paper cylinder of tobacco drops off the blonde's lips, sliding perfectly between her perky, tanned breasts.

I reach into her dress and pull out the cigarette, turn to get a lighter out of the purse closest to Cara, and light the smoke in my mouth.

"Really," the blonde says. I reply only with a grin, and blow a little smoke out.

I hand her the cigarette and hold back from choking. I hate cigarettes, but I can chain smoke joints. A sip of whiskey rescues my tongue from car exhaust tastes and back to caramel, toasted oak. Bass, high heels and chatter swirl around me. The whiskey is hitting me hard and the blonde girl is smiling at me intently. She takes a long drag and whips her head back, her satin angel blonde hair returning almost magically to salon form. She is standing with most of her weight on one leg and her bottom leans to one side, her hand runs through her hair and ends up on her hip.

"So I don't know your name and you've had your hand in my shirt and my smoke in your mouth, I'm Liz."

"Dylen," I say, offering my hand.

She takes it and I pull her into a spin. The small of her back touches my left hand and her right shoulder is just below my mouth. Our eyes make contact for a second and she spins herself back to where she was. I smile and ask her where her drink was, and she replies it's flowing through the pipes somewhere, as she throws up every time she drinks and does blow. For a split second there I feel pangs of regret as I lose all interest in her. She's probably just like me. I hate me. I instantly queue in that she's probably down to fuck, and I smile again.

"More room for another drink," I quip, a quick mouthful of whiskey gets knocked back and I turn to open the fridge. Liz half slides, half steps in beside me and says "Hmmm …" Her petite left arm wraps around herself and her right arm points up, her hand playfully scratches at a non-existent beard. I grab her redbull to go with stoli, the frosted glasses sit inside the fridge on the door. I take one and pour her stoli until she says when. She doesn't speak until I pour her a half glass of vodka. Crack the can and she has a killer cocktail of 50/50 energized booze. Passing her the drink, she is tapping out a little container on the counter top, a blank plastic card lays flat while a rolled up $50 stands on its end, a rocket ship to pleasure prepares for launch.

Liz takes her drink and swallows nearly half of it in one chug, putting it down only for a cocaine snack. Her nose finds the bill, ant eaters in a hive of marble counter-tops and stainless steel, heads down to work on making rails disappear. She throws her head back, belts out a loud squeal, and one of her eyes squints and closes.

"What the fuck Matt, this shut is CUT!" she groans.

"It's right from a brick," Matt hollers back, laughing while bouncing a girl on his knee.

Liz steps over to the couch. "No, no, NO! I'm not buying any more unless it is in a big chunk like your old shit." Matt laughs and bounces the blonde girl furiously. She shrieks and raises her hand to hit him before he stops. I turn back to the counter and spot a fat, juicy line. My nose is a starving, diabetic man at a BBQ, tucking in his bib, his feast awaits.

The rolled up $50 bill is crusted around the edges, matted cocaine doubles as glue to hold the bill together from spiraling out. I hold the bill between my thumb and middle finger, pull the bill taught, and feed my ego. The line is rough, eyes both water, the left nostril catches fire. Rush.

Liz and I are in bed. She's naked and I'm drawing little circles on her back. She purrs and smiles, dry lips smack together. Her skin looks young and so soft in blue tones of dawn.

Fantasy escapes as Liz walks over with Matt in tow. "Soooo, last time I ordered a party pack and I only got a g. I know it was a g because a party pack goes into six lines, not four."

Matt and Liz bicker back and forth for a few minutes, my nose protests and my heart thunders inside of me. My mind touches its ceiling and breaks through into a beautiful euphoria. This is what being in love feels like.

"A ball for $200," Matt says, Liz is getting visibly angry. Matt teases her with a tiny flap in his palm.

"Fuck off Matt, I buy so much shit from you, I practically pay your child support you ... Dickface!"

Joellen's laugh is heard above a Kanye track.

I sip my drink and notice my teeth want to clench. That was a huge line of some potent shit, my foot is tapping and my right hand is in my back pocket to keep it still. I'm so fucking high. Matt takes out a handful of baggies from his oversize jeans, puts them on the counter, fingers run slalom through them for Liz's request, gently tapping each for the prize. One baggy doesn't squish flat immediately and is pulled off to the side for inspection. Matt's fat fingers pinch together and hold the specimen up for more light. With the care of a drunken watchmaker, he flicks it with his finger and smiles. The little ziplock has a large jagged rock in it, off white, with very little powder in the bag. "I told ya, it's right off the brick. I pick this shit up in Delta fresh from the border." his voice is hoarse and frustrated. Liz hands him $200 in cash, opens the bag and puts the rock on the marble counter top.

Sun bursts through the window and Jitterbug comes on the radio. The entire apartment is awash in golden light. Liz is wearing an apron, a smile, and nothing else. We're alone, together. She's using a rolling pin and a fresh greased tray sits on the counter.. My arms are around her and I'm kissing her little ear, and nibble on her neck before telling her how good it smells in here. She's baking cookies for her yoga class tonight, I'm going to play hockey, we kiss and tell each other how nice it will be to cuddle later.

Liz snorts back a huge line and Kanye tells me about how she don't date any broke ass niggas. My mind tries to fill my empty shelves. Liz rubs her nose, gleefully pointing at the half-crushed rock and giant line she cut for me. "Try THAT!" she exclaims, "es primo!" she says in her best attempt at an Italian accent.

Cara says "it's a-me!"

Joellen, Cara, and Liz sing "A-Mario!" and laugh.

Joellen claps her hands and says "I think I'll mosey on down that rainbow road!" her upper body gracefully swings down to snatch a line with such poise, an elegant dance for drugs. They line up and queue for lines, I smile. I'm floating on a high that I never want to come down from. My world isn't bliss, I am bliss itself.

The girls start to gab on about their rings and their purses, my teeth grit as I lose my interest and think about getting another whiskey. Liz locks eyes with me a few times and I go in for a kiss. She gives me a hesitant peck and turns around for a line. Cara is showing off her ring again to Joellen, they compare it to the colour of white wine. Liz drinks some of my whiskey, turns around with newfound confidence, and kisses me deep with her tongue. Vanilla chapstick mixes with the whiskey. A deep breath out through her nose sweeps my cheek with warmth. I lightly bite her upper lip, the sour taste of blow soon freezes the tip of my tongue and front teeth. Dougie taps me on the shoulder. Liz has her arms around me, but she lets go when I notice him.

"Whoa I thought I was your date?!" Dougie jokes with his hands out and palms up.

Cara walks from behind the kitchen island, "Dahling" with the thickest English accent yet, "you do a better job admiring me than talking." The girls laugh. Dougie is far more handsome than I am, and in better shape. Cara's eyes fall below his face, she wants him, if only for right now. That yellow diamond set on platinum didn't buy her fiancé any faith, while the much cheaper rock smashed on marble, might have just bought Dougie a lover for tonight. Dougie grabs Cara in his arms, begins to exaggerate a dance with her as he sings "Moon river, dada, da da da!"

Cara howls with delight.

The best looking man in her arms and the highest status ring on her finger.

Liz takes another swig of my drink. Wrapping her arms around me, numb lipped kisses a prequel to her tongue violently thrashing around my mouth. Not guided by passion but by instinct. Things seem like they're going well tonight, arriving in hell and finding it balmy with strong piña coladas and girls in grass skirts. The only trouble is, those piña coladas turn into shit once it hits your tongue, and the girls have rattlesnake mouths for vaginas. I smile. Cara isn't letting go of Dougie and the soiree has just started. The night roars on past 11, the music grows louder and more aggressive. I briefly talk to the quietest girl in the group, Rebecca. She's Italian, a bit chubby and plain, with long, curly brown hair. She spends much of the night on her Blackberry on plenty of fish. I get the feeling the other girls keep her around to make them look better, it's not the first time girls I know have done that. I'm not surprised any of these chicks are hanging out with Matt, him being a small time coke dealer now. His friend doesn't say much at all the whole night. He's on mushrooms.

The girl that bounces on Matt's knee is his girlfriend, Sylvia. She's so proud that she's pregnant with her second child, and is quick to turn down drinks, point out when drinks are too close to her, when she can smell second hand smoke. It's for the safety of her child she says. Then she starts doing a line or five. Bouncing on his knee turns into a public lap dance between queuing up for a bump. Dougie and Matt hit off on a long conversation over musical tastes, the debate being Snoop Dogg VS Ice-T. He's always been better at making friends and meeting girls, I've been better at relationships than he is, or was, until I stopped trying. Liz is out of her head drunk and high, she sneaks off to the bathroom and throws up a few more times. Her whiskey and bile flavoured kisses add to the gutter bouquet of coke now dripping down the back of my throat.

It's after midnight and a few more people show up, a joint is smoked and Sylvia gets upset. Joellen's other friends show up in rapid succession and soon the apartment is full of strange faces, forcing the coke plate to be banished to the bedroom. A secret meeting, six of us huddled around a plate, all trying to talk at once. Stragglers from the new party prove themselves soft, timid people trying to find the bathroom walk in on us, and exit without a word. Matt suggests all of us head to his place, and it's quickly decided that we'll go. Liz and Cara are relieved that Matt has gum for their teeth grinding. The sketchy, rag tag crew gathers together their belongings, Matt's friend on mushrooms is coerced into moving from the safety of the couch. "The ducks!" he keeps saying. Whatever.

21 Snortmare

Out the door, down the elevator, my ears feel nothing, I may be too high. The mirrors love us all as we all look so good. I squeeze Liz's ass and she presses it into my crotch. The door opens and we step into the lobby sometime after 2 AM. It's a different doorman, this time he's older, with sagged shoulders or maybe just a sore back. He spots us and his grin is a little tired looking. His crisp red jacket with gold details give him an air of dignity, I'm guessing he eats cheap bologna sandwiches, no name soups, plays crosswords, and lives alone. I smile at him through my 32 little pestles. Two cabs swing up and friendly Indians scoot us off to Matt's.

I'm flying. This metal and glass madhouse sprints through the streets of downtown Vancouver, Liz digging her hand into mine with the first of several ran yellow lights. Between my fingers I feel moist flesh interlacing and squeezing reassuringly tight. The cab flies over a speed bump going fast, the car bucking hard enough to make my stomach do a back flip. With my head buried in the headrest, city lights and skyscrapers flow faster, then slower again, coming to a stop at lights. All idea of time is lost while soaking in the ecstasy of world-numbing cocaine highs that elevate with each passing moment. Exhaling between shivers, I expect to see my breath. While Liz squeezes my hand hard, her mouth finds my neck, a gentle suck and a giggle. Lights streak overhead. I never noticed lights this bright. I have to sit up, a trap door opened in my stomach, nausea from the blow down the back of my throat. How long is this drive going to take! *Fuck!* A pang of panic hits and fades fast, my focus drifts back to Liz's hand in mine, the sensation for a moment that we're both feeling happy and giddy. A honeymoon couple, if only for one night, strangers meeting to share a moment and at least pretend we're in love.

Turning away from light streaks to look at her, we're stopped at a red. Cara's nose is sniffling as it has been for hours, but I think I've only just really noticed it now. Dougie is talking about the Canucks while my tongue is buried in what's-her-name's mouth. Oh yeah, Liz. Cara protests and the lower lip my teeth are holding struggles free into a belly laugh. Cara says something, I can't understand or don't want to, Liz shifts her body closer to mine and her satiny lips hit mine passionately. The hair on the back of my neck sticks up, shivers rush down my spine and my cock struggles against blow sedation. Streetlights strobe by overhead with buzzing eyelids trying to hide from them, red and black tones fill my non-sight.

Scents of her sweat, breath, perfume, and hair soak into me.

Beard stubble reddens her face, a fuschia hue seen in between the splash of headlight and neon street glow. Sour and frozen, my lips would ache from her biting. Maybe I'd trade the dull throb of swollen lips to think that what I have here is real, but who would deny that lust in the moment feels better than lonely in eternity. Her hand grabs at my dick, she's unreserved in showing me what she wants and how she needs it. Cara and Dougie talking blends in with Liz's breathing, the cab driver must have put on the radio, my hand cups Liz's breast and I squeeze. Cara chuckles. Dougie yells "Whoa, whoa, whoa!" I come up for air and laugh. We're here. Dougie checks his wallet and he's out of cash. I give the driver a $20 and thank him for the trip. He looks at me like I'm a piece of shit.

I close the door and the cab pulls away, an ugly yellow stain among a convoy of black Mercedes and silver BMWs. Inside fancy cars ride a cargo of wealthy Asian sons and daughters living a life so completely foreign to mine. A rush of jealousy is quickly washed away with the thought of how much fucking better I am.

Thanks, cocaine.

Liz hugs Cara on the sidewalk, it's late, but Asians and dog walkers poke up and down the street, they shuffle around our enthusiastic motley crew. Dougie dances and sings "cuhcuhcuh-coooocaine!" Michael Jackson would be proud. "Nononose in paypaypayayyain!" Cara freaks out and screams about missing her purse, I point to Dougie as he strolls up the street with chutzpah only possible through copious amounts of liquor and drugs, a little black purse over his shoulder. Liz leans against a tree and slips her shoes into her left hand, her feet slapping the concrete as she starts running to catch up to Cara. I speed up my walk to match theirs while the tension in my chest keeps me from running.

Chased by security while high one time, my teenage self got caught skinny dipping at 3rd beach pool. Flashlights and yelling, dodging through bushes trying to find my car, I lost my shoes that night. Hard to forget how I couldn't catch my breath for an hour, the sensation of my chest nearly exploding. I promised myself I wouldn't do blow again after it took two hours for a normal heartbeat. Not doing coke turned into just little lines, the catch being none after midnight. Then it became none after two. I did stop for long periods of time, at a time when most of my friends were also shut-ins.

I'm watching Liz's ass. The way her dress sometimes rides up her crack. Her perfect looking toned legs glowing as headlights of a starting Audi shine onto her. A larger man is getting out of a taxi a half block down. It's Matt. He is with Joellen, Sylvia and the fucked up guy on 'shrooms. Cara, Liz, and Dougie start waving wildly at them, I smile.

Matt staggers over to an iron apartment gate and fiddles with his keys. This must be where the party continues, a low rise condo unit off Robson Street. My teeth grit and clash against each other, I shiver and feel hot at the same time. The crew follows Matt through the front gate, up a shabby elevator that feels a bit cozy with all of us inside it. My crotch presses against a girl and my right hand finds the middle of Liz's back. I'm antisocial and everyone's chatter and laughter grinds inside of my ears. Penthouse level, down the hallway and another door unlocks, Matt's place is spacious. Two large rooms form the kitchen that doubles as a bar, and a living room with a glass coffee table. A small office leads out to a balcony while the bedroom has a hot tub and mirrors on the walls.

We all queue and Pacman up through our noses, briefly taking turns sitting on the couch. Matt lights up a fat joint and passes it around. The girls decline, but I take three large hits and pass it back to him. My tongue curiously laps my mouth for a taste of smoky teeth and gums while a thick rope of saliva binds my oral organ. Smoke, spit and sugary sweet cranberry tones mix together into a viscous blob and I swallow it in hopes of clearing the taste of blow from my throat. High as fuck while stoned and drunk, I reach a peak and feel like tripping out. Liz sits on my lap and grinds her little ass on me until I have to push her off and step out of the living room, through the office, and out onto the balcony. Lights twinkle everywhere. A landscape filled with so many shuttered windows and dim condos. I'm standing facing a hotel across the street, blocks and blocks of apartment buildings are behind it, to my right, and to my left. A valley of what the modern man considers a home, certainly not a castle and not the Canadian dream.

I inhale sharply, frigid air is coughed back out. I can't remember if I had been breathing. My chest feels tight and I steady myself on the balcony which is covered in light layer of frost, flirtatious lights of the city watching my every move. Music booms behind me, closing my eyes, a gentle numbing euphoria rolls over me in waves.

Why am I here?

I open my eyes and city lights blend and swirl together, waves of calming warmth and a deep sense of satisfaction bathe my brain in powder fueled pleasure. I'm in a paradise of self-loathing.

I breathe out through my mouth, the steam twists and curls into exotic, flowery forms. Liz steps out behind me and puts her arms around my neck. I can't fake any interest in her no matter how genuine my intent is to flirt, my hand finds her fingers together at my collarbone and unbinds them. She mutters something about drinks and I think she walked away.

I draw a little smiley face in the frost, what little happiness there is in the world is probably chemically altered. Two, six, no, fourteen. Fourteen of my friends are on or have been on anti-depressants. I was even on them before, a little pill that helps you numb biting reality. A layer of gauze over all of your senses, a gag on the voice inside that calls out to you when it senses something is wrong. Sex isn't fun, but you don't need it. Food all tastes like plastic. Spooning that girl you like, she might as well be a mannequin. My heart is racing, a sharp cold stabs into my forearm and I breathe in sharply. It's Liz, she brought me a big glass of vodka on ice. Perfect store-bought ice O's pop and crackle in my nearly clear beverage, the cranberry barely lends it a pink tone, its more vodka than cran. I guess when 50/50 blackout mixes aren't enough, the ante gets upped to a split that favours the house over the player. The house, in this case, is the floor. Drinking is a game, seeing just how close to blackout you can get, finding that party-veteran point of being not-too-much-but-just-right fucked up.

"Cheers!" she stutters while shivering from the drugs, the cold, or both.

Our glasses clink together, glass to chin, head dips back to take the numbing cold vodka in my mouth. Cocaine's bitter aftertaste haunts the back of my throat, only easing up after dancing with the vodka going down. Liz stumbles into the patio furniture and knocks an ashtray off the table. She giggles and pulls up a chair to be beside me. The drink finds the railing and I can't bear to face her. I don't want her here. This is all fake. This is the drugs and alcohol acting inside me, making me want her. Second hand smoke wafts over and invades my personal space. Litter and neon light hum, the slums of thoughts, a grimy dive, alcohol, blow, smokes, and the thought of Liz's pussy. An award-winning high. My heart feels like it's going to give up, I breathe in and feel like a king, beside me sits the queen of this evening, the ace can be found up my nose.

Liz says something, I can't really hear her. My stomach flips in a knot from the vodka assault, or I could have snorted the coke back too far and swallowed a lot of it.

"Wha ... What?" I barely manage to choke out.

Nausea hits me hard.

"They're listening to fucking dubstep, I hate it. Sounds like a robot being tazed taking a shit." Liz flicks her smoke with panache. I don't know if this is how she is, or she's trying to impress me. So high, so cold, I'm shivering almost to a beat.

"I'll be bu-ba-back" I croak out to Liz, my legs feel like lead, back into the office, through the archway to the living room. People are lined up around the snow pile, conversations everywhere. Boastful hand gestures, a 60oz of vodka is half finished on the counter. Melted ice runs out of a bag on the counter and into an ever-growing puddle on the floor. A few people acknowledge me and I push passed them, eyes glazed over and my stomach turning upside down.

22 1994

My stomach barely makes it to the bathroom, my foot kicking to close the door, and I puke into the sink not a moment too soon. Puking again and again, the sour mess of cocaine coats the inside of my mouth. Metallic and dirty, a lemon made of old car parts and kerosene. I barely catch the feeling of my guts ready to explode. My right hand slides the bathroom lock into place as my left hand fumbles at my waist. Shaky hands tear my belt open and I slam my ass down on the toilet while removing my pants in one fluid motion. My ass hits the seat, almost instantly a shotgun blast of shit torrents from my overwhelmed bowels. I feel amazing. So high, my teeth chatter and my belt tinkles together as I shudder uncontrollably. The door handle rattles, a muffled voice. I don't care. A few pushes and some semi solids hit the water. Wipe, flush. A snot trail of vomit and cocaine must be on my lips, my tongue finds it and explores the taste again. Bitter like crushed aspirin, but it makes me want to do another line.

I stand up and get my bearings, the euphoria is back in full force and I check myself out in the mirror. Looking as handsomely fucked up as ever, a few moments are spent fixing my hair and face. Pounding back another mouthful of vodka, I open the bathroom door to several people I don't recognize from earlier. Leaving the ruined shitter behind me with big striding steps and a smile on my face, haters gonna hate. The first poor guest after me will get intimately close with the odour of my bowels. Down the hallway and into the snow nest, Matt is opening another flap. Three large rocks fall out and he chuckles. "Shit he was right! These are fucken beautiful!" Cara squeals in delight, Dougie looks at me with shifty eyes and looks away immediately. I think for a moment if he feels as sketchy and shitty as I do, but that goes away when Matt hands me a rolled up bank note.

Matt puts a coke rock on a glossy black plate, ceremoniously holding it up to one of his kitchen track lights at eye level. "Come, look! This is pure, totally pure. They call this el puro in Latin America. See that sweet off white and the crystalline sheen? This is the best shit. It's not like that fucken bullshit Cara's ex gets."

Party members nod, some laugh, a few conversations float on around us as Matt rants on about cocaine. He takes time to crush the rock up fine before cutting me two huge rails. I briefly worry about my heart until it's all in my sinuses. Matt is sweaty and dancing about, he grabs the plate from the kitchen counter and does a monster half gram line. Another pile of blow is being tended to on the couch. I begin to peak again, looking to sit on the couch and chill out with my drink.

I feel like I'm swimming, my whole body sinks into the couch, I tumble into the soft mouth of practical European design, and I'm eaten by leather. My jaw clenches in time with the beat. Coloured lighting flashes through the room and cuts ribbons of smoke in its rays. Laughter and fast talking voices spill out into the music and creates an anthem in my head. A few tight bodied girls dance and writhe in front of me, one is sliding down the knee of the other, ass stuck out and splaying apart her hips. The womanly figure of the upside-down heart shape created by a woman squatting or bending over, strikes my instinct ablaze. The familiar snap of a match, the pop and hiss of an angry fire elemental summoned. I feel it in me. My body feels furious and I sit up, unable to sit still. I pat my leg down, still have my phone. Wallet? I reach back, wallet. Keys? Do I need to leave, can't remember the plan.

Liz walks in from the office, she's bitching about something. A blonde girl is behind her, her eyes wide and apologetic. The two seem to make up, pounding bass and voices in a roar to drown each other. My face is completely numb, gritting teeth the only option other than grinding them. My pulse is racing and I can't sit still. I get to my feet, feeling my heart hammering against ribs and feeling as though the room is on top of a colossal-sized tuning fork. Every conversation and each note of the music seems to reverberate through reality, my shoulders and back nod, music washes over me, my arm raised and I'm a fucken cowboy now. The world in front of me throbs with a zeal for life, Liz's smiling at me, Matt just cut up a huge couple of lines and I'm about to put on some Pitbull.

Shit's cool. The Music is bumping. Chicks are dancing. I dance while a few girls grind, Liz bumps one out of the way to dance with me. Liz spills her drink on some guy. Faces are familiar whether I recognize them or not when wandering around drunk and high, I don't know who Liz just soaked with her drink, but I'm glad he's not freaking out. Smiling faces, hugs, shots, bro fists, Matt gets out a hockey stick signed by Kirk McLean. The party grows rowdier with guys showing off new choke holds they learned from a buddy, several rounds of high fives, drinking, drugs and laughter at a frenetic pace now.

"Fuck where were you guys during '94 that night? Check this shit out." Matt turns his hand so his palm is under the coke plate's light, showing off a noticeable burn scar.

"Dude we stayed down there for hours just throwing the tear gas cans back at the pigs. I learned fast they are fucking hot right after they're launched!"

"Haha! Fuck yeah!" parrots some random.

That must have been fun, running under streetlights, throwing shit. For one day being able to smash what little order there is left, rejoicing at the smells of tear gas and ash, a fucking symphony to my ears when glass breaks. Batons, shields, Guy Fawkes masks, little green tear gas mist men dance to the songs of crackling buildings. Anarchists cheer as it all falls down.

Dougie hands me a shot. Bam, done.

My mind evaporates.

"Matt, you got any ice left?" Dylen asks. A melted bag of ice sits in the sink, Dougie taps Dylen and shows him the awful news. Groans are heard and warm vodka breathes a sigh of relief. Shoes snuggle with feet, tagalongs are gathered, and the first expeditionary cocaine commando party recon team descends in the elevator.

Dylen cracks a joke loudly and old people on the 3rd floor just made some angry faces. Dylen somehow realized this and wishes they were high too. This elevator has been in service for decades, but it hasn't seen such juvenile jubilee in years. Dougie somersaults out of the elevator and Cara jumps on his back. Liz and Dylen embrace in a kiss and push several buttons on the elevator. Quantum entanglement or coincidental timing, Cara and Dougie turn to witness elevator doors closing just as Liz's skirt lifts up. Cara and Dougie sit in the lobby, hands and arms interlocked. Dougie wants to kiss her, but knows his coke breath is disgusting. He hopes Cara can't smell it. Cara's wondering she should have worn her bronzer, Dougie obviously thinks she's not good enough. Fuck him then, she thinks.

Two humans in the elevator wiggle and thrash their tongues, clothing disarrayed and Liz has two fingers inside her. Her hand slides across the front of Dylen's pants. Two more floors open and close, bottom lips are bitten tender and Liz's panties cup wet girl parts. Dylen's brain a maelstrom of highs and higher jagged peaks as her musky scent lingers inside his nose, heaven on earth. The mission to get ice crosses his mind again and he hits the G button with a free hand while internally hunting for her G spot with the other. Drinking warm vodka is simply not partying responsibly. Liz assembles her shirt and helps Dylen with a few button snaps. The elevator thuds to a stop on the ground floor and the doors rattle open, Cara and Dougie in an awkward drug fueled embrace.

Out on the street, streetlamps and shadow give everything an orange and black tiger stripe pattern. ATM signs wave at jonesing stragglers, a club across the street uses curvy neon and pulsing bass to entice drunks to cups, bottles, and bitches. A number of people are smoking outside, rowdy and boastful to the night. The darkness smiles and will hear about their hangovers from a girl he's been chasing forever, Morning. Dylen and Liz dance up the sidewalk in imaginary Hammer pants, moving and clapping wildly to a beat only they cam hear. Cara can't get her lighter to work while Dougie looks around nervously for a corner store.

"Sev's down this way Dyl," Dougie calls out while pointing.

"Yeah bro we're grabbing cash and meeting you there," Dyl yells back, already a quarter the way down the block.

The two couples split up and Cara and Dougie walk up the street together, Cara's lithe figure hunched over her phone, slender fingers tap on her Blackberry and inspire names for firecrackers. Lady fingers thread words with the careful and elegant motions of a spider weaving a web. No way is she going to fuck this Dougie guy, he's handsome and all, but he doesn't even own his condo. He's a renter and she needs security. Her girlfriends have found guys who will let them live in condos and not have to work, while the men work jobs that require travel. Her friends live the life, shopping, partying, gossip, and seeing who has the dirtiest stories to tell. Here she is 27 and still working on her degree while 60k in debt. Fuck that, she isn't even going to look twice at Dougie. She clicks send as she finishes explaining to her friend about how hot this guy she just met is, and sends a photo of her and Dougie kissing to her girlfriend.

Dougie takes a flap out of his pocket and stuffs one of his house keys inside. He said he wouldn't buy any more of that shit on Thursday, but Friday had a different idea in mind. Forty in party powder usually leads to a good time, eighty guarantees it. The paper pouch is in his palm and concealed, he glances around, just Cara, a few Chinese people, some taxies, a girl walking her dog a half block up. Dougie stops and looks down into his palm. Taking a key, he digs in, slowly pulling the key out while balancing the coke on its side. Up to his nose and he feeds himself some brain candy. Dougie puts the key back in, back out, and lights up the other nostril. Damn smooth, going to get more of this guy's stuff.

Cara didn't notice that Dougie wasn't there, causing a startle when he jogs up beside her. "Oh Doug, it's just you," Cara's hand half sarcastically falls on her chest, tips first. Her nails are a deep azure. Dougie thinks inside of his mind what a beautiful, but stuck up bitch Cara is. She's smart, ladylike, graceful, and not normally easy at all. She thinks she needs money over love, and that's why he's going to fuck her brains out and never talk to her again. Dougie says nothing and offers her a key hit. She stops and glances around quickly before loading both of her nostrils. She giggles after both. Her smile is from ear to ear and she holds on to Dougie's arm the rest of the way to 7-11.

Women's heels and acceleration from engines, crowd murmur and a siren blocks away, Dylen and Liz share the moments. Liz mentions to Dylen what to buy at 7-11, no ice is an unforgivable party foul to her. She digs through her mini black purse and finds her bank card. Dylen plugs away at the touch screen and soon a fat wad of cash is in his hand. Liz slides her plastic inside, types a couple of buttons wrong, Liz giggles because Dylen had his finger inside her, having reached up her skirt and finding her silky pink thong easy to slide under. Dylen is so high he forgets that those fingers were just used on a public ATM machine. Liz turns around, kisses Dylen deeply, and gives him her cash for the next round of booze and drugs.

A group of wealthy Asians walk by, dressed very conservatively. Liz feels almost slutty for wearing such a short dress. Almost. Dylen pulls down on his jacket with his hands in its side pockets, which hides that he has a half chub going on. Liz and Dylen head toward the 7-11, both smiling and closing their eyes occasionally, a bit longer than a normal blink, to hold onto that cocaine-fueled bliss. A Nissan GTR flies up the street, mechanical noise and race exhaust echoing down through the buildings and alleys. Liz hates the sound and her face grimaces. Dylen smiles and dreams of wheel spinning 2nd gear shifts, sore necks going into 3rd, and chirping the tires into 4th. Fast cars and beautiful women, feeling rich. Chemicals rush positive thoughts into their brains, the short walk to 7-11 is quiet, but deafening inside their heads.

Cara and Dougie stalk the isles of convenience, each of them oblivious to why they even came here. Eyes fidget in sockets as the group tries to recall why they walked here in the cold. Dougie buys a slurpee, Cara buys some chips and grabs a coconut water. Dylen and Liz walk in just as they finish paying after waiting in line. Dylen bee lines for the ice, and has to walk by late night food. Greasy tubes of meat, zombie poultry wings, oxidized corndogs. Sugar hints sweetly in the air, pitted apples under the Fresh Food awning, a row of sandwich clone soldiers rest on their backs. Subs with grey meat have labels like 'Roast Beef Supremo' and 'Ole! Tex Mex chicken fiesta wrap.' Taco bell used to advertise to make a run for the border, most who eat ten day old 7-11 fiesta wraps will be running for the bathroom.

Six bags of ice. Dylen's hands are freezing after holding them while in the line. He's pissed Dougie forgot to get the ice. Ice in bags, Liz, Cara, Dougie and Dylen are back on the street. Liz leads the group down the end of the block and turns the opposite way back. Cara calls out to Liz and she doesn't reply. Dylen is so high he doesn't notice and stays quiet. Dougie stops and snorts another key line. A quarter the way up the block, Liz turns and darts into a McDonald's. Cara says out loud "What the fuck," and is obviously pissed off. Dylen puts the bags of ice down. Dougie walks over to Dylen and puts down the loot he's carrying.

"I'll see what's poppin," Dougie says, Dylen nods. Cara lights up a smoke and stares into Dylen's glazed over, high as fuck eyes. Inside the McDonald's, Liz just wants chicken nuggets. She couldn't resist and hates to ask. She was on meds for anxiety related to her weight, and has struggled with eating as long as she can remember. Her doctor recommended that she quit her vegan diet as it had been making her have dizzy spells sometimes, and she stood up a little too quickly months back, passed out ,and hit her head. She would die if someone made fun of her eating, especially at McDonald's, but she couldn't ignore two day old hunger pains any longer.

Dougie walks up to her in line and asks "What's up?" Liz has her arms folded and stares ahead "Chicken nuggets! Want anything? I'm buying!" Liz replies in her sing songy tone, secretly hoping Dougie wants to eat so she doesn't look like the only fatty. The line is pretty long and a couple people seem restless. "Yeah, uh... fries?; Gonna ask Cara and Dyl if they want anything." Dougie notices a fat guy in the lineup talking loud on his cel, a spike of tension and his voice is loud and arrogant. A shitty little goatee and the way he sips from the straw in his large drink is pissing Dougie off, fast.

Dougie steps out of the McD's and Dylen looks agitated, Cara is getting a light from a stranger. "You guys want anything? Liz needs food."

"Aww it's so sweet when she eats too!" Cara purrs, "She takes little nibbles! Yeah I want a shake."

Dylen turns to Cara "Watch my shit, I need to see a menu!" and leaves through the door into McDonald's.

Dougie shrugs, Cara points back towards the McD's and tells Dougie she wants a chocolate, no, no, strawberry shake! Dougie nods and ducks back in, and down the long, corridor shaped urban McDonald's. Dougie can't understand how these people want to eat, the drugs in his system working to ignore all needs to dine or sleep.

Liz and Dylen are lost in conversation. The fat man on the phone is talking about eating pussy. "Hey, hey man, your girl on the rag and you never had your red wings? Haha bro! Bro it's fucken' choice bro!" The whole restaurant can hear him.

Dougie looks around nervously, he knows Dylen can be the hot head sometimes, that bipolar maniac has some serious attitude problems some days. Now it's Dougie acting the fool and getting all bothered by some fat d-bag guy yelling into his phone. Dougie can't believe Dylen hasn't said something. Dylen is laughing. He can totally hear the fat idiot describe how the side to side motion of eating a girl out on her period would leave red blood in a wing pattern on your cheeks. Funny though, on drugs he knows he has a much higher tolerance for getting pissed off. Dylen is thinking of how sexy Liz looks.

Liz is horrified. Dylen mentioned how he wants to steal a couple nuggets, somewhere inside Liz's mind it translates into her being fat. He wants to eat her nuggets because if she eats them all, she'll gain weight. Liz takes all of her focus to not run out of the lineup while laughing nervously at the chicken nugget theft comment. Dougie is staring at some fat, annoying greasy East Indian guy. Liz hates East Indians, but she's not racist. She had her car hit and ran twice by brown guys, and when she worked at the keg in Surrey, East Indians would give shitty tips. They would rev the engines of their Mustangs in the parking lot before leaving, assholes. Maybe this guy had a Mustang, she thinks anyone who drives one is an automatic cheesedick. Liz would tell anyone that she hates racists if they asked. Liz thinks to herself how she was so fucking thin back then and sighs.

Dougie is pissed. The fat guy is now yelling at the McDonald's people to hurry the fuck up with his meal. His attention diverted for a moment, he screams "Yeah I fucken know, 15 minutes for a fucken' burger!" The scurrying little immigrant Asians working behind the counter dash and spin aimlessly while beeps go off on the deep fryer. One of the older ones is the only one actually doing anything, firing fries and burgers into bags, a shadow passes behind the food chute and another couple burgers slide down to fill waiting orders. Dylen shifts his weight onto his right leg and sighs.

Liz grows impatient and pulls out her phone to text, Cara is on her 3rd smoke, high as balls, and freezing cold. Liz texts Cara that she's getting a nice strawberry shake and to chill out. Then writes back and apologizes for the choice of words. The line shuffles forward and fat phone guy is two orders back in line. A tray sitting with fries and a pop gets a burger on it, finally. Liz swears it was on the counter when they first walked in. Fat phone guy starts waving at someone in the back, "Hello China? Where's my burger? This is fast food, stop cooking like you're driving!" A few people laugh.

"Sir, please stop," the littlest looking Asian grandma working the counter looks tired. She's not working the 3 AM shift for fun, and the pleading look on her face says everything. Dougie and Dylen both glance at each other and think the same thing. Liz is looking a little panicked, her fingers text away to calm her. Fat phone guy walks over to the woman at the counter and barks a few f-bombs about his fucken burger and fucken fries. "You what? Fuck this!" fat phone guy says as he throws his cup on the floor, the lid flies off, and ice scatters everywhere. Shoulders fall down and sag on the older woman working here, she looked a little down when Dylen walked in, looks like clinical depression now.

Dougie feels a surge of empathy and growls, "Dude you're a real piece of shit."

Dylen's face lights up in a maniacal smile.

Fat Phone looks at Dougie, "Hey buddy you could end up cut up for that, Sicilian neck tie mother fucker!" and draws a line across his throat.

Dougie laughs. "Bitch, *please*, cheeseburger gangsters don't scare me."

Fat Phone takes a couple steps forward towards Dougie, ice crunching underfoot.

"You have no idea who you're fucken with," Fat Phone's face goes completely blank, a psychotic look of rage in his eyes. His hand lifts up the corner of his shirt to reveal a sheathe tucked into his waistband, a finger flicks the cover open.

Dougie's face a portrait of tension, the whole restaurant goes silent save for the beeping of french fry alarms.

"That's what I thought," Fat Phone sneers, Dougie unwilling to risk getting cut over nothing.

Dylen throws his arms in the air wildly, "Ohh pick me! I already want a makeover and a painful death!" and kneels in front of Fat Phone, arms outstretched to the ceiling, chin up and back offering the neck for a willing blade.

Liz's mouth hangs open, these guys she just met are fucking crazy!

"Just fucken' do it you fucking poosaaaaay!" Dylen screams while slobbering drunk, eyes closed and kneeling.

Dougie and Fat Phone sort of stare at each other, each turning to look at a frantic, almost possessed-looking Dylen.

"Fucken clowns," Fat Phone mutters, his eyes glancing in the direction of the exit.

When Fat Phone guy finally tries to step around Dougie, he slips on some ice. As Dougie has trained in martial arts for years, the sudden movement Fat Phone guy made is mistaken for getting swung on, and Dougie quickly throws an overhead right while ducking. Audible popping as flesh sandwiched between knuckles and cheek does little to protect bone. Faces in the crowd widen with shock of spectacle, Fat Phone staggers back slowly while his snapped jaw looks inhuman. Ice cubes form a slippery minefield underfoot, sending Fat Phone flailing and crashing headfirst into the fountain pop machine. With a huge smash followed by a brief stunned silence of the crowd, Fat Phone lands in a barely coherent pile on the floor. Dougie grabs Dylen and rushes him out the front door of McD's fine restaurant-turned-dojo. Cara isn't at the front door. Dylen looks around in a haze as Dougie spots her nearby with and cops coming up the street only a few meters away. Thinking fast, Dougie says "Dyl, move," and walks with him in the opposite direction. Cara is a few meters from the opposite side of the door, opening it for the police and pointing in. "Cara! Here!" Dougie's voice says in an anxious whisper, his arm flailing franticly to motion her over. Cara holds up her phone and grins, "Guys, Liz said there was going to be a fight and I told these cops that the guy had a knife!" Cara's phone goes off, "Oh my god! Haha! They just threw him down on the floor and are all laying on him. Knees all up on his back and everything haha!" Cara cackles in delight, her head peeking around the side of the door. "Yep they are working him over good, haha!" Cara is enjoying this a little much. Dougie and Dylen grab the bags and tell Cara to walk back with Liz, fast. Dougie and Dylen book it the fuck out of there to avoid charges, but mostly because it shouldn't take 30 minutes to get some fucken ice.

23 Jaw Boogie

Ice water runs down my forearms which mimic jogging sniffles up my nose, I'm a mess of leaky fluids, no dignity and numbed flesh. The back of a cop car would at least be warm right now, but the drunk tank is never as fun as my bed with a girl in it. My hands are freezing and my nose is simply arctic. Liz is smoking and stumbling every so often. Dougie and Cara look like an old couple the way they stroll together arm in arm, if only for tonight.

We get back to the party, greeted with shifty eyed people strung out on speedy E, or that's at least what they're complaining about as they rip open bags of ice, taking handfuls and rubbing it on their chests and necks. "That's for drinks guys, FUCK!" Matt says as he grows more frustrated, his brow glistening and his movements twitchy. Dougie and Cara move out to the balcony, through the sliding glass door I can tell he's kissing her with his hand between her legs.

"Here," Liz passes me another drink. I take it and suck back a mouthful of vodka that wasn't stirred at all. A hint of the mix keeps me from gagging, fumes into my frozen nose flow with the subtly of chainsaws on fire. Liz sneaks a little plate over to the couch and calls for me. I'm laughing and nodding at Matt, I haven't understood a word he's said since he did a monster rail a minute ago. Time gets lost, I sit on the couch and do lines with Liz, my hand slides back up her dress and I dip a finger back inside her wet warmth.

She squeals and is oblivious to anyone around us. A girl sitting across from us smiles while watching with lust in her eyes, a curiosity fueled by drugs, liquor, and a need to get off. The party is raging and Matt yells out "Yo we gonna pop a bottle in the tub!" I turn and see a champagne bottle come out of the fridge, a few people disappear down the hallway towards the bedroom where the fun is.

I feel Liz's hand on my wrist and she gently pulls my finger into her deeper, her hips slide forward and back on the couch. Liz's skirt rides up and her panties are visible, the girl across from us sees my finger sliding in and out of Liz's swollen, juicy lips and her mouth drops open a little. Liz lets out a little moan and arches her back, a few people are watching Liz enjoy herself, as she drops her head behind her shoulders with eyes closed.

I pull my finger out of her, thick, clear juices coat my finger and I stick it in my mouth to clean it. She tastes so delicious and my cock stirs from a cocaine coma.

The brunette across from us squints at me with a look of jealousy. I slide my hand back up Liz's skirt, her inner thigh soft and hot to the touch, her waxed labia invites my finger to play and find her petite opening. Inserted to the first knuckle, her pussy tightens and squeezes on me, second knuckle and I have to push harder to bury it all the way in. I make my favorite come hither motion inside her with my finger and Liz muffles her enjoyment with only the slightest hint of shyness. I pull my finger back out, coated again in Liz's cum, turn, and offer it to the brunette. Without a moment of hesitation, she jumps out of her chair, sits beside Liz, and performs fellatio on my finger, sucking it hard and cleaning it of any trace of Liz's cream.

A couple people in the kitchen may have noticed, but mostly there are only a few girls in the living room where we're sitting. The brunette looks down at Liz and says "Hi!" with such enthusiasm. Liz looks at her, bites her own lower lip, grabs the brunette by the hair, and begins the longest and most passionate kiss I've seen in a long time. My dick roars to life in my pants and I almost feel light headed, euphoria takes over and my hand slides up the brunette's dress. For a moment I feel like I'm intruding on personal space, but she spreads her thighs enough to get my fingers to her panties. Her soaking lace panties are easy to slip my fingers behind and a small amount of course hair scratches the cuticle of my fingernail. A little wiggle to find the passage inside her and she finally stops tongue kissing Liz long enough to give out a "Wow ..." my finger slides in and out of her, she's wetter than Liz was.

Liz smiles and says "You're hot," to the girl, my finger pulling out of her and I offer it to Liz. She licks it from the 3rd knuckle to the top, and then the brunette puts her mouth down on it and sucks the rest of her own flavour off.

Liz giggles and hugs the brunette girl, "New bestie!" she purrs.

The brunette smiles, "I'm Alicia, you guys are?"

"Dylen," I say, hoisting my drink to my mouth and sipping.

"Elizabeth, but my friends call me Liz; my lovers can call me anything they want."

Liz bites her lower lip, her eyes squint to almonds while gazing at Alicia's body, sizing up her prey.

"Here, have some," Liz sits up, snatches the little plate from the table and offers Alicia a rail. She accepts a pinner sized line while I put my drink down to snort back another small one. Liz loads both of her nostrils with a couple of towering snow drifts. With an orange peel throat and wild eyes, I lean back and hold my jaw in place from grinding. Liz lights up a smoke. Alicia goes in and loads her other nostril before making a little scowl. "Wow. Fuck. This stuff is smooth." Alicia bursts into a giggle and her scowl turns into a smile. Liz laughs "I know eh? The fucker I buy from snuck in a batch of whack shit last time, this is his best and I don't accept anything less."

Alicia looks back towards the crowd in the kitchen nervously for a moment. "I've uh, only done this stuff a couple times before and it just made me feel anxious and it hurt my nose." Alicia talks a little quieter than she did before. She looks younger than Liz; I'd be surprised if she's a day over 23."Yeah we were all rookies once," Liz quips as she OCD relights her still burning cigarette. "Once you get to where I'm at, you know what you like and where to get it." Liz tilts her head back and blows a few smoke rings.

Matt stomps over from the kitchen. "Fuck off Liz; you know you can't smoke in here." Matt powerwalks with gusto to the balcony door.

"Here, this, this place is where cigarettes fucking go, Ok? Fuck. *Fuck!*" He throws his hands in the air and laughs, then scowls again.

"F-F-FUCK!"

"Yo Matt, chill!" I hear behind me from the kitchen.

Liz jumps up and goes outside with her drink, turning around to pop her head in the doorway.

"Alicia, wanna smoke?"

"Sure!" Alicia replies, shooting me a smile as she gets up and walks towards the balcony. She has thicker, shorter legs, a wide ass, and a narrow upper body. Very fuckable.

Lens flare over a beach of white sand, Alicia's bikinied ass. A bright yellow dot of sun in a sky one shade lighter than the water below. A stereo beside me belts out California by Phantom Planet, grit under the cap of a Corona bottle crunches as I pop the lid off.

My wishful future life as drawn by MS Paint.

Matt sits down across from me. "Fucken bitches think they just own this place, Liz knows we're cool, but fuck man, the 'tude on her." Another fresh pile is on the plate and Matt goes down for another bump. I think my heart would explode if I did another. I nod, which then turns into a head bob to the music. Matt smiles at me.

"Buddy, we should hang out more, it's been awhile! Remember our last party? Haha ... SHIT! You were in the tub covered in bubbles and you made out with that cute broad with the curly hair. She was supposed to come tonight too, fucken reunion!"

I nod, I really don't remember what he's talking about. My eyes close to allow my head to flow with the music, vanguard of my euphoria. My body doesn't so much as sit on the couch, as it sucks the comfort from it. Matt rambles on and the words blossom into laughter and high fives. I don't know if I forgot what he said as he said it, or if the words just fell apart in mid-air.

Someone yells from the kitchen. Matt catches his phone. Hollywood Undead fills the room and Matt jumps up and down on his couch. Berserk laughter tilting my head back, light sprays across the stucco ceiling.

Children in summertime, running through rainbow prism water spray, mutt dogs in tow. Sunshine through lemonade, watching rind dance and swirling around on its own. Ugly bugs, your first bee sting, those scary times of learning how to ride a bike. Those pure days of innocence might be lost by giving smartphones to kids. I'll have to remember that. Will I ever have a family or kids to call my own? These girls are what, 20? Practically kids themselves, and what am I doing here? Who am I kidding, this is my fate, this is where I belong, not fucking for love, but to see what's behind her thong.

Noise blends together into a force that keeps my head nodding and my foot tapping. "Dylen," Liz jumps into my lap. "Dylen!" Disco lights. "Dylen!" Liz sits sideways across my legs. A smoky kiss glides across my lips, and 50,000 stories up my mind registers pleasure. Alicia giggles, "He's so high!" I smile, turn my head, and look at her down my nose.

"Dyll-en ..." Liz whispers.

I can't take my eyes off Alicia.

Liz bites my ear.

Matt's sweaty, meaty head appears in front of me.

"Dude, we have some great E on its way! Hehehe!!" he laughs maniacally and I sit up in time to see him jump on the couch beside Alicia and then jump over the back of it. A couple dudes I don't recognize walk by with a fat chick in tow to the balcony.

"Dyllll-en," Liz whispers again.

"Yeah Lizzy Lizzerson?" I reply.

"You're such a poo-say! I'm done my drink before you, again! Here I thought I met a man ..." Liz has put half her hair into one demented looking ponytail, crosses her eyes, and sticks out her tongue before bursting into laugher. I take my queue and finish the rest of my now-warm vodka cranberry.

"It's a good thing we're having a tough guy competition tonight Liz, you're going to earn your Fuckstronaut badge tonight when we each rail a cap of E." I wink at her.

"Ooh! Pinky swear we will Dyl?" Liz offers me her little mini pinky finger, hooked to complete my promise.

"Pinky swear."

"It's a deal!"

"Ok, but you have to keep one side of your hair in pigtail. I think it suits you."

Alicia laughs from the other couch.

"She should do one too! She's just a rookie, let's *brrrrr*eak her in!" Liz growls the r and points at her. Alicia feigns shock and giggles, meanwhile I'm fantasizing about how wide her hips are compared to her waist. She doesn't have quite the body or daddy issues to be a stripper, but she would make one boner-fueling burlesque dancer.

"Hey Dylen! Get over here!" Matt yells from the hallway.

"I take a couple uppers," Matt sings, as he closes the door behind his delivery man.

"I down a couple downers!" echoed by a couple of ball capped guys from the kitchen.

"But nothing compares to these blue and yellow purple pills!" Matt hollers as he skips to the kitchen, Irish-clicks his heels, and tosses a huge zip lock bag full of pills on the kitchen counter.

"Whoa," says Raiders cap guy.

"Fuck yeah!" says a skinny blonde next to him, as she lifts the zip lock up to admire the easily five hundred or more blue pills.

Matt snatches the bag from her hand. "NEVER touch my drugs," he hisses. For a moment things seem sinister, but Matt's face relaxes into a grin as he opens the bag, and hands her a blue cap. Matt again reaches in the bag, takes three caps out, and swallows them with a straight vodka chase from the bottle. "Yo everyone, I need $10 per cap, no exceptions!" Matt yells as he hands me a cap. His hand was a little sweaty and the cap bleeds an M&M candy blue in my palm. Then he gives one to Raider hat. He takes a couple pills and walks to the couches to give them to Liz and Alicia. I watch as Matt hands out at least a pill each to the dozen or more people milling around the kitchen and living room without taking any money from them. Did he forget already? Fuck it. I pour myself another drink and return to the couches.

Alicia is sitting on the couch with Liz, blue pill on the table, eye fixed on the prize. I take a seat on the couch across from them, careful not to sit on Matt's dirty shoeprints. "Alicia do you want me to wait for it to kick in, I'll let you know if it's speedy," Liz says so sweetly. Alicia glances at her for a second, and looks back at the pill. "No, it's not that, I just know that people die on this stuff. What if I have an allergic reaction or something?" Liz smiles.

"Look honey, I'm almost a decade older than you. I've seen my share of drugs and nobody has allergies to this stuff."

I raise my eyebrow. This is like The View, only leading to a drugged up threesome. I knew a girl once who overdosed, she died after working as a hooker for a couple weeks on Kingsway. Did too much down and slipped under the bathwater.

I miss her.

"Yeah you're probably right. You only live once right? I like that song by Drake," Alicia picks the pill up off the table, her eyes widen with excitement.

"You guys will stay with me tonight?" Alicia says with a sultry tone.

I can already see what's coming, and I'm not even that excited.

"Yeah, for sure," Liz says, and puts her drink in Alicia's free hand.

"Oh god I'm not washing down my first pill with vodka and cranberry!" Alicia protests.

"Yes!! Yes you are!" Liz takes Alicia's hand and nearly forces the pill into her mouth, Alicia chases it with Liz's cirrhosis special and chokes on the drink. Vodka and cranberry spray from Alicia's face, some landing in the coke, most of it on Liz.

"Oh SHIT!" Liz squeals, jumping off the couch.

Alicia pats her chest and coughs. "It's, ah ...stuck!" her face and brow contort in discomfort. I get up and briskly walk to the kitchen, pour a glass of water, and bring it to Alicia. She puts her arms out for the water as I walk back towards her and hand her the cup. She finishes the glass and smiles when it's down the hatch.

"Haha! How will I know when it kicks in?"

"Ali, remember when you licked Dylen's finger? When it kicks in you'll want to do more than just lick," Liz smirks as she pulls out a smoke. Alicia coughs and giggles again.

"Uh, Liz-"

"What?" Liz replies, thumb flicking a lighter, her eyes aligned perfectly to stare at me down the fag's body.

I take a big chug of my drink. "Well, Matt's more your friend than mine, but he already warned you about smoking in his house. I'm a guest here too and I don't want him to think I'm disrespecting his place by not reminding you not to smoke." I swear, cocaine makes me more eloquent.

"Aw, *fuck Matt*, I buy enough sneeze cheese from him to pay for his mortgage," Liz lights up and flicks her zippo closed. "If Matt wants to kick me out, he knows I can just get a new dealer." I shrug.

Alicia looks like a deer in headlights. I can't decide what Liz looks like right now, pencil thin legs and arms, a cute little egg of a body, drugs and sex sunny side down. $C17H21NO4$ puts my mind into overdrive, countless spiny looking molecules coursing through my brain, synapses clutching dopeamine tightly. I hope my dick works later when it hears its call of duty, most likely the sound of these two getting it on. Alicia and Liz yip and yap back and forth about the most trivial of shit. Matt's nowhere to be found, Raider hat and his friends mill about the kitchen.

"Hey Liz, where are Dougie and Cara?"

"They were on the balcony making out, and then they left. Cara said she needed to be up early and Dougie was going to walk her home."

Yeah right, guarantee he's digging her out right now. I wonder if she's still wearing her engagement ring.

I finish my drink while Alicia talks about shopping at Forever 21. Apparently Liz gets her eyebrows threaded on Robson and according to Alicia, pays $15 too much. A 10 year younger me might not have recognized the potential big time party foul of telling Alicia that Liz's eyebrows look better. Then again, if I really, really wanted to fuck Alicia, that's exactly what I'd tell her.

Liz is giving her tips on clothes shopping even though she's probably 8 sizes smaller. Makes me think of how ineffective it would be for a body-builder to tell a bowler how to work out. Peeling myself off the couch, the kitchen and the last of the vodka lures me away from conversation about Liz's favorite dress. Raider's hat nods to me as I pour my drink. "Dude, nice work with that chick in there bro," he says, hand offered for a grip handshake. I shake his hand and he leans in with a hug. "Oh man I couldn't believe it when that other chick licked your finger! That shit is freaky man!" I nod. "Thanks man, haha!" I half-heartedly chuckle. Once the kitchen is a total sausage fest, I know a party is turning to shit. Nomad thoughts abandon the dick party in the packed kitchen while curious feet want to check out the hot tub action going on down the hallway.

"Uh-dude?"

I stop. "Yeah?"

"Matt said they're getting freaky in there."

"I'll take my chances!" The door is closed. I knock.

"Who's that?"

"Hey it's Dylen!"

"Yo come in!" Matt's muffled voice yells. I hear splashing.

I open the door and a bunch of water and suds flood into the hallway. Matt's bedroom is half carpeted floor, half tile near the rectangular shaped, double-sized tub. The tub has almost two feet of bubbles over the deck height, two chicks heads barely poke out of the soapy hurricane. Another two girls are leaning up against a wall passing a bottle of tequila between them. Matt's holding a bottle of sparkling white wine, looking sweatier than ever. The floor is a dynamic carpet of wet towels and discarded clothes. Matt's girlfriend is horizontal on the bed looking grumpy, no doubt feeling sore from Matt's eyes on the two tub nymphs. "Sup buddy!" Matt bounces in place. "We're having a bubble party in here!"

24 Dragonborn

Bubbles. Bubbles, bubbles, and more bubbles are popping and floating around everywhere, a soft hand gives my cock a small squeeze. Her hand grips the head and slides back the foreskin, I feel it barely stir from its blow induced hiding. I don't know what overcame me, but the moment I heard bubble party, I kicked my shoes off, stripped butt ass naked, and jumped in the tub between the girls. I thought Matt was going to flip shit with the tsunami of water I spilled all over his floor, instead he had been feeding his girlfriend drugs and not noticed. At some point before the underwater stroke job, Matt had noticed the suds and water all over his floor, soaking everything. Drugs are great, instead of freaking out he just put on 'Rasputin' and danced Russian, splashing water around and squishing wet towels. The pill. The pill must be kicking in. A slightly zit faced blonde chick is rubbing my cock, I can barely see her face from out of this prison of bubbles. When I first got in the tub, the girls were laughing. It's not often that I suffer from micro dick, but the blizzard in my nose will do that to me. Penis size and masculinity are linked for sure, being a grower over a shower, I hadn't thought about the consequences of dropping my pants. They must have all noticed, it sort of looks like a tiny little nub when cold and so fucking high. The brunette girl to my right was laughing, and then apologized to me. I didn't realize it at the time, but she said that she was sorry and that she shouldn't laugh at a small dick. Maybe it's the drugs I asked her, the blonde saying she's never seen smaller. The power of pills used to hide the ego. Right away I can tell the blonde is the friendlier of the two.

"I am the king of bubbles!" I proclaim.

One of the girls against the wall coughs.

"Shells, pass the teccy!" the brunette squeals as she bats soap suds from her face.

"I decree there shall be tequila in the tub!" I bring my fist down hard enough to splash the water back up into my face and eyes, blinding me.

"You can't be a king without your crown," the blonde says. She puts her hands together and cups some suds and places it neatly on my head.

"The king requires this, this teccy. My kingdom for a bottle! And a line!"

Matt grunts and leaves the room in a hurry, all he's been doing for the last hour is helping get people more fucked up.

The brunette next to me swigs back tequila and passes the bottle.

I take a drink and nearly gag. Tequila and soap add to the coke drip going down the back of my throat. I pass it to the blonde but she declines, the brunette snatches it from my hand and takes another drink.

"I bet uh, I bet you'd build a big bubble castle to compensate." The blonde is still busting my now warm and comfortable balls about my shrinky dink. I can feel the water has warmed it up, and every so often her smooth legs rub up against mine. I'm pretty girthy when half hard and in need of some face-saving.

"The bubble king has ample weaponry to impress any princess," I say in what I'd like to pass off as a British accent. A sudsy hand reaches under the bubbles and takes her wrist, slowly guiding it to the premature baby arm floating in the tub. Her eyes catch mine and she glares while smiling. The lights reflect off her braces and her hand explores my Pink October. Matt walks back into the room, stumbling into furniture and carrying both a plate and bottle. "Breakfast guys!" he sounds chipper. Politely declining a line, vodka ends up as my immediate poison of choice. My heart is just pounding again, dancing in my ribcage the way a fish flops around the bottom of a boat. Shit. I take a deep breath and relax. My cock is getting rock hard from the blonde slowly tugging on it, and nobody realizes anything is going on. Brief anxiety passes as euphoria returns, I feel nothing but pleasure.

Cold glass brushes my shoulder. "Here," the brunette says as she passes it to me. I can't refuse such a polite invitation. I take a swig.

"What's your name anyways? How do you know Matt?" the brunette asks.

"Dylen, didn't we meet earlier?" I have no fucking idea who she is.

"No, we supposed to?" I think we may have danced to Pitbull and talked earlier, but shit is a blur right now.

"Yeah, I'm Navi." Now I see some slight desi features on her. She's beautiful.

"-Morgan!" says the blonde with a handful of my dick.

Navi takes the bottle back and has another pull. Robert Miles plays over Matt's bedroom stereo, one of the girls against the wall comments that she thinks she's back in grade 9. "Yeah, Matt, what smash hit you going to put on next, something from Big Shiny Tunes?" the others snicker. Matt looks confused. He knows he's being made fun of, but changing the music means he takes a break from feeding his girlfriend drugs and alcohol. That wild eyed bitch on the bed looks like she's going to snap if he leaves her side again. "Uhh one minute baby!" Matt exclaims. He walks over to the stereo and doesn't even put the coke plate down. With Matt not looking, I seize the opportunity.

"From tiny egg, the mighty dragon," I whisper in my best wise Asian guru accent.

"-SOARS!" I yell, standing up from the hot tub with a stark erection for the girls to witness. My proudest achievement of the night, a full erection while high as fuck, drunk as shit, and rolling on E. Suds drip off my veiny dick and the girls stay stunned for a moment.

"Oh my," Navi says. "Never would have expected that from what you were packing earlier."

The girls against the wall laugh. I sit down and cause another splash out of the tub.

"You guys saw it too?" I ask, honestly wondering.

"Yeah, didn't you hear us laugh?" Shit. I'm totally losing bits and pieces. Maybe I shouldn't have another drink. "Who showed who what?" Matt asks, still fucking around with the stereo, the music flips through ancient tracks.

"Bubble King showed off what makes him a king, Yeah!" Morgan chirps as she puts a fist in the air. I laugh.

"I saw it too ..." Matt's girlfriend coos.

"What the ... fuck what?" Matt stops changing the music. Navi laughs. One of the girls against the wall giggles. "Oh shit, you've got her started now!" the fatter girl against the wall says. Matt turns around and looks pissed. "You showed my girlfriend your dick? What the fuck dude, what the fuck!"

"Not on purpose man! I thought she wasn't looking!" I totally forgot she was in the room even. Now I'm naked in this hot tub with a boner and some guy is getting ready to freak out.

"Well ... fuck this, fuck this ..." Matt looks at his girlfriend and grabs his head. He steps out of the doorway and immediately back into the room. "You ... OUT!" Matt is choked, sweaty, and looking deranged. He ducks back out of the room and I slowly climb out of the tub. Attempting to dry myself off with a wet towel proves as futile as sunbathing in shade. My clothes are soaked in a pool of water I spilled earlier. I wring out my underwear and put them on.

"FUUUUUUUCK!" echos down the hallway. "What the FUCK did I tell you about smoking indoors?" Matt is probably ready to snap at this point, the E has me mellow and the situation just went from bad to worse. I throw on my soaking wet clothes and make for the door.

Morgan squeaks a quiet "Bye."

"I'm Dylen, add me on twitter @sicklove if you want Morgan," I say while smiling at her."It was nice to meet you!"

Morgan grins and says "Ok, I'll tweet ya!" while I throw a wave at Matt's girlfriend. Navi points me towards my shoes, but my socks are hopelessly lost.

"Cya!" I say to the rest of the girls, ducking out of the bedroom in waterlogged shoes. I leave a trail of wet shoeprints down the hall.

I'm so friendly when high, the once-anonymous hot tub handjob didn't hurt either. I can't believe I just gave a girl my twitter to remember me by, seems appropriate for hot tub socializing. The hallway seems to go on forever.

I'm back in the living room and Liz slings her purse over her shoulder. Alicia is standing in the kitchen looking worried. "Fucken bitch you never listen, never listen," Matt makes a nasally sounding voice, pacing angrily around in a circle.

Stumbling over to Alicia to hug her, "Let's go," I whisper in her ear. Liz says nothing and walks towards the front door.

"Yeah get the fuck out, and take that shithead with you, he tried to steal my fucken girlfriend," Matt mutters.

I wave at Matt and turn around to avoid any conflict. I'm so fucking high and freezing cold. The door shuts and my shoes sog down the hallway with the girls, their jaws grinding in time with my squishing steps. The elevator takes us to the lobby, the air outside shivers me into spasms. Liz hugs me and Alicia shivers.

"C-c-cab, now," I say through chattering teeth. With luck, a cab rolls by in a few seconds. With luck, only bad this time, the cab driver says I'm too wet to get in, and drives off.

Shivering, Liz hugs me and yells, "Fuck off!"

Three seconds too late for the driver to hear it.

What seems like a week passes as I shiver and shake. Alicia and Liz hug me from both sides and keep me from completely freezing. It's almost hard to breathe. Behold, the glory, a minivan cab drives up and we're offered a ride. "Gastown, C-c-cordova C-c-arrall" I say, taking a deep breath in. "Can you turn up the heat please?" The driver turns up the heat one notch. I feel like such an asshole, but it feels so good.

25 Tight

My door cracks open and I feel relief. Home. My chest felt tight the whole ride here, my eyes felt like dancing in their sockets, this E is potent. Alicia is holding hands with Liz and smiling. Staggering to my shower, my hand cranks it on full blast on high heat. The purple leather couch makes fart noises as the girls crawl on it, and each other. A blast of hot water hits my face and the shivering finally stops. The bitter coke taste runs into my mouth and the residue cascades down my body. I blow my stuffed up nose slightly. With one hand I rub my upper lip and then grab the head of my cock. I try and numb it a little so I can last a bit longer with what we're about to do. The water calms, hitting my back to do battle, heat hammers coming to smash down goose bumps. An ice-blue goose stepping army fowl jabbers on in angry bird song; as eloquent as Daffy Duck on bath salts. Flaming righteous winged mallets burst from a sky where the air itself is a wet fire; liquid heat flattens skin, chases chills, a massage for tripping and tangled nerves. Finally I feel warm and clean again, who knows what the fuck goes on in Matt's tub most nights, and with who, or where they've been.

Just before I switch off the hot water, the girls stop talking. The water goes off and I reach to my sink and get a towel. Padding myself dry, my curiously begs me to look at the couch. One peek and I'm rewarded with a beautiful sight, Alicia is laid back with her eyes closed and legs spread, Liz is rubbing a Corona bottle on the middle of her panties. "Like that?"

"Like that," Alicia repeats in a whisper.

I smirk and feel warmth flooding into my hanging meat, the girth quickly starting to swell again. "Don't start without me or nothin'," I say with a hint of sarcasm. Stepping slowly behind Liz to get a better view of

Alicia being teased with the bottle, my body is electrified with anticipation. The room is silent except for Alicia's soft moans. She draws little circles with the rounded edge of the bottle, occasionally pressing the tip a little into her venus mound. The panties have a wet spot in the middle from where Liz has probed some of Alicia's honey out. I'm half-mast and pulsating with excitement. I feel the blood rushing into it, a strong pulse in the base. I swing it into Liz's arm and it makes an audible thwack. Liz turns and grabs it with her free hand, looks me in the eyes, and then runs her tongue from the base of my cock to the tip. Alicia sits up a little and watches as Liz's tongue glides up and down the bottom of it, across the head and down one side, then down the other. She spits onto it with a raspy sound that would make a pornstar blush. A thrust with my hips forward and Liz opens wide only to gag on it. "Not so fast," Liz chokes, pulling a few of her own hairs from her mouth. Alicia sits forward and puts a hand on my shaft. Liz lets go.

"If I'm doing this, no sense in holding back ..." Alicia says with a smile as she brings her mouth down on my pole. Her pale soft tongue and thick red lips ferociously attacks the top of my penis, sucking and slurping it hard enough that I throw my head back. A few rakes of teeth hint at inexperience. The ceiling stares back at me, perhaps in jealousy as it witnesses me in absolute ecstasy, the intense physical pleasures from cocaine and E fuel my sojourn to carnal paradise inside my head. My knees quiver and my cock pulsates with intensity. I feel precum flow out of me and into her mouth, she smacks her lips and makes it obvious that she's sucking it and tasting it. I look down to see her open her mouth and lick her lips.

My ears are filled with Alicia's lips slurping and pulling on me. If I close my eyes, colours and sparkles decorate my darkened eyelids, a shooting star opera composed by the specter of an acid trip. Alicia is sucking my balls, and I hate having my balls sucked. "Here," I interrupt, sitting in between Alicia and Liz with my back against the couch. Alicia goes right back to work and Liz holds her hair for a few moments before stopping to take her own top off. Liz's breasts have the nicest puffiest nipples, peach and tender looking. Alicia closes her eyes and does a great job using her hands to stroke my shaft while using her mouth. She slobbers and leaves a thick coating of saliva, it squeezing through her fingers that hold a firm grip on the base of my shaft. She's pretty good at giving head, probably didn't fuck a lot in high school, but put her mouth to work for sure. The earlier raking may have been from nerves. My short memory of high school involved a lot of fingerbanging girls and getting head every chance I could.

Liz sits beside me and spreads one leg over the right side armrest, leaning on me a little. She lifts up her skirt a little and rubs herself through her panties, Alicia opens her eyes and sees her doing this, gets embarrassed, and focuses back on the blowjob. Every moment feels like an explosion of senses is going off in my brain. A matrix of nerves being stimulated at the speed of light up my spine, my cock a receiving point of absolute physical bliss. Alicia is sucking what feels like a pint of precum from my throbbing, granite hard shaft. "Aw fuck it," Liz groans, as she lifts her legs and pulls her panties off. Her hand goes right back to work rubbing herself and I see she has a bare waxed slit with a glowing red button of a clit sticking out. "Alicia, look," I say to her. Alicia opens her eyes and sees Liz for a moment, then closes her eyes and smiles. She rakes me a little and I tense up for a moment. "Alicia, you said you were ready," I taunt her. Liz lets out a soft moan. "I can't ..." Alicia pulls my dick out of her mouth long enough to answer. "I can't, I've ... I've never done that before!" I laugh a little. "Haha, come on, you have to start sometime!"

"Yeah, but ..." Alicia won't even look at Liz.

"-but what?"

"What if I'm bad at it?"

Liz sits up for a second, pussy still pointed towards Alicia's face. "Honey, even a bad pussy licking is still good. Come have a taste of this, I know you want to try it," she coos.

Liz makes an upside down peace symbol with her index and middle fingers to spread herself open, inviting Alicia to taste her inner nectar. I thrust my cock toward Alicia's face. Alicia gives it a lick and a tug, a small bubble of precum flows from the opening of my penis which Alicia promptly licks off. Alicia looks at Liz and smiles. She blushes for a moment and then just dives into Liz's crotch. I hold Liz's left leg open and she throws her head back in a loud moan. Alicia has a little nervous laughter before moaning herself. Alicia is kneeling on the floor with her Brazilian sized ass pointing out towards the green heart neon on the wall, what a Kodak moment.

I slide myself out from under Liz and lean forward to slap Alicia's wide ass. Her waist is narrower than it looked earlier, but that might be the liquor talking. My hand finds the top of her thighs from behind, rubbing her moist panties until her hips are grinding with the slow motions I'm making. I look at Liz and she's staring me in the eyes, her right arm draped over the back of the couch, right leg over the side arm. Liz's left hand is holding Alicia by the hair and grinding her face into her pussy, her left leg twitches with pleasure. Liz closes her eyes and all I can hear from Alicia is hard breathing and the sound of her lips sucking lips.

I'm breathing hard, my finger slipping into Alicia's soft wet folds and finding her clit. She lets out a muffled sigh. First I rub her clit to make her groan, then switch to a shallow, slow fingering of her hole for a bit before getting on my knees. Alicia's beautiful backside is staring me in the face, reward circuits in my mind race with activity. Switching to my thumb, I start slow and rub her gently on the inside, pressing down and pulling back on the inside wall. Her hips react and she arches her back and shudders with sensations. "Uhnn!" Alicia moans, pulling her head out of Liz's pussy. "Oh I love that ..." she barely says as Liz yanks her by the hair back into her crotch. Liz's face looks serious when she's getting licked. I thumb fuck Alicia for a few more moments, Liz's lips and face need some cock.

I stand up off the floor and put one leg on the couch. Leaning over I brace myself up against the wall and put my dick right in Liz's face. She leans forward and pulls me closer with her free arm. One of my hands holds Liz by the hair, with her hand on my ass cheek to clawing me and pulling my cock deep into her mouth. A three freak circus, choruses of sex sounds play out from a big top, I'm the ringmaster of this coked up fuck fest. Concrete wall dust dries out my hands and distracts me from the fun, I pull back just as Liz moans. Penis spills out of her mouth and leaves a trail of spit on her cheek, both women let out gasps followed by low, horny growls. Liz pushes me to lay down on my back, while Alicia giggles as she pulls me towards her at the same time. "You go ... here!" Liz pushes me with a fist in the gut.

"Turn ... haha, this way?" Alicia's chin is wet with some of Liz's honey.

I ignore them both, bend down and flip Liz onto her stomach.

"That tickled!" she giggles, while sitting back up on her knees to expose her spit glazed swollen pussy.

I grab my shaft and it's a bit less than fully hard. Right index and middle fingers find Liz's opening and start to penetrate her deeply from behind, while my left had holds the back of Alicia's head to get my cock started again. Alicia gets back to work and her spin cycle tongue works my dick into a fury, fast. I pull it out and it's almost glowing red with an intense pressure inside of it. What power I feel. I pull my fingers out and line the head of my penis up with Liz's pussy. She moans as it plays around inside of her folds and bumps up to her tight opening. She pushes back with her hips slightly and I'm lined up to go deep.

Alicia stands up beside me and holds Liz's ass cheeks open while looking inside.

"So that's what it looks like in person," Alicia says with wonder. I give her a WTF look. "I mean, how it looks, not what, yeah!" she stammers.

Liz rocks her hips back and forth, the head falling out of her lips and then back in again. The head is lined up again, feeling the ring of her inner muscles clench up and release. Hips pushing forward to get the head to slide inside, the ring of her pussy clamps down again much harder this time. I pull back and try and pull out, the inner ring of her pussy muscles holding me in. Incredible sensations shoot down my penis and into my balls, which send back a squirt of precum as I lose control and moan out loud.

"Fuck!" I cry out.

Liz turns her head back sharply "Fucken want that do you?" she barks back at me.

I say nothing and Alicia reaches towards my balls and rolls them in her hands. Her narrow waist and round, bubble ass penetrate into my mind and capture my focus. I push with a little force and the ring around the head releases and I slide in halfway. Liz moans and I feel liquid run down my cock, Alicia's hand finds my shaft and begins to rub Liz's leaking cum down to the base and back up. Liz pushes back and I can feel my cock pulsing with pleasure again, my back arches and I slide in deeper, Alicia's hand trapped between us. Alicia lets go and stands up, looks me in the eyes and kisses me. I reach down and move aside her panties, fingering her hole. My right hand slaps Liz's ass and she pushes back down on me until I'm buried to the hilt.

I fuck Liz doggystyle for the next fifteen minutes. Her tight pussy relaxes as its fucked open enough for a little air to sneak inside, sloppy wet sounds of crude and real sex fill our ears. Sweat streams down my back as my senses relish in these raw moments. My sexual gluttony aware of its own non-limits, my cock probes Liz's insides, the sucking and slurping of her vaginal opening pulls a load of cum out of me and nothing could stop my bestial fucking, our animal mating. Fantastic new highs are reached while orgasm grips the body, my mind takes flight and I envision the pleasure centers in my brain.

A mountain tall piano making Everest a small hill. German engineered, with slick Cupertino design queues gleaming with monochromatic appeal. Cut and polished platinum keys nuzzled together with the narrowest of tolerances between them, the ebony grand frame they rest in looking solid enough to support Atlas. Cocaine, the King of Titans, body muscled as a Greek god, carries two hammers of diamond. Black and white marble handles drilled through thick, rectangular bricks of polished clear carbon.

They all come together in a symphony of destruction.

Cocaine swings the hammers together and diamond pulverizes precious metal with each note. Platinum keys thundering as they are smashed, cataclysmic notes of pleasure reverberate in my brain. Cracks begin to warp the black pillars holding the sublime instrument up, the hateful conductor reaching his mighty crescendo. A final, deafeningly loud crash follows a double overhead swing that nearly vaporizes his hammers, the piano perishes into broken powder. I fall back on the couch mission successful; my second load inside Liz's mangled cum ditch.

Liz falls onto her side breathing heavy. "Oh fuck, I was just about to cum again," she sighs. I can barely breathe. Sweat from my back soaks into the couch. Alicia has been watching and masturbating, now that we stopped, she pulled her hand out of her panties and walks into the kitchen. Moments later, she is back with a couple glasses of water. She's still wearing her top. "Here you need this!" she hands me a glass of water, I pass it to Liz. Alicia passes me the other glass, reaches to the side of the couch, and grabs a blanket before sitting down on my left. Liz sighs and giggles, fanning air to her face with her free hand. Alicia cuddles up to me a little and closes her eyes. "That was hot, now I feel so snuggly. Lights flash behind my eyes when I close them." Maybe we did M and not E. I breathe in and out deeply, still trying to catch my breath from the enormous orgasm I just had.

On coke, it takes a little while to go from spent to ready again. I cuddle Alicia and cover up Liz with another blanket. We rest in the dark for nearly ten minutes before Liz sits up again.

"Hey Dyl, remember she said she wanted to try everything?"

"Yeah?"

"She didn't get fucked," Liz states. Alicia's eyes stay closed.

"I think she's sleeping anyways," I wonder if I could go again, my cock is flaccid and I'm not feeling horny just yet.

Liz leans over and looks at Alicia's face. "You know she's just shy. Just get on her other side and spoon fuck her. I'll let you know if she starts smiling," Liz is such a dirty bird. Alicia was listening the whole time and she smiles with a giggle.

Standing up I survey the scene. Liz is covered up and watching, Alicia is under a blanket and now looking at me with nervous excitement. I pull the couch out from the wall and fold down the back rest, converting it into a bed. "Nice trick!" Liz is impressed, whoopie. Offering my naked body to Alicia, she sits up to bend over for me, rubbing her pantied tush against my flaccid cock. Her large, round ass feels so warm, and her narrow waist makes her look ultra-feminine. The familiar rush of blood below the waist, the thick saliva taste in my mouth, both signs of a sex drive signaling that it's ready to go.

"She's smiling Dyl, you rubbing her yet?" Liz asks.

My index finger goes down and pulls aside her panties, the head of my cock finding a wet spot. Alicia sits up on her elbow and looks back at me with a smile. "Go gentle ... this is my first," she whispers. I pause and look at Liz, her mouth wide open in shock.

"What?" we say in unison.

"Yeah," Alicia looks down and closes her eyes briefly. "I watch a lot of porn and I've been on the pill since 16!" she says, perking her head up and opening her eyes.

"I don't know why I waited, I just did, now I'm wondering why I did?" Alicia smiles and her eyes open wide.

Liz laughs. "Well, that shouldn't stop you Dyl, what are you waiting for?" Liz sits up and holds Alicia's hand.

I'm starting to feel like this is really fucked up, but I'm suddenly too horny to really care.

Feeling her tight opening, I slide my cock in her as gently as I can. Dipping it in to make sure it's wet enough, and just going a little deeper each time, then giving it one hard thrust to pop it and it's done. I'm buried to the hilt, and with one little shriek, Alicia moans and smiles. Liz offers up a high five, which I smack hard. Liz watches intently as my hips rock back and forth at different angles, finding that the pain of losing it only allows for one angle that feels good for her. The tightness fades a little as she relaxes, wetness soaking the front of my legs, and my right hip feels wet from being in a pool of her juices. She reaches back and holds onto my left forearm "Finish, soon ... it hurts, feels good ..." she moans. I sit up and straddle her sideways, my tempo rushing to a frantic pace for about

10 seconds before I spray inside of her virgin prize, and fall off the couch onto the cold concrete floor.

Heavy breathing fills the room. I feel aches and pains, the drip in the back of my throat still lingers. Vodka taste coating every surface of my mouth. Pussy smelling lovely on my fingers. My nose stuffed and certainly bloody tomorrow. That salty, sweaty taste mixes with the unforgettable flavour of cocaine and snot running down my face. A cornucopia of party flavours only missing the taste of girl. Alicia and Liz embrace in a hug, they mumble some small talk and Liz congratulates her. Alicia giggles and describes how it feels to leak for her first time. My body may be on the floor, but my mind is soaring.

Euphoria and Bliss are embracing on a patio at dusk, Chinese lanterns sway in the breeze. A brown silhouette of an old oak tree, branches swaying and blowing an ever growing 'shhhh' through leaves at the couple slowly dancing. The kiss they have in the moment is just that, a mere moment and nothing more. The fleeing experience of such a high only invites the storm coming on the horizon. The sky discolours from what a pretty sunset should be, turning to a shit brown and toxic green. Euphoria vomits on Bliss who falls down. Bliss turns to gaze up, green eyes hemorrhage and boil, the blood runs black under a defiled twilight sky.

"Dyl? Dyl?" Liz is shaking me. "We're grabbing a cab. You were snoring haha! Like a fucking chainsaw!" Liz is laughing. She's back in her sexy blue dress. Alicia says she put a blanket on me, I don't remember.

"It was SO fun meeting you!" Liz says.

Alicia laughs "Did that just happen? Did we all meet tonight? Haw!"

Alicia snorts while laughing, Liz laughs.

"I'm fucken tired and this couch isn't my thing, it's all wet, haha!" It takes all of my effort to push myself up and move from the floor to the couch. Liz was right, I just laid down in a damp spot.

"Bye," Alicia whispers in my ear, hugging me. Liz's high heels tap their way to the front door, and I hear Alicia scampering her way to meet her. I can't even muster a goodbye. Colours dance a little on my eyelids, they soften, grow drab and tired. I just want the colours to stay with me, please. I turn my head and vomit a little onto the floor. A weighted head free-falls back down as heavy eyes shut. Pressure in my stuffed nose the least of my worries, dangerous chemical cocktails in my delirious brain with a heart of mine that beats on in an off rhythm. The storm is getting closer and the colours give up on me.

26 Animal

Nothing isn't black, it's grey.

I'm down, down deep in my bed. My body spent, my soul tired; tired of all of this.

A cocoon of self-loathing and disgust, my own self-doubt and apathy planted me here, a garden shod with the ashes of my future. Purpose long left my life, drugs ride shotgun while alcohol gives directions from the back seat. Flat tires rumble on as an empty tank pushes me along on fumes. How long have I been asleep at this wheel for is anyone's guess, one headlight illuminates the path ahead. Concrete to gravel, gravel to dirt, dirt to a dead end. A rectangle on the ground, my grave.

"No," I mumble, in bed, safe.

"Fuck no," rattles from coarse chords as I flip onto my other side.

Shivering doesn't stop no matter how tight I pull these covers. A seagull mocks me in the distance, my snot and cocaine sniffles echoing through the loft space that extends on empty for far longer than it should. If I rolled out of the bed in this condition, I might just fall into the sky. Images of my lost loves rush into my head, the dam of emotion gives and I see their faces. Julianne, one of my first longer term girlfriends, I hear her ask me why I kept fucking her if I didn't love her, tear stains drawn down her face, shrunken, reddened eyes from my lies. She was bored one night and came over for a swim, I held her softly in the pool, kissing under moonlight. My roommate had been gone this weekend and I chased her playfully naked through the house, she pinned me down on the couch to make love, and I rolled her on her stomach and fucked her.

Immediately after sex I climbed off of her, went to the bathroom, and cleaned up. Minutes later, returning to her sobbing, trying to find her panties in the dark. "Why? Why use *me*?" she whimpered. I couldn't recall ever knowing why she was blowing this out of proportion. Maybe then I meant something to her, now nobody means anything to me and I mean nothing to anyone. Bones. Dust.

The equatorial heat stirs with feelings of warm sand underfoot, the joy of full glasses of rum. Some girl and I are spending a happy week on vacation, somewhere in my past, somewhere tropical, Mexico this time. Her face fills my vision, I recall she was always jealous of my wandering eye, another girl I never really loved but who followed me and loved me conveniently enough. I hadn't believed in love, I wouldn't for years, but it doesn't cover the crushing guilt of knowing I used her. No makeup on her, she fumbles with her cute cowboy hat, pudgy thighs and a white skirt. She cried a little on our trip when I told her I thought she looked bad in her bikini. I danced with a Mexican cabana girl in front of her and saw her heart break. I meant so much to her. I took advantage of her and shit right into her heart.

I don't miss her, but miss what she represents.

Photos. A photo can speak a thousand words and then some. Native Americans believed that a picture could steal your soul. I now look at photos to prove I once had one. I'm rolling around in my bed, my nose plugged from last night's snowstorm, my stomach protests as if it's full of broken glass and snake venom. Lips are dry and cracked, this heart pumps dirt. I feel like I have nothing left in this world. Rolling over in my bed and escaping wet spots becomes impossible. Whether it's from the girl last night or my sweat this morning, I don't even know. A chill shakes me to my core and nothing comforts me. The blanket chokes me when it's on, the nip of open air digs into my skin when it's off.

"Why," I whisper.

Last night my body was quivering and lit up with pleasure higher than I've ever reached. I drained myself into Liz two or three times, I'm not even sure. Somehow it comes back to this, seeking out this short term rush of pussy, liquor, partying, and laughter in packs, rebelling from any sense of duty or need to obey laws and customs. My goals are purely selfish, indulging in moments of instant gratification and ignoring the damage wrought upon myself and anyone around me. I can imagine Liz right now, in a cab or on the bus home, looking haggard and feeling deranged. Her groin being sore for a few days is the only thing she'll remember me by.

Nausea washes over me and I freeze, my battered body tenses up and I almost gag. I have nothing to throw up anymore, might be my soul that finally wants out. Waves of heat roll over my body and shivers follow. I don't know if I've even slept.

Time doesn't pass unless I feel something that hurts.

My dick aches, swollen and tender from destroying Liz. A slow crawl out of bed, pausing every couple seconds to avoid gagging further. Back to this, crawling to the bathroom after the same old, same old encounter. I used to keep people together and people happy, now I'm back on a floor alone. There was a time where I could remember every girl I kissed, where sex felt like it had purpose, rather now it's just something to do to kill time and achieve social rank. Raiders hat guy talked to me like I was a hero for what I did with Liz on the couch. Left, right, left, right, keep going Dylen. The floor is something I'm familiar with, I retch and throw up clear fluids only feet from the toilet.

I miss the reason behind love. My mind is obsolete, a relic from the past. Leftovers from a time of purpose, I'm a washed up husk of a person, no fortitude to stick to any beliefs and no spine to deny the easy route. Even if I married any of my amazing ex-girlfriends, I would've cheated by now. I'm so basic and all too modern human, no ability to resist the urge to bury my cock in another available woman, fulfilling my animalistic pleasures. What I did last night, fucking and cumming inside into those two girls, had no purpose beyond saturating nerves with a fluid swap.

Vomit mixed with cocaine and blood runs down my upper lip and into my mouth, freezing the curious tip of my tongue with a terrible chemical copper taste. Sore elbows and red knees carry me into the shower, having shaking hands on the shower knob is getting a little too old hat. Frozen skin burns and cold bones rattle, the steam rises and I fall over onto my side. The idea of having a responsibility to a woman, to a son, a daughter, is not even a seed in my being. I live purely to reach highs of physical pleasure and ego stroking, encouraged by my peers, cheerlead by a society that doesn't want me to care. I believe in nothing and it shows.

The shower acts as my loving nurse until the hot water runs out, and then some. My skin wrinkled, shivering, I turn off now-cold water and collect myself. Tired legs struggle to stand for hands to grab a towel, drying myself with minimal effort before stumbling to crash back on the couch. The fuzzy blanket hardly warming, the leather smells of booze and cum. The dismay felt over that next day odour, is a more than subtle reminder of overcast skies and quiet hung over mornings. I hear rain begin to tap on the window ever so lightly. The couch hates me, every fiber of wood frame stabbing into my bones, the metal spring coils have turned to concrete. I shiver, pull the blanket to my chin, and close my eyes.

27 Rain God

For eight days it's poured down rain. Eight days. I haven't left my house in as long, and I had to order food for the last four to keep myself fed. My phone blows up in texts from artists needing to use their space, my explanation is that I'm sick and nothing they can do will help. One girl texts that she made me my favorite cheese bread, after that I turned off my phone. My skin wants to blister if it spends another moment under halogen light or in front of a monitor. It takes me an hour to get ready to leave, even the breeze outside is ripe with angst and the pedestrians out today aren't much better. Faces on people under umbrellas keep their eyes down, people in cars petrifying in traffic. Poisonous cities smell of hot brakes, exhaust, feces and idle buses. Sneers across druggies' faces still a week away from their welfare cheques. Two blocks to get a coffee and the rain melts my hair onto my face, in the future I'll remember to never lend out my umbrella.

The coffee shop is lit in bright yellow, eager young women greet me with beaming smiles, full of joy. Ordered a drip coffee, I can't tell the difference between an Americano and a drip coffee half the price. I thought I noticed her smile fade over a $2.25 order. The barista finishes making some broad in yoga pants and cowboy boots her soy chai latte. Extra foam. Her vegan organic cranberry salad neatly packaged in a clear plastic box that will outlast her. The next guy puts in a $60 order of brown wake up juice and baked sugar, the girl smiles extra hard. Bitch.

My coffee is slid across the counter top and the barista turns away without a word, no flowery announcement of "large drip," nothing close to how soy chai latte rolled off her tongue. Aural silk is her voice, this pretty bird comes packaged with her own sunny day. She smiles and puts happy thoughts into her movements behind the counter, her energy matches her vivid exterior look. With brown hair holding streaks of red, hourglass figures look a little tamer under a turquoise v-neck. She used to chat me up when I ordered a mocha, even drew a vagina in foam last time. I grab the milk jug from the sugar and sticks counter, filling it near the top for a chocolaty brown colour. After snapping the lid on, I already want out of here. I try and remember that she is busy and I'm not exactly friendly. I catch my face in the stainless half and half bottle, sneer and rain smeared below my nose, cross eyebrows. Eight days of rain, Dylen, just the eight days of rain.

Outside the door, the dull, numbing drizzle is falling heavier, popping and snapping from larger drops off the awning, cars drive by and spray water over the curb. Can't say why, but I turn the opposite way from home and begin to walk. Anticipating a long journey, I reach into my side pocket, grab my phone, and put it into my inside jacket pocket, the driest spot I can think of. A few sips of my coffee periodically and my mind drifts off. My entire body is soaked in a few blocks, a few more and my shoes squish and weigh a ton. Without any destination, my legs carry me to the seawall near Stanley Park, it's deserted. My coffee's done and I carry the cup to find a garbage bin. A low fog hangs over the water and the rain is even harder now. Sometimes getting lost is the only way you can let yourself be found again. Whipping my soaking hair back and forth, a smile cracks across my face and a fit of giggles begins to take hold of me. Soaked to the bone, laughing at this mad man walking in the rain.

The seawall is long and my feet are getting sore. The Lion's Gate bridge looms out of the fog, green on grey, and I take a seat at a bench where I can look out over the water. Few birds in the air, a ship blows its horn as I think of post cards in my mind. Resting my arms outstretched, a tilting of neck, and surrendering to the rain. Here I am, do your fucking worst.

I can't sit inside hiding from this, the stain on my mood of eight days of solid grey showers. I give up and give in.

Puddles form in my eye sockets and rain ticks through my empty ribs. I feel my bones are wet, no flesh to keep them dry and warm. Ragged, torn clothing fall off me in shreds, drip after drip falls from my white bleached ribs. The rain no longer looks like it's falling, but coming out of the bones themselves. The act of giving myself to the rain isn't one of death, but of rebirth. If I died right now, would I be happy with the time I was given? My shirt sticks to my chest, the warm layer of water pushed up against me with the most subtle of heat. Pants feel like they're bunched up and chafing at the crotch. Feet numb like stumps, what must be worn skin burns my heels. Time makes itself known as flesh returns to rain scrubbed bones, while wooden benches press chilly spines into crooked, wicked shapes. Skin, bone, and organ are useless without purpose coming from soul. The pain of my back drowns into a background of showering clouds and soft inlet waves. This crashing cloudburst is a strange remedy.

My fingers are whitewet and wrinkled, when pressed together they are irresistible to not rub them for that sandpaper tickle. What seems like days passes in minutes, my body and soul feel cleansed. I stand up slowly as my frozen body protests, geriatric movements sluggish at first, but the thought of a hot shower sends a rush of desire through me. Drenched legs snap forward with motivated thrust. Back around the seawall and I'm nearly in my home turf, bums looking at me with fear for my mental state. I smile. My hair is matted against my head, catching a reflection of myself in a mirror and I could be mistaken for someone who just climbed out of a swimming pool. My inside coat pocket is soaked, hope my phone isn't fucked, but if it were, that's OK too.

Slogging through Gastown, feeling like a million bucks and giving zero fucks.

My feet want to double stamp every puddle spotted by manic eyes, a professional dog walker ahead crosses the street to avoid me. Friendly Dachshunds and French bulldogs even look the other way. A bus driver honks at something and I give him a wave, a couple of jumping one-legged strides through a deep sidewalk lake produces a loud plop-plop-plop. Tech professionals in tight black turtle necks gawk from the inside of the coffee shop. I stop and see a trash bin, my hand helping the cup find its way from my coat pocket into the bin's slot. I glance back into the shop and the counter girl looks at me in horror; an honest smile pulls up the corners of my mouth and I realize, I've never felt warmer.

28 *Unlove Letter*

Heartfelt messages through email never quite work. That disconnect of my message moving through the keys, becoming 0s and 1s, and sitting on a server somewhere for her to click the bold link titled "I miss you." It could easily end up in her spam folder purgatory. I can count dozens of times I've been spammed with that message from supposed overseas brides. Just 0s and 1s carefully arranged to get my forlorn heart to pay.

I've written a simple email.

> I remember last year when you called me around Christmas, we talked for hours. Then you sent photos of your cats and the spilt milk on the counter top, and photos of you at the mall with your nephews. I really liked that, it made me smile for days and days. Even though we were thousands of miles apart, I had never felt closer to you.

> I hope your Christmas went well, and that you're looking forward to making 2013 your happiest year yet. Yeah, I know, you probably feel some anxiety when you think about me, or talking to me, and I feel the same way. The anxiety I feel is because you actually mean something to me, regardless of if you still hate me more than you've hated anyone else before.

> Maybe you'll remember this photo, it was the last time I saw you happy.

Leaning over my desk with my chin in my left palm, an autonomously chewed middle finger leaves a painful hang nail. I must have lost track of time completely. A pen and a book of lined paper sits before my keyboard, I had begun to write her a letter telling her how much I've missed her, how much she actually means to me. My normal recollection of favorite females is by the shape of their genitals, images of countless vaginas and the faces they're attached to having been fucked into my memory. With this one, it was her smile. Her laugh, her little quirks, holding her hand, the way we talked together, and the way my soul caught fire when our lips met. Nostalgia fills my head and I swim in the endorphin rush.

I haven't finished the letter yet, the final paragraph is supposed to be where I ask her if her life has been going the way she wants it. If I could just talk to her again, maybe she'd see that this time I've really learned. Maybe she'd see I really want something with purpose, to build a life together. My hand picks up the pen and comes to a rest on the paper. I can't handwrite this right now, emotionally I'm drained. I could easily type or text it, but writing is different. My hand forms each and every word, my heart connects with my chest, my chest to my arm, arm to hand, hand to pen, pen to paper. If I really believed in myself, and my ability to make her happy, this should be easy, right?

Right?

I wish there was a manual that came with your life, something that explains when you should listen to that little inner voice inside you. Laying the pen down gently, my stomach twists and I take a deep breath. At night, the stars twinkle and shine light from history in the same way that love from your past can be seen. A faint glow of something far away; inaccessible but felt, impossible yet known, a framed memory lit up in gold light, hung in my mind's innermost sanctum. The glow from the monitor makes everything look a dull light blue.

Earlier in the day, I was hanging out with a few wild artists. They are a couple of stars from the local fashion scene, never a boring moment while around crazy lesbians with style to everything they do. Jane Dough and her girlfriend won't show me the matching tattoos they got, but her girlfriend showed me her jungle cat spots while Jane was in the can. When Jane came out she packed up her stuff and left angry while Jaguar girl chased after her.

Art supplies are scattered everywhere.

Dirty dishes pile up in a sink littered with coffee grinds and pipe ash. A broken bottle of Jack has retired on my black photography backdrop, I don't remember what I was thinking when it got smashed. My track pants bottoms are too loose on me, and the draw string turtled back into its hole. I have to hold my pants up when walking or the ankles drag on the ground. Fucking artists, I feel pathetic.

The dimly lit studio has a small fridge tucked in a corner, clutter forces me to carefully tiptoe around a canvas drying on the floor to get to it. A tube of paint explodes under foot, I can barely make out that it's blue, and has just created a giant fucking mess. I sigh. What could make this go away? I pour a little bit of a full glass of Jack on ice. My cellphone jingles. I walk back to my desk, pick up my phone, and noticed a thick blue paint trail across the floor of the entire studio. Fuck it, half a glass of Jack sent straight to the liver for some calm.

A normal person wouldn't drink like this.

I got a text from Hanna, she said she's stressed and wants to come over. For weeks now I've been blowing her off, she stayed with me for a ten day romance about a month back, even kissed me when I had morning breath. I felt a bit used when she left me to fuck some hipster that lived across the street from her, but how can I blame her? She's just repeating what she's grown accustomed to. Throw away friends, throw any relationships, throw away sex, throw away future. Can't say I haven't done the same. That other half glass of whiskey goes down smoothly as an ice cube wanders into my mouth only to get crushed. I text her back and let her know she can come by if she wants. She texts me back immediately to say she's heading over.

I comb my hair and make myself presentable. A little more grey hair adds to the slight salt and pepper look, a few wrinkles line my face. Just a couple months ago I was getting it on with a solid 9, Hanna is pretty hot herself though. Maybe I feel this way because I feel like I've done this before, and I know I can't stop.

Whiskey pilots its familiar course through my system, no icebergs tonight to be wary of. I smile and start to lighten up. A few clicks of a mouse and I'm relaxed by some ambient tunes, taking a moment to wash my dick in the sink. Back to the computer and I review some art tumblrs to keep track of what's hot. Someone I'm following has posted a bunch of tattooed up suicide girls, looking more like aliens than women. High saturation photos are trying so hard to look edgy and sexy, most people probably like these. Their faces are all smiling. The flesh and colours of a group of tatted up girls pulling the panties off another girl. What whores, but could I blame them? Trading pussy for cash has never been easier, a generation of men self-defeating and jerking themselves into oblivion. I can't even imagine the number of guys right now that are Alt-tabbed out of a video game, jerking to porn, returning to their digital escape.

I flip through a few more tumblrs. Art gets predictable when it's popular, just like people. Tow the hivemind narrative and don't question it. Be a cheerleader for the current trend. Sometimes I wish I could wipe my mind clear, forget about the Internet, and live in a small town where people didn't check their phones at coffee. Where internet dating didn't turn our courtship into sending dick shots to get women horny. Funny how times change, a man used to show up at a woman's house with flowers and a smile, now that guy is a creeper. I send girls photos of my dick, and more often than not I get back sext messages with a spread open pussy and a question of when I'm available.

I'm the new gentleman.

29 Chump Taxi

The whiskey is giving me superpowers again. I look at my phone and a second later it's ringing. She's here. I buzz her up and next thing I know she's walking in and taking her coat off, she's always dressed so smart. Yellow rubber boots and a cute ponytail. White button up shirt and a pair of blue jeans.

"Hey," she says to me, her smile beaming. She rests on my couch and spreads out, looking exhausted. She sighs and looks cold. I bring her a blanket and tuck her in, I soothe her with some small talk of my day and put on some ambient music. Two glasses of whiskey are promptly poured and I bring her one. A carefree caramel glass of let's fuck. I sit at my desk near the couch and open up some of my latest photography. "Oh that's nice!" she parrots occasionally. I'm looking through a folder for some more impressive shots and I feel her arms wrap around my upper body from behind. She's so warm and smells so pretty. I take her hand and walk her from behind my desk chair, in front of it, and sit her on my lap. "Wait a second," she gets up and grabs her coat, and digs through a pocket.

"Here," she walks over sits back on my lap and lights a small joint, "I brought this for you."

I smile. She's not the type of girl you can hold on to, but not the type you don't want around.

We smoke.

She sits up and leans over my desk, her hands on my keyboard and mouse looking for a song to put on. Her gorgeous round, beautiful ass is right in my face. Her blue jeans fit her perfectly. Some more upbeat tunes kick in after a double click, and she sits back down on my stiff lap. I'm so turned on and there is no way she can't feel that. She starts talking about her fears, all her fretting would wear on me but it's nothing I haven't heard before. I kiss the back of her neck and lightly stroke her thigh. I hug her and hold her close, it doesn't feel forced but it doesn't feel right. We aren't even dating, just socializing our genitals.

She grinds herself a little on my lap, her playful grin shows me what she wants me to take. I put on Netflix and put on the stupidest movie I could find. Air Bud. We stand up from the chair and then lay on the couch, she's such a fun little spoon. We cuddle under a blanket and she holds my arm across her chest. Sweaty palms like in grade 9, perky B cups and a permanent boner pressed into her lower back. Both of our bodies are getting used to the climate and soon my hand is in her shirt. Soft breasts and a nipple that would cut diamond, she pushes her ass into me and my hand explores south to play with her clit.

In almost no time her pants are off and I'm inside her. She is a little sore she says, I bet she's been fucking a lot, and I'm wearing no condom. Whatever. She's so good with kegel control, her tight opening squeezing down on the middle of my cock and it pulses in time as I cum. I just drained myself into her. Heavily breathing, we embrace, my penis still inside her. Sometimes we just like to fuck and not kiss during sex. Air Bud is playing to only my hydro bill's benefit.

The dog is carrying a football down a field with the ball in its mouth, and suddenly out of nowhere, a huge football player tackles the dog hard. I laugh and my penis comes out of her, cum squirts out of her pussy and I feel it running down my thigh. I really hope that's just mine and not some mixture of mine and someone else's. We sit up and have a couple sips of whiskey, I lean over to put my drink down and I spill some on the sofa and her shirt.

"What the fuck Dylen!" I've never seen her mad, but she's pissed for sure. "Fuck!" she looks away and is silent. Her half nude body looks beautiful in the light cast by retriever with football.

"What's wrong?"

"I'm going to my friend's house tonight, and now I smell like booze," she says with a sigh. I recognize that sigh. It's half I-don't-give-a-fuck, and half how'd-this-happen-again.

She wipes her shirt with the blanket, sighs again, stands up and takes off her shirt.

"Where is your dryer?"

I point towards the utility closet on the far wall behind her. She tosses her shirt in the dryer, her cute naked butt turns me on again, but with a dulled ferocity. She walks over to the small sink near the shower, picks up a handful of kleenex, and begins to wipe her leaking vagina. Bowlegged and furiously wiping herself, Hanna lets out an "Ugh! There's so much!" and shuffles to the stainless trash basket where she discards the semen I gifted her. What a waste.

Hanna walks back over and has a seat on the couch, her hands quickly find her phone and she starts texting. I smell her musky scent mix with the hint of whiskey and popcorn, between her folded legs a tight pink slit peeks out. My hand can't resist sliding along her inner thigh, her fingers texting rapidly as my dick hardens again. Alternating small strokes with my index and middle fingers, I draw little circles near her upper thigh, occasionally sliding a finger close enough to feel that she is still wet. Her texting doesn't slow down and she never looks up, her hips start to grind with the motions of my fingers and I move higher up. Soon my fingers spend half their time on her upper thigh and labia, half their time teasing her clit and opening. She is soaking and yet continues to text. She looks up for a moment, smiles at me, and is back to texting.

I move my body sideways on the couch while my hands guide her into a doggystyle position. She tosses her phone down and acknowledges my actions with bedroom eyes and a single "Oh …." Now here I am, behind her cute little bubble butt and petite waist, staring down her puffy and pink waxed pussy. I feel a huge rush of excitement and I'm already rock hard, a pop of my hips forward and the head slides in. I grab the base of my dick and stir it around inside of her as if it were a spoon in a mixing bowl, making a sex fluid omelet to coat my shaft. She lets out a little moan and a deep breath, and surprises me by sliding herself down on me, my right hand grabbing and slapping her ass. She lowers her head and puts her hands out in front of her, bracing herself on the armrest of the couch. Her motions backwards become harder and more violent, my cock getting even harder and more aroused than I thought possible, I feel the head hit something inside of her and she begins to whimper and moan with each thrust.

The couch behinds to slide along the floor and the blanket drops from the couch. All 105 pounds of her are pushing into my double weight frame and almost knocking me over, I lean into my left knee, the sucking and slurping sounds of her pussy mix in with her moans, I feel so primal. My right leg swings out and kicks over my whiskey tumbler, probably shattering pieces of it into my foot, but I can only feel myself inside her. Slapping her ass and grabbing the back of her hair, she sits back and squats on my cock, turning her body enough to push me into sitting on the couch in the position that you'd normally be in. She straddles me facing the other way, squatting. She's in complete control.

Her palms hold onto my knees and her pussy clenches tight around me, her pink lips stretched tight flex and release slowly. I'm in a euphoric spasm of pleasure as she slowly tightens and releases, grinding her hips with precision control side to side, back and forth. I feel her lips slowly milking precum out of me as my cock pulses what feels like a mini orgasm inside of her. Her nails dig into my leg while holding herself steady, a faint sweat shines on her back showing the effort she's putting in. Her motions forward and backward are visually hypnotic, from her arched back giving me a beautiful look at her pink asshole and swollen lips, to being tucked forward and having hidden her softest bits.

Her odour tickles my nose, her moans a delight to the ears. Closing my eyes for a moment and the sensations run wild in my mind. Each sense taking input at once, overloading my mind with savage fucking. My hips thrust upwards and penetrate her deeper, she lets out a gasp, her legs quiver. Sharp nails burn into my skin and she thrusts back. I pull my hips away as does she, almost uncoupling, then ramming together again forcefully. Groaning and breathing deep, she pushes herself up and leans her back into my chest. I sit her thighs on mine and lay flat on my back on the couch, her on top of me, both facing the ceiling. I kick her right leg onto the backrest of the couch and grab onto sweaty hips. Back arched, screaming as she feels the head of my cock nudge her insides.

Sweat slides between our steamy bodies, her salivating vagina takes a fast pounding that violently echoes in the studio with the beating of meat wet together. The couch slides again, her arm comes up and grabs me by the back of my head. Deeper, harder, her ass banging hard into my hip bones, faster. She groans and turns her head and bites the leather of the couch, her legs begin to shake. My body tense, our tempo building and building to finish, she sits up and braces herself with her hands, "Oh .. Oh ..." she holds her breath. I'm drilling her as hard as I can, my dick buries itself in her with each thrust, pulling back until I'm almost out of her. She lets out a fluttering "Ohhohohhhhoo," and she moves barely off of my shaft, her hand grabbing her crotch as I feel a splash on me. My arm pushes her down and my cock finds its way inside her, about to cum myself, she groans and snaps her legs together and pushes her pussy down on me. It's so tight my cock has to literally explode inside her to ejaculate and I count over a dozen strong pulses, filling her completely with my load. She collapses on me, wet from sweat, breathing hard, and shaking.

Moments pass and our breathing slows, she lets out a few sighs and giggles then rolls off of me to go clean up. "Toss me a towel!" I yell before she throws one over. The couch and I are soaked. Finishing the clean up, turning to see she is already dressed and spraying herself with perfume. Being naked and totally spent, my penis grows more flaccid with each passing second. She picks up her phone and says "Oh, shit!" then turns, and runs towards her boots.

"He's been waiting!" she smiles as she says this.

"I feel so bad!" I raise an eyebrow and smirk.

No you don't.

She grabs her purse and gives me a hug, turns, and walks out of the studio.

The falling back on the couch is turning into an art form. Laying on the warm leather, sex drive totally satisfied with my nerves now able to feel the sting of my sliced foot. Loneliness encroaches from the little death of ejaculation. My mind is going through the immediate post-coital clarity and I can't help but think we just used each other for sex, again. I barely know her and she barely knows me. Well, could be worse, I could be the guy picking her up after waiting for her to finish banging me.

30 Wound

I can't go too long without some drama. It's been almost a full week of positive thinking, and now this. Misha is heartbroken. Her new boyfriend was caught cheating on her, what a plot twist. I've been on the phone for twenty minutes trying to console her. Noticing my socks smell like a freshly opened bag of doritos at around the 5 minute mark makes me a bad listener. Between sobs a fresh pair is put on. By the 15 minute mark I was picking at a hangnail while telling her to calm down.

Apparently she did so much for him and had been the best girlfriend she could. She described how she even looked past his one misshapen ear, and his back hair. I think she forgot how she also bragged about his job and how much money he made working the oil sands. She's going to get off the phone as Kiki showed up at her place with some Valium. I tell her we'll grab a late dinner after I finish work and hit the gym.

She whispers "Ok, call me, bye," and I hang up. How can't Misha see that without any shared values, relationships are pointless. She encouraged him to go to Vegas and party with his friends, and then is shocked that he has ass on the side? Not to mention the fact that she's been talking about how much she wants kids, and this guy isn't the settling down type. Maybe you always want what you can't have?

Human nature at work pushing and pushing us to get what we want, not wanting what we have.

I've fucked Misha at least a dozen times. She has a beautiful petite body, one tit is a little lopsided but I still even like the smaller titty. Her kiss is soft, she never forces her tongue into your mouth like so many club tramps and party skanks I've met. I remember when I had bound her wrists together under the ottoman for my couch, had her ass in the air naked and her face pressed against the purple leather. Her tanning sessions paid off well, a bronze body and silky waxed girlflower right in front of my face. She gasped and moaned when I blew gently on her clit. I put my mouth an inch from her opening, my nose almost tickling her asshole, and I dart my tongue inside her. She writhed in pleasure, grinding, my tongue a torch dropped into a pit of snakes. Her body moving all around, in and out of shadows cast from her thick ass cheeks, the ottoman skidding on the concrete floor. As far as sex goes, she's amazing, it's too bad that's all we've got.

Does it always come down to sex? I wonder if there is a healthier way to date. She met this guy online. Online dating allows for people to come in and out of your life with very little actual investment, as their lives and social circle are completely independent. I can't blame the guy, dating these days is a game, for sport. Who has a plan to look for a wife? It's a free for all, have fun, do whatever. The pattern formed in my early 20s continues in my life, and the men around me.

Find, fuck, dump. What threw out the expectations of how I should date? I sigh. I've been staring at the ceiling again. The sex I had with her was very pleasurable but ultimately hollow and meaningless temporary pleasures. Debating philosophy with myself is worse than masturbating with an angle grinder. Shuffling over to a mirrored cube near my window, a zip lock bag, scissors, and rolling papers are used to bring calm to my ruminations.

I'm sitting in a haze. Tapping of rain and the backup beep alarm of a truck pierces my veil of solace. Smoke makes sure there are no worries and no cares, soon I'll be thinking of food. Yeah, I think this is why I can't get those nice abs I've always wanted. Misha would be a great girlfriend for any typical douche. I particularly enjoyed the sex, her company, her looks, her smile—when it's genuine. I noticed she didn't think like me, and we didn't have any real common values. When I was younger people mattered more, women really were individuals and not just pretty things that I knew how to talk to so I could fuck them.

Misha never seemed interested in knowing who I am and what I stand for, instead she just seemed to want a good banging. I was just something to do, someone to occupy her time and vagina. I never got beyond seeing her as a fuck buddy as a result. We're just sexy strangers sharing a bed.

A sigh coincides with the knowledge of what The Right Thing To Do here is. It probably won't make a difference but I have to try. Unplugging my phone from the charger, I send her a text and ask her to meet me for a drink. Walking across the studio, I pick up one of the sketchbooks left randomly about, bring it back to the couch, and begin to doodle. I draw a rose and write a few words of encouragement. She needs this.

For every alpha that pumps and dumps a woman like her, they are helping to create a world I don't want to be in, full of people like me. It's not when you make your bed that you have to lie in it, but eventually you'd get tired and regret the way you made it. A world where the notion of love is laughable, people leaving and lying on whims, abusing each other and tearing down what could have been in order to pursue a piece of ass. Meanwhile, those same women can become so heartless in their dealings with men.

I finish the sketch and fold it so it stands on its side. Who knows if she'll keep it or throw it in the garbage, I'm doing my piece to make her feel like she has some value outside of being a convenient cum dumpster. A quick comb of my hair follows finding clean pants and a shirt. Kiki texts me and says Misha is getting ready. She apparently had taken a ton of sleeping pills earlier. She's ok though, Kiki made her throw them all up and most of the gel caps were still intact.

My heart skips a beat and I feel genuine empathy. I'm not in love with her at all, but it can be hard to see someone you care about hurt themselves, and over someone who doesn't care about them either. I'd feel like such a white knight pussy if I hadn't already been inside her carelessly so many times. I hate how I view caring for a woman as friends seems so weak, but the gender war rages on, and it's eat or be eaten.

Soon I'm out the door and waving for a cab in a light rain. A stroll by the coffee shop and Natalee shoots me a smile and a little wave as I pass. She's been even more friendly to me after seeing me soaked outside her shop awhile back.

The thought of her makes me grin.

A taxi pulls up and I take a ride in what smells like someone's armpit. Ten minutes later I'm at our favorite restaurant in Kits, along the beach, from the street it looks completely packed inside. It takes me a minute to work through the crowd around the front door, recalling the food and drink here it's no wonder it's packed. Walking inside, light shines off blue gem eyes shining wet and pretty inside nubile hostess skulls, their bodies in skin tight dresses. My mid-thirties penis aware of every fold of perky, full breast, the way the dark fabric highlights thin, petite waist above full, round fertile hips. The waitresses have some age on their faces and busy determination on their brows. The bartender, she looks like the grizzled mama-san. The place is stuffed full and Kiki and Misha are holed up along the back wall, Misha looks ridiculous in dark glasses near dusk. I walk up and a solemn Misha stands up and hugs me. We stand at the table hugging and blocking surly waitresses for a good ten seconds.

We sit down and I place my rose sketch in front of her. She cracks a little smile and her chin shakes a few times. Kiki puts her arm around her and Misha sighs. A waitress takes my order, double ja no, I'll get a pint of beer. I get a pint of beer. She vanishes and Misha speaks through sniffles "I'm so sorry you have to see me this way. I just…" she takes a sip of a Caesar; it comes in a bootshaped mason jar. "I just snapped when I heard he did this. I spent so much time and money, spent so much of my heart to make him happy and he wants to keep secrets of getting laid in Vegas from me. Then I find out he's also been seeing another girl here. Am I shit? What's wrong with-"

"No no no!, Mish, You're a good person!" Kiki interrupts.

This conversation goes on like this for quite some time.

I try my best to listen to everything before speaking. It sounds obvious that this boyfriend of hers is still having fun and playing the field without a care. I've been there and I probably have no idea how many kleenex tissues have been soaked over my actions, or how many Caesars have been drank as a result of mean texts I sent.

"Misha, you are a really good woman," I lead into what I really want to tell her.

"I don't think he can appreciate you yet for who you are, a caring and loving woman. He wants the side of you that wants patio drinks and a good fuck when it's easy. Did you ever talk about what he envisions for his life?"

Kiki frowns.

"What does that have to do with him cheating on her?" she states, tilting her head to one side.

"Everything" I reply. "I have this idea that people who don't know what they want and don't see where they are in life are the blind leading the blind. Misha, trust isn't always believing what comes out of someone's mouth, but rather, a complete assessment of their character and moral fiber."

"Yeah, I guess," Misha whispers.

I take a sip of beer.

"Think about it, at one point in our culture, being a womanizer was seen as universally bad. Now, I know you Misha, and this guy is probably pretty cocksure and has money. Do you think he has much respect and belief in the values that lead to long term bliss?"

"You're being an asshole, Dyl!" Kiki is glaring at me.

"No. I'm not. I'm trying to be as real as I can be with you. Look at how we date and fuck each other without even knowing much about who we are as people. Women just give up the sex so easily and a few men get all of the available tail. How long was it before you guys slept together Misha?"

"I thi-"

"Dyl she doesn't need a lecture," Kiki cuts off Misha and glares at me. If looks could kill.

"No, it's ok Kayla," Misha seems to have calmed down a little.

"We slept together on our first date and we had been just hooking up for a few weeks before he made it official. I did all the work to see him and paid for most things."

Sitting back in my seat becomes an attempt to not look like such a smug son of a bitch. It's not working. I'm not *really* trying.

"I'm not saying you're to blame here, but make yourself the prize, Mish. When a guy can go around getting what he wants with so little effort required, can you blame him for taking what's offered?"

Kiki kicks me under the table.

I feel like such a dick, but I think she needs to hear it. It's not wrong to date assholes, but just know what you're involved with.

Misha drinks back her Caesar. I want to explain to her that the way we date is poisonous. Lying and keeping secrets is the norm. We don't need each other, so we don't act like it. Then when you do meet someone who can openly talk about their desires for courtship and romance, they are the weird ones. I'll keep it to myself for now.

"It's so hard to see myself as a prize when he just goes and does this to me. Why? What's wrong with me?" Kiki hugs her and she sobs. I don't think she can understand what I'm trying to get out there. Our methods of dating and loving are coming apart at the seams. It's leaving plenty of people popping pills, drinking alone in their bachelor suites watching porn, or giving up on the opposite sex and going gay. Let's get faaaaabulous! Can't blame anyone for trying anything to find someone to love.

Kiki scowls at me. "Some fucken friend you are Dyl. You say you care so much and you come here and blame her for this, real classy." I roll my eyes and give palms up dismissive shrugs to both of them. Misha continues to sob on Kiki's shoulder. My work here is done, my hand pulls cash from my jacket and slips it under the beer I just slammed. Walking to Misha's side of the booth, I kiss her on the top of her head and squeeze her elbow.

"Take care Mish."

I hope she heard me say that, I know I care. It's just that it's hard to show in a way she can understand.

Hostesses wave at me and tell me to have a good night. Those girls are so friendly when paid to be that way. Out in the street, I'm happy to find that it's not raining anymore. My place is a good long walk from here and I need the exercise. Before long I'm walking over the Burrard Street bridge and looking out over the water, the vibrant city glowing at night, the marina below scattered with hundreds of boats worth more than I can imagine. Down the other side of the bridge and along Pacific, the city goes from wealthy, to wealthier, and finally into rock bottom shit when I turn the corner from Rogers Arena. Down Carrall and I'm soon back in the land of sidewalk pudding and hands looking for change. Almost home. A bus blows the red light as I prepare to cross onto the street my studio is on. If I had been wasted that could have been really bad. Across the street a girl steps off the curb, it's Natalee from the coffee shop.

"Hey Dylen," she says, almost passing me now.

"Hey Nat," replying as I walk passed her. One foot on the opposite curb and a hunch turns me around. She's quickly disappearing into the night. "Hey Nat!" yelled from my curb perch. She turns around on the other curb "Yeah?"

"A snack, you and I, right now," my face bursts into grin.

Nat's lips turn into a slow smile, "Mmm, ok!" she yells back.

A woman walks by me with incredible body stench, a menthol cigarette hanging off her lip and holding a styrofoam cup. A couple dressed sharp, walking an energetic French bulldog, the woman is beautiful and has the face of a model. The man is much older and looks wealthy. A man walks up next to Natalee across the street and spits a few feet from her. The light changes and I walk back across the street.

"I've wanted to check out this new place for weeks, right here," she points to a little hole in the wall that I hadn't noticed before, almost next door to the coffee shop. I turn and walk with her towards the door, about 50 feet from us.

"Yeah? You don't have anyone to go with?"

"Na, I'm still a student and most of my friends aren't into trying new places. They have their favorites and they stick to them." I nod. "I'm still trying to get used to living somewhere with so many choices, so many places to go, people to meet. So many things to do! I'm from a pretty small town." We step up to the door and I hold it open for her, she smiles as she enters, waits for me, and I choose a table by the window.

"What took you so long to ask me to do anything? You've been coming into the shop for like a year now," she smiles and takes off her coat, revealing a blue buttonup blouse.

"I have a thing about meeting women at work, I can never tell if they're being themselves or have their work-personality on. I don't want to hit on someone when they're under pressure to be nice and friendly to customers."

I can't even remember why I started thinking this way.

A waitress comes over to greet us with a couple of glasses of water, and a couple menus. "Thank you," Nat says to her, so polite. I like a woman with courtesy.

"Thanks," I say.

"Yeah I know what you're talking about. You know the blonde I work with? She is such a rude person but you'd never know from her work face. Her personality is completely different. I try to be me all the time, why be anyone else?" I smile and nod, thinking back to everything I know about pickup artists and how they work. It's like personality steroids to try and trick a woman into sleeping with you, rather than using merit and a genuine approach. It works better than anything else, especially honesty. I can't fault guys who do that though, as being yourself just doesn't have the allure of a peacocking, negging male.

"I guess people act different than themselves because they want to conceal their motives? Imagine if you knew from the moment you met a man what his motives were, exactly what was going through his head. That would take the challenge out of dating, right?" She cocks her head a bit to one side "Hmm, I think it would make things easier, yeah-buuut, uhm," her face grows puzzled and she looks up at the ceiling.

I remain quiet as her eyes drop back down to meet mine. "What would you think if I told you what I want, Dylen? Wouldn't that scare you?" Our eyes are locked on each other, her little gems look so beautiful in this soft light, a yellowish sheen from the streetlights giving her skin a bronze tone. I want to tell her it wouldn't scare me, but that would make me seem desperate. Fuck it, I'm done hiding my intents. "No, no I don't think it would. I'm looking for a real partner that wants to love me as much as I love her, for the long haul. I want to have that adoration and not just another relationship of convenience. Does that scare you?" I grin and feel my palms sweat, blunt honesty is a workout for my soul. "Well, I've heard a lot of bullshit from guys trying to fuck me!" she laughs nervously and then covers her mouth. "Oops, hehe," she blushes. Taking her menu she looks at it and says "Oh wow, it all sounds so good! Tomato saffron mussles, or the arctic char graxlax?"

"Hmm, something that goes well with white wine."

"Okay!" she puts the menus on top of each other and takes a sip from her water. I figure she thinks I'm desperate to get laid.

A few moments pass and the waitress comes over, "Yeah, can we get the Ogopogo's Lair pinot grigio, and the hummus please?" I hand her the menus and she replies "For sure, that all?" A silent smile and she walks away.

"I haven't had the best of luck in relationships Dylen, my experiences in Vancouver have been anything but romantic," she says without a smile, her eyes looking out into the evening street.

"When I had first come to Vancouver I thought, wow, the big city, so many new friends and precious moments to be had, and instead of finding romance or even a few good flings, I've just felt like, isolated from men."

Her eyes peer deeper into my own.

"I guess it hit me last Valentine's day, I was seeing this guy and, looking back, I should have seen this coming. I wanted to make him feel like we were really going somewhere. As soon as I got off work I rushed home and started prepping dinner. He comes home and he's dirty from work, so I tell him to take a shower as I leave to pick up a couple of filet mignons and a bottle of wine for us. I go out in the pouring rain and pick up everything for us to celebrate the night together, the thickest, juiciest steak for him to enjoy! I mean, these steaks were beautiful!" She beams a smile. "But what happens when I get back? He's on his Xbox playing some stupid video game. I understand people want to relax after work, so I just cleaned up his pile of clothes in the bathroom and threw the steaks on the grill. I then go into our bedroom and get my lingerie ready so I can serve him dinner in my newest little lacey number, just for him," She sighs.

"Then what do I notice? There is a towel on the floor beside the bed and his laptop is open, he just jerked off to some porn on Valentine's then went to play video games!" I laugh. She smiles and laughs too. "So yeah, picture me, this 24 year old girl who spent her entire last week planning and budgeting out this night to make him feel wanted, made his favorite scalloped potatos the night before so I could throw it in the oven, the best steaks I could find, the hottest little crotchless pair of panties-uhm, I don't know why I'm saying so much-"

"Honesty is in short supply these days, keep going, this is me getting to know the real you," I blurt out.

"Ok, I just wanted to feel like I wasn't the only one celebrating our time together, and then there I was, standing in the bedroom thinking that I was just some bitch. Someone who didn't need romance, but I do." The waitress walks up and puts down a couple of wine glasses, "Good pairing with the hummus," she remarks, pouring two glasses of pale yellow social lube. "Your hummus is coming right up," she politely informs us as she walks away.

"Cheers, Nat, to being wanted."

My hand takes my glass and raises it, our eyes meeting and her lips part.

"To wanting and being wanted," she replies.

248

The glasses chime together and she takes a small sip, never taking her eyes off of me.

"I've never just offered that much so fast to someone, about me, about my fears," she gets comfortable in her chair and pulls her long, brown hair back over her shoulders.

"I bet you've never had a conversation like that with a man, about the end goals, the purpose of even being together. I know I've never really been able to articulate how I feel about modern love. Why two people would choose be together when the options are unlimited and we don't really need each other. Is there anything you can't do on your own Nat?"

She pauses and looks down briefly. Without looking up at me, she whispers, "You're right, there is nothing I need a man for. I make my own money, I will have a career soon, my light bulbs are all changed and I have a deadly spiderkilling aim with throwing heels. Hiya!" she makes a couple of karate chop motions with her hands and laughs. I pretend to duck as the waitress walks up and I nearly put my face into the hummus and pita bread.

The hummus is placed on the table and the pita bread steams. Soft bread dipped into mashed chickpeas, garlic, and lemon juice delights the tongue and compliments the wine. This not-so strange woman's company, the food, wine, this table by the window, it feels like a new beginning.

"Mmm!" Natalie smiles, unfolds her napkin, and dabs the corner of her mouth.

"Delicious," Nat says, taking her second piece of warm pita bread. I manage a grunt to acknowledge my satisfaction. Our faces become a commute for wine and hummus, occupied with food and grins until nary a drop remains on the plate or in the bottle. She folds her napkin on the table, crosses her arms and bends forward. "I'm supposed to be studying right now, and I really shouldn't have come with you, but I'm so glad I did."

Finishing my wine gets difficult through such a big smile.

"I have to get home and get some stuff taken care of myself, let's get the bill," I say, our eyes locked for more than a moment. I turn my head and attract the waitress, who instinctively brings the bill over.

We could be mistaken for eager lovers.

"I got it," Nat says, putting a couple of twenties to cover the meal. She turns her body and puts on her coat, I look outside and it's showering rain, she has no umbrella. We both stand up and walk out the front door, the awning of the restaurant barely sheltering us from the downpour. Her phone comes out of her pocket for the first time and she says "Shoot, my bus isn't for another 15 minutes," her shoulders ride up her neck and she puts her hands in her pocket with a little shiver.

"Hold on," I step out from the awning, into the street with my hand in the air. A yellow cab squeals to a stop, my hand finds the back door's handle to open.

"Where you going?" I call out to her.

She steps over to me holding the door. "Commercial near 12th, you don't have to."

I kiss her, and she pulls back.

It's raining hard and we're quickly getting soaked, she looks a bit shocked that I would kiss her in the middle of the street against a taxi. She grabs me and pulls me close, our lips meeting again for a moment, and my eyes close as my heart opens. A car horn interrupts this blissful moment and she gets into the cab. I pass the driver a twenty through his cracked window and the cab pulls off. Her eyes meet mine from the back window of the taxi, then she's gone.

31 Pill Ow

I forgot to dry my hair off after I got home, my head soaked as I watched her get in the cab, her face turning to smear and reflected light as it drove off. I even watched it turn the corner. A honk from behind startled me, I guess I was standing in the street still. A waved and I hopped over a puddle and onto the curb. Crushed shit and discarded gum flow into a constantly changing mural, a boot print and a couple of little logs form a demented smiley face. I swipe my way in and pass by a few unhappy faces exiting the building. One guy remarks on how I must be cold, but I can only smile and try and catch my breath still. My elevator comes and I'm soon back on the 5th, skipping down the hallway and doing airplane wings.

Peaks of happiness stand on either side of a valley of reality. I'll never be able to support a family, afford a house, live and love normally, but kissing her is close enough for now. I unlock my door and dance inside, it will probably close itself. Dancing half Fred Astaire and half Snoop Dogg, I kick off wet shoes while grabbing dirty dishes off my coffee table. I can do this because I'm happy and excited. Loading the dishwasher goes smoothly, the buzz in my head keeping my hands deft and my mind focused. The last time I felt like this I was ready to fall in love. The kind of love your friends make fun of you for. Being giddy, being unable to hide your happiness. Making stupid faces in photographs, your face flush with colour and lit up with a grin from ear to ear. I laugh at the irony of how most men would think I have the ideal situation, meanwhile I'm happy at the thought of getting to know a woman a little now *before* I put my penis inside her.

I turn the dishwasher on and it whirrs away. I lay down on the black leather couch that I earlier moved into the middle of the room, kick some

251

brushes and a paper pile off seat, put a pillow behind my head. Sighing, searching for peace with heavy eyelids. Even with this huge rush of endorphins I'm experiencing right now, this incredible sensation of happiness, I know it will crash back onto a thundering depression. How many other times had my lips touched a woman, how many nights had I held one close, been inside of, kissing and cumming inside of, just to have the relationship burn out. Where does actually believing in love begin again?

John Candy. If anyone knew about love it must have been John Candy. Netflix is my favorite source for campy shit, as the selections of TV shows are so out of date. I spend the rest of the night watching Uncle Buck. Flashes of my childhood rush through my head. I had a neighbor growing up, Gordon, that I remember. He was big like John Candy, and rode a Harley. I end up pouring a drink, Jack over ice, and sip it slowly. The pillow has an wafting smell of wet hair and is a bit damp on my neck. The way people love each other in the movies isn't real, but I so wish it were. A few drinks later and my pillow is dry. I find a long blonde hair on my shirt and lay it in a wide coil on my coffee table.

I hope Misha is ok.

32 Sting

Your bed is universally the most comfortable at noon. It is typically found to be the least comfortable past 2 AM, but only if you need to be up by seven. Chinese-eyed and drowsy, I fling out an arm for my phone. A couple blind sweeps of the bedside and I have a handful of halfhearted communication. Dougie sent me at least a dozen texts. The first couple read:

> holy Shut bro shut just went down
> your Fuken bitch Misha and Kiki vouched for these dudes they brought with them to my party last night
> they invited more sausages and filled my apartment with fags in cashmere and old hipsters holding onto the glory of living in e van basement suites
> so ya these tools stole all of the coke and a few left then we noticed the flaps r gone and we ask them what's up and then they get all defencive and accuse me of being crazy

I have to shit so badly. I know I've been trying to lose weight, but last night I saw a video on Liveleak of a live wolf pup being run over on purpose by an asshole on a snow mobile, I ate a whole pizza out of depression. Maybe I had a double Jack and coke, or five, to wash it down. This is going to be a disgusting, greasy mess. I go to the toilet and shit faster than what could possibly be recommended. I take my smartphone with me and read on:

> yeah then I chill out and my girl is in the bedroom with me saying shell boot everyone out and I'm cool
> then I get a text from your buddy Matt who was just coming back from a booze run and he sees mish and k walking out with those guys and one of them throws empties against the side of your building and they all laughed
> so wtf dude that's like an 8ball GONE and those notches fucking laughs while their friends trash my building!

I've been staying at home even more lately, feels shitty man. In this case I'm glad I missed out on what was sure to not only have been a sausage party, but a loser sausage party. Misha and Kiki probably hooked up with one of those d-bags last night after stealing Dougie's blow. Maybe they took turns. Not whatever this time, fuck it, fuck that whole scene.

I finish my business and flush. The process of life stinks and disgusts me. I brush my teeth, comb my hair and flex a bit. Not bad, a bit chunky still, maybe I've been drinking less. I notice Dougie also left a voicemail:

"Dyl, it's Doug. Give me a call man, those crazy bitches of yours started major shit here last night. I'm done with'em bro. Call me for the details, you won't fucking believe it."

I don't want to have to deal with this. Can't people act with some standards? I laugh at asking myself that, a man who laughs in the face of standards to begin with. I don't have any booze left to numb my hypocrisy, so frowning will have to do. Wait, fuck that. I open my phone's contact list and hesitate over deleting Misha's number. I should wait for her side of the story. After that little drinking and driving before the fashion show, and now this embarrassment, what's going on with those two? Every moment I spend with them is some sort of fucked up shit, drinking, drugs, and the mindless fucking of Misha. I briefly think of Misha, panties around her knees, face down and ass up on my couch. I clear my mind and no longer want to think of sex as just something to do. Easy enough now, I'm not horny; just pissed off.

Removing people from my life has never been simpler. My Facebook went from 700 friends to 80 in about a half hour of furious clicking. Who are these people? Yeah that girl I fucked in 2002 against a cutlass supreme while camping. This guy here I worked with and haven't talked to in four years. A distant cousin, we never talk. Delete buttons are used to cut ties with them all. These people might email me and ask me why I deleted them, assuming they'd notice.

Cellphones are even easier, as who actually remembers a phone number anymore?

Just delete the contact info and don't answer strange numbers.

Delete the voicemail and you'll never have to bother telling them why.

In this case, I need to seriously cut back on the number of people I know. The first step to avoid being trapped by wine, song, drugs and sluts is to stop going where they're going to be. Drug dealers and skanks are obliterated from my phone, its contact list looking bare bones. Gone are the numbers such as 'Blizzard' and 'Jenni nice mouth', what's left are 'George H' and 'Julie from school.' Sigh. I'm going to miss a few of these people, but sometimes without striking it out on your own and casting off from familiar ports, you'll never discover who and what's out there. Maybe I need to discover what I have inside me, if there's anything left.

33 Church Rat

I hadn't been in a church in 25 years. I remember it smelling the same, and these benches never ended up getting any more comfortable. The wood is smooth to the touch, polished by tens or hundreds of thousands of asses.

I almost forgot why I came here today, to sit alone and be with my thoughts. I cross one leg over the other and lean back with both of my arms outstretched over the back of the bench. My right index finger twirls in the air, and when I shut my eyes I can feel her curly blonde hair. I'm smiling and remembering her with such fondness I forget that twirling my finger and smiling like this in a church could look pretty strange. It's strange just being here.

I remember falling in love like it was yesterday. She called me first thing in the morning to wish me a happy birthday. I remember the sun peeking through my window, being groggy as the phone rang. "Uhhnnff ... Hello?"

I knuckle my eye to remove some crunchy night goop from it.

"Hi!! Happy birthday!" she exclaimed with a smile I felt through the phone.

"Wha ... Yeah hey thanks," was all I could muster.

"Ok! That's all I wanted to say! I hope you have the BEST day today!" I smiled so much that morning. I hadn't felt those muscles tire in ages.

I think we hung out off and on for a month, but I couldn't really get close to her. There are things I just didn't want to burden her with, and as strange as it sounds and feels to say, I'd feel guilty if she loved me. There was this perfect girl with all of her perfect family and so many accomplishments, and then there's me. A janitor stabs a mop into a bucket and lifts it out, the splashes echo in the empty hall. I move around on the bench, one of my ass cheeks is completely asleep.

I started realizing that I loved her when I held back. I didn't want her to be in my world because she's better off without me. It was when I realized this that I had to come up with an idea for change, but into what? My nail finally finds a rough grain on the back of the bench and I pick at it gently. Soft lemon is such a pleasant scent. The janitor is old and looks so frail that a good sized fart might tear him in half.

I don't really have a model for a man to emulate or admire. I know if I'm the type of man that women prefer, I'd be gay or a complete womanizer. Being gay would make your sexuality a complete non-threat in their eyes, being a womanizer also helps as your sex becomes utility to them. Just a dick attached to a non-threatening man that will leave or call them a cab.

I used to enjoy singing hymns in church. It seemed like a fun thing to do and to hear words of praise seemed to reinforce the beauty in life. As a child I was really happy until I began questioning if God was real. Santa was a lie, how do I know you're not lying again? I never got an answer from my parents and soon after they divorced. Santa, God, and Love were never real. Until I met her.

Tall with a dancer's body, a beaming smile, her real genuine sense of love for the world around her could bring the sense of being found to even the most lost. I could feel this deep well of energy in myself with her around. I can still draw on the power of that love to move me when I need to. I need to now.

The word love means nothing without action, same with God and Santa. Yes, Santa is a commercialized whore, but the smiles on the faces of children give him soul. I long for a Christmas like a Coke ad, a house covered in snow, soft lights twinkling on the roof. The children are asleep in their beds, while mom and dad are excited for the morning to come. I would hold my wife close to me, flannel PJs and her hair in my face. On the roof, that fat bastard pops the lid off a Coke and ho-ho-ho's into the clear winter night.

The janitor has barely moved. I don't think he's cleaning, just enjoying the lemon scent like I am.

I can't help but think God and Love are intricately linked. What I feel when I feel love is a great sense of responsibility and caring. What I think people typically hate God for is the perception that this benevolent force that created us, abandoned us. Music that curses God always ends up referencing all of the suffering and disease, war and pain. I'm slowly coming to terms with my agnosticism, that God is just interchangeable with a reverence for love. Wanting love, giving love, being in love. Love is the only way humans have of manifesting whatever God they have into reality. A life without love and there is no joy, alive without even love for yourself and you could end up drinking a cup of antifreeze.

I wanted to give her so much of my love, but at the time there was no possible way to explain how I felt about her. I hadn't found the distinction between lust and love, instead being stuck in the uncomfortable space between. I'd grown up being told that any kind of sex was good, in the last decade of porn saturation I had lost all of the connection between sex and love. The very basis for sex is procreation, now it's beautifully marketed to my generation to sell porn subscriptions, and penis enlargement pills. You can find webcam chat websites where you can spend 15 minutes watching a girl double penetrate her holes for you. Maybe sex is interrupting your playoff game with a raunchy car wash video, trying sell a hamburger.

Now I go around in circles, I've had sex with so many women and came inside so many vaginas without any thought. I sometimes ask myself if my brain is subconsciously suffering, thinking that I'm infertile. That craving for more than fluid swap fucking now drives me towards getting closer with love. The heights which I reached with her, holding her petite hand while she drove me home, drunk in my own car and in her care. I even taught her how to do a clutch drop. I grin when I remember her excitement over that.

I've been living without that reverence for love, instead choosing peak moments of physical stimulation. I now realize none of my fears would have come true, if she had loved me the way I loved her, she could have accepted me for who I am. Maybe if I had learned that lesson the first time, I wouldn't have let Dark Heart slip away.

Both of my ass cheeks are completely numb. I stand up and talk the old man into taking a break. The rest of my afternoon is spent mopping the floor of a church. The old man sat on a bench, eyes closed, smiling.

34 Connection

It's a big day.

A gorgeous yellow sun hangs high overhead, the sky a radiant blue canopy. Two rental bikes on deposit, and a pocket full of BC's best electric lettuce, Natalee is meeting me there for a ride and toke. Yeah I'm excited, but it's nothing I haven't done before. Sure dating is fun, the chemicals from flirting, the conversation, the unknown. These things have grown numb over time. I sometimes wonder if it's just me, as much as Dougie disagrees, but I have to say it's my own personal problem. Dating gets repetitious, but just relaxing and getting to know her wouldn't be. The pain of sitting through another conversation with a bitch I don't like by the second drink, and I'll break a bottle and ram the shards into my own eyes before I say again the shit I need to in order to fuck her.

I hate thinking bad things.

When I confront myself with the reality of not being able to afford it here, I want to call the whole day off. Falling for a girl is the last thing I need, but it's everything that I want.

Stop.

I close my eyes.

I need to remind myself that it's one day at a time.

Deep breath.

Spring in Vancouver and the air can still bite, so I put a couple of sweaters in my backpack in case we get cold, tossing in a cable bike lock in case we stop somewhere. Natalee is a smart gal and I'm sure she'll bring a coat, but I want her to know I thought of her. Wallet, check, keys, check, phone, check. Lights go off and I'm on my way.

CITY OF SINGLES

The streets in Gastown are flooded with a different breed of people when the sun is out, making everything and everyone look pretty. The trees just start to green around the time bums dress a little nicer, spit a little less, smell a little more. I walk to Canada Place and find the little bike shop underneath it, right at the start of the seawall. Just as I finish paying for the rental, Natalee pokes her head in the door and says "Hey!" in her sing-songy voice. I smile from ear to stupid ear. I hug her and we go outside to grab our bikes, I steal a kiss just before we ride.

We make a couple of stops for photos, and once we reach the park we start smoking the joint I brought. Her kiss is playful and soft, arms around me squeezing me close. I lose my balance and end up in a pile of girl and bikes, Nat skinned her palm on the way down, but she's so proud that she saved the joint from going out. If the Beetles had been formed in 2012 Vancouver, they'd probably write a song about seawall biking with beautiful, happy women. Natalee puts her arms out and flaps them like a bird. Not a dirty Gastown pigeon, but graceful as a crane on Xanax. We talk a little and laugh a lot, I've been smiling the whole time and I even got pooped on by a seagull with a bad diet. Natalee busted out her water bottle and some napkins to clean me up quick. She charges me two kisses, one paid up front, one for later on. So demanding.

We ride to the other end of the seawall and end up sitting in a little cafe on Denman Street. Two large hot chocolates and some small talk fill us with joy. Stories of her friends and family come out of her smiling face in just above a whispered tone, but shout to me her values and what matters to her. Photos of her nephews briefly remind me of a dark hearted girl I once loved, for all the same reasons. Natalee radiates femininity from every pore, and she's doing a great job of speaking to my heart and mind. A few jokes and she's laughing, my phone comes out and I show her the art I'm currently working on. Her eyes focus in and she asks 20 questions about it, and by the time we're done our cocoas, the sun has set and we're late taking back the bikes.

I tell her that I'll walk them over in the morning, and we could use them to bike to get groceries. "I hope you like spicy!" I say, to which she replies that she makes a killer Pad Thai. She's a little shy about the PDA, taking her hand and gently putting flirty lips to it. She blushes for a moment before grabbing me by my ears and giving me a kiss on the cheek before standing up.

"Well, what are you waiting for?" Nat happily quips, "Shrimp and noodles don't cook themselves!"

With that we're out the door and on our bikes. She's plenty fast on wheels and it almost takes effort to keep up, her shopping is a Tasmanian devil whirlwind of shopping, flirting, and noodle choosing. She hides something from me in the yellow basket under a package of salad. "Don't look!" I love surprises so I don't.

The girl at the checkout counter rings dinner supplies through and Natalee pays for it. The store is close to my house and she walks the bikes while I carry the food. She accidentally drives them over so many logs of shit on Cordova that the bikes drag heavy from all the extra rotational weight. We get to my place, wash the bikes off quick in the courtyard and Nat goes to lock them up. She bends over and I leer significantly less than normal, but I do check out her fine caboose.

Up the elevator and into my studio, the groceries go on the counter and we prep dinner. She demands that I sit down and relax while she cooks, and pours me a glass of wine from my fridge. She makes a salad with apple slices, dried cranberry, almond slivers and a little goat cheese. Yum. I flip through Netflix and find something to watch. The Leprechaun looks really ridiculous. Dinner comes to me on a steaming plate, the curry sauce looks and smells red hot spicy, just the way I like it. Nothing is said during dinner but I moan from flavour stimulation the whole time.

"Oh my god this is so good," slips out three or four times, and I think I must have told her she is the best chef *ever* at least a half dozen times. We both finish the plates down to the last bite, and toast to a beautiful day. We kiss.

She takes the plates to the kitchen and comes back with two strawberry tarts as the surprise. We devour them and fall over together laughing at how good they taste. She's held in my arms and we're both so satisfied and tired, the kissing turning into a slow, hot make out. Our tongues crash together and her fingernails dig into my side, I bite her lip.

"So," she whispers, "Where are the blankets in this place? I won't let you walk those bikes there alone tomorrow." She hops up to look behind the couch.

"Ah! Knew it!" she grabs a pillow and a big fuzzy blanket and wraps us in it. I put on The Leprechaun and she giggles.

"Oh this movie looks terrible!!" She says, turning her head to me, kissing my neck.

"I don't think we'll watch this movie much anyways..."

I feel her hot breath on my neck, and her hand slides down to my zipper.

I'm tired of doing the same thing over and over, I don't *have* to fill the same mold, or ride the same rail. My dick is ready to roar like a lion, but my heart can wait. I reach down and move her hand away.

"I don't do that right away," I state.

She is in total shock.

I stay spooning with her and I hold her hand. Softly kissing her cheek, I whisper in her ear. "You made my day so wonderful."

She smiles and gives my hand a little squeeze. I wait for her to fall asleep and turn off the world's worst Jennifer Aniston movie. I slither out from behind her warm and welcoming body, with a face so peaceful, chest rising ever so slightly with each little breath she takes. My beard stubble gave her a little sandpapering. I walk to my kitchen to pour another glass of wine, and light a joint. I can't help but think what I did seems like weakness, but for once I feel an honest strength.

I'm in control of what I want now.

Walking over to the window and I take a seat overlooking Burrard inlet; watching as lights from Vancouver's north shore twinkle on the water. Warm port yellows blend fuzzy oranges, blue hues and ski hill whites. A bum scream echoes in my alley. Turning back to look at Natalee on the couch, a little disappointed she already tried to fuck me, but I couldn't blame her for thinking that's what I wanted right away. Maybe the tramp on my couch tonight will wake up the lady I've always wanted tomorrow.

Probably not.

Life imitates art, if you change art, you change the world.